A MAN OF ACTION

"Indeed, your poet friends and I are as different as flock and herd. If I were in love with you, if I desired you, if I intended to *elope* with you, mere words would never be enough. I'd make sure you understood what I expected in our relationship as husband and wife, man and woman." Adam's other hand drifted along the edge of Becca's bodice in a slow sensual pattern, lightly skimming her flesh. His gaze slid from her eyes to her mouth then to her breasts. "I would need to touch every delicious inch of you. That tiny mole behind your left ear. The tender pulse point on your wrist. The soft flesh of your thighs. I'd make sure you realized that passion runs deep within your soul."

"This discussion is inappropriate," Becca gasped.

"Inappropriate? You just claimed to scorn society's rules, to frown on the virtue of innocence. Remember?" He allowed her time to withdraw, but when she did not, Adam slowly lowered his head. He gently pressed his lips to hers.

Peggy Waide

Mightier Than the Sword

LEISURE BOOKS   NEW YORK CITY

*Special hugs to Angie, for making me read my first
romance, and all my Jazzercise buddies
who have been so supportive.*

A LEISURE BOOK®

March 2001

Published by

Dorchester Publishing Co., Inc.
276 Fifth Avenue
New York, NY 10001

ISBN 0-8439-4842-6

The name "Leisure Books" and the stylized "L" with design are
trademarks of Dorchester Publishing Co., Inc.

Printed in the United States of America.

Visit us on the web at www.dorchesterpub.com.

Chapter One

Eastern coast of England, 1816

Traitor. A disgrace to king and country.

The loathsome accusations skittered through Adam's mind for the hundredth time, freezing his blood to the temperature of the water swirling about his ankles. Around him, waves crashed past onto the rocky shore in a relentless rhythm, gulls swooped and soared, and yet he stood motionless, longingly staring at the gray stone walls towering high above the cliffs ahead. A deathless well of emptiness opened in the pit of his stomach. Adam Horatio Hawksmore, fifth Earl of Kerrick, soldier, lord and gentleman, was finally home.

But to what end?

To be scorned? Ostracized? Hanged like a criminal? A particularly unfitting punishment, he mused, for a man who'd been raised to follow in his illustrious ancestors' footsteps and serve king and country, a man who'd been trained to kill ruthlessly in the name of honor and tradition.

Mac, Adam's trusted friend, sat in the small boat behind him and pointed to the red stain seeping through Adam's woolen jacket. "You're bleeding again."

Fighting for balance as another wave crashed past toward shore, Adam held the skiff in place in the shallow water and shrugged his shoulders. There'd be time enough to see to his wound and cracked ribs once he reached the safety of the castle. "I've had far worse."

Digging into his pocket, Adam removed a marker for one thousand pounds. It was the only thing of value he had to offer, and it seemed a pittance. When Adam needed help, Mac had willingly come to France and procured a safe haven until they could sail back to England. The man had hidden Adam on the *Fleeting Star* and reconnoitered Kerrick Castle to ensure its lord's safe arrival back home. He'd discovered the details of Adam's supposed treason. And never once had he questioned Adam's innocence. Money was a small price to pay.

Holding the note in his outstretched hand, Adam said, "Take it, Mac."

"I don't want your damn money."

"Don't be an ass."

Yanking his woolen cap from his head, Mac dragged his hand through his unruly auburn curls and narrowed his eyes. He was obviously stalling, searching for some plausible argument to sway Adam's mind.

The effort was appreciated, but a waste of time.

Once Adam set himself to a particular way of thinking, it was easier to sink a fleet of ships than change his course. "If I find myself in Newgate Prison," he said, "I'd much rather you have the funds than that fool cousin of mine. Cecil will squander every farthing on whores, cards or horses. Besides, you need the money. It's the least I can do. Contact Lord Wyncomb if I'm indisposed."

"Dead, you mean."

Mac had never been one to mince words. Adam shrugged again. "There is that possibility. But I refuse to leave a black mark on the family name, so I have no choice but to try and clear my own. Now go. And don't be risking that worthless neck of yours. Remember, you've not seen me since that night at the Horned Mermaid."

With a curt nod, Mac slapped his cap back on top of his head, stuffed the marker beneath, then shoved the boat from shore with a single oar. "And what a night that was, my friend." He gave Adam a pointed look. "Watch your back. You know how to reach me, if need be. Best of luck."

Adam didn't argue, though luck had never once helped him in his life. He certainly had not survived for twenty-eight years—three fighting in the Peninsular Wars and the last eight months in a French cell—due to luck. Wits, patience, training, skill and logic had saved his life. Those, and a hefty dose of determination to return to England and find the bastard responsible for his imprisonment and tarnished reputation.

Alone on the beach, he watched Mac's boat disappear into the foggy mist. Nearby, seabirds welcomed the day with shrill cries as they rode the winds blowing off the cliffs, soared freely above the sea. Adam envied their freedom.

Threading his way across the rock and sand, he wedged himself behind a huge craggy boulder that acted as a giant sentinel to the narrow, slitlike opening of a small cave. He pulled a candle and flint from his pocket and lit the tallow stub. Its offensive scent filled the small cavern, stirring the memory of endless hours of waiting and wondering, the isolation and emptiness that never seemed to leave him.

Shaking the vile thoughts from his mind, he used the light for the final climb to his bedchamber. His side throbbed and sweat beaded his brow and upper lip, his body's own heat a sharp contrast to the cold, damp walls. Grim with purpose, he forced one foot in front of the other. After all, he hadn't escaped to perish in his own castle's damnable secret passage. The crumbling steps rose gradually, then veered sharply to the left, ending at what appeared to be an oaken wall.

In the corner he found and pried loose the two bolts that held the wall in place, then he thrust his shoulder against the solid barrier. His muscles screamed with the effort, yet the blasted wall didn't budge. At last, with another hefty shove and an unrestrained curse, the two-by four-foot section of wood shifted. Adam closed his eyes and exhaled a deep, self-satisfied sigh. Then he stepped into his private sanctuary.

Opening his eyes, he saw everything was where it should be. His favorite oversized chair made of soft burgundy leather with sturdy armrests made to his specification was still placed by the fireplace. The carved family crest, IN HONORE DEFENDIMUS—in honor we defend—hung above. A matching padded footstool and mahogany table sat beside his chair. The armoire stood as it always had in the opposite corner. A small writing desk, another comfortable chair, a large wooden trunk and an enormous bed completed the room's furnishings, sparse in number, but just as Adam preferred. As a soldier, he disliked clutter or chaos. As a man, he enjoyed luxury and detail.

The faint odor of shoe polish and the smoky residue from a fire reached him, causing him to wonder about the amount of blood he'd lost. The castle should be somewhat deserted, and certainly no on should be building fires in his bedchamber. He had to be imagining things.

His bed was positioned on a mahogany pedestal enclosed on all sides by a navy velvet drape, and it called out to him. Surely, once he lay down, he'd sleep for a week.

Stooping to set his small knapsack on the floor, he felt a stabbing pain in his side from his wound. Gingerly peeling the jacket from his shoulders, he stumbled toward the bed and parted its drapes. He blinked once, twice, at what he found. "What the devil?"

Incredible golden eyes in the face of a heavenly angel rounded in shock and glared at him. Her blond curls hinted of gold, brown and, he supposed, even honey, and tumbled wildly over her shoulders and down her back. The lustrous cascade framed a heart-shaped face with a determined chin, flushed cheeks and full lips that currently frowned in an unwelcoming manner. Most disconcerting was the pistol aimed directly at his chest. The woman gasped, dropped the weapon to the bed and smacked Adam soundly across the face.

11

"Why did you do that?" he snapped, still trying to overcome the shock of finding a woman in his bed. Not just any woman, he amended, but Lady Rebecca Marche, the daughter of Edward Marche, Earl of Wyncomb, and the man who had agreed, as a personal favor, to handle Adam's affairs in his absence. Becca also happened to be the girl he'd refused to marry before he'd left for France.

"First, you frightened me near to death, and secondly"—Becca narrowed her eyes to slits—"because we have worried about you for months. You are supposed to be dead."

Dead? He wasn't quite sure how to react to that news. It had been disconcerting enough to discover himself branded a coward and a traitor. But dead?

"Sorry to disappoint you," he said finally, still trying to reconcile the stunning beauty before him with the skinny, freckled, flat-chested child he'd known when he left for the continent. Where the devil had those delightful pouty lips come from?

She now had breasts, too. And by his estimation they would fit quite nicely in the palms of his hands. This was not good. Not good at all. One simply did not covet an old friend's daughter's breasts—unless perhaps the daughter was one's fiancée. But Becca and Adam would never marry; they were as different as two sides of a coin.

Still, she was attractive. And Adam was a man who appreciated the fairer sex as well as the next. "I thought the place was vacant," he grumbled, chagrined by his wayward thoughts. "Are you alone? Are your parents here?"

"No. Though, once I notify them that you are alive, they will surely come. At least Father will be pleased to see you. For me . . ."

12

The pain in his side intensified, and Adam raised his hand to dismiss what was sure to be a lecture on his past sins. She frowned, and he said, "I know. You would rather see me banished to the farthest colony in the Americas. . . . Better yet, the frozen wastelands of Russia."

She wrinkled her nose. "What is that stench? Where did you come from? And where have you been, for that matter?"

"France," he said simply. Becca's mutinous expression blurred about the edges as the room spun. To his mortification, he felt muddle-brained. He'd never fainted in his entire life—even as a young man, with his hands bloodied from his first battle. He had emptied the contents of his stomach that day, but he hadn't passed out. Not even when he'd taken that bullet in his leg or the saber in his shoulder. When his parents were murdered before his very eyes, injured himself, he had helplessly watched them die, but even then he had not fainted. "I'll be damned," he mumbled and crumpled to the bed.

Leaping to the side, Becca reached for her robe and shoved her arms into the sleeves of the garment. "Don't you dare fall down," she cried.

" 'Tis a bit late for that," he groaned.

"Well, climb back on your feet."

Adam managed to open one eyelid. Had he the strength, he would have shaken his head. "I should have known, Becca. Even as a child you always managed to complicate my affairs. You are one of the few people who could unwittingly spoil my plans. I swear you do it on purpose."

"Thank you very much."

"It was not meant as a compliment."

"I would not expect compliments from you, anyway, a man committed to more masculine pursuits such as war."

His head throbbed mercilessly. "Why the devil are you here in the first place?"

"For your information, your cousin Cecil, the tallow-faced wretch, is impatient and wants his inheritance. Father has delayed the inevitable for months now, claiming that without a body or some sort of proof of your death, he cannot release your holdings. Cecil is planning to present his plight to the House of Lords, though. Father intends to argue against him, but he sent me to prepare the estate . . . just in case."

Adam shook his head, trying desperately to clear his thoughts as the last strength seeped from his body. He was so bloody tired. "Please, for once in your life, do as I ask, Becca. Tell no one that I am returned. I will explain after I rest."

"If you haven't noticed, you're in my bed."

"*My* bed," he reminded her softly.

"You know what I mean."

"Actually I do." He smiled weakly at her. "It must be the loss of blood. I certainly never did before." Becca had always been a conundrum, a puzzle too difficult for him to assimilate. A green group of corporals were easier to understand than she.

"I'm no different than most women," she said. "You never listened."

"Never listened?" he repeated in astonishment. He was about to respond when he was overcome by a particularly eye-crossing stab of pain. He really did not need this discussion right now.

"Yes. You were always too busy offering advice on my . . ." She trailed off as she saw how truly weak he had become. Scampering over his body, she jostled him and the bed in the process. He groaned. Her hands flew to the buttons of his shirt. Once she revealed the nasty bloodstained wrapping about his waist, she uttered a small cry. "Oh, Adam, what have you done to yourself? Let me call for help." She crawled to the edge of the mattress.

With the last remnant of strength he possessed, he grabbed her wrist and clamped down. Becca had always been willful, impatient, impetuous—the list of her recalcitrant qualities was endless. He needed to eliminate any possibility, immediately, that she might seek help. He needed time to decide what to do before anyone knew his whereabouts. His fingers loosened and slid from her wrist. "My life depends upon your silence," he whispered.

Praying those words were enough, he sank into unconsciousness.

Chapter Two

"Don't you dare do this." Becca leaned over and shook his shoulder. "Adam?" His eyes remained closed, his breathing faint and raspy, his skin pasty. She pinched his cheek. "Adam?" she called again.

The blasted man had fainted dead away, collapsed on the bed in a heap of filthy clothes with little explanation. How typical, she thought. He'd always done exactly what he wanted, when he wanted. And still she had once thought she loved him. Then again, those feelings had only been the product of a young, infatuated mind.

"Damn and double damn. Spit. Mercy. Damn," she cursed. She had acquired the habit from her father, but because it was frowned upon by her mother, she exhibited it only in private. Sitting on her heels, she brushed a strand of black hair from his forehead. "What am I suppose to do with you?"

His face, a handsome mix of angles and planes, was leaner than she remembered, and hidden beneath a dark scraggly beard. Had she not seen his silver-blue eyes for herself—eyes she'd once dreamed about—she might not have recognized him. His brows arrogantly arched on his forehead as if, even while sleeping, he dared anyone to question his authority. Reedy breaths of air escaped his mouth, drawing her attention to it. His lips were full, and, even in slumber, were incredibly enticing. Sensual. Even bloodied and sleeping, this man exuded a maddening self-assurance.

Her gaze drifted over his broad shoulders to the opening in his shirt. His muscled chest was dusted with crisp dark hairs that trailed down his belly and, she assumed, below the waist of the trousers that rode dangerously low on his narrow hips. The dratted man still had the ability to take her breath away. Becca muttered one of her father's favorite curses, then reminded herself, "He also broke your heart."

She steadied her resolve against any romantic feelings toward Adam and renewed her vow of independence. That vow was the real reason she was here at Kerrick Castle. It and a silly note scribbled by Barnard Leighton, a young poet and neighbor of the family who believed he was in love with her.

She remembered that final letter, a flowery epic of Barnard's devotion and his suggestion they elope. She had never dreamed that one simple note could turn her world upside down. Although, when she thought about it, most parents would be furious with their daughters at the appearance of a note entreating her to elope to Gretna Green.

Imagine, she thought. *Banished from my own home.* Oh, her father claimed he needed her to supervise the preparation of Kerrick Castle, but Becca knew this to be a fool's errand designed to separate her from Barnard. And her public denunciation of marriage as a form of slavery for women—proudly proclaimed while wearing a pair of men's breeches before several dozen lords and ladies—along with her decision to forego the upcoming season, hadn't helped the matter. Her father had sent her away for a few weeks to reconsider her wild ways and ruminate on obedience. And whatever he called it, Becca called it banishment.

She wasn't likely to change her mind. She would always wonder why men thought they must dominate women's lives. Honestly, Becca really wasn't averse to marriage; she simply wanted a man who considered her an equal, someone who truly appreciated her worth as an intelligent woman good for something more than as a brood mare. Love, of course, was a must. But not at the expense of forfeiting who she was.

She understood his aggravation regarding Barnard, but her father's displeasure at her decision not to marry had surprised Becca. While she was accustomed to his bluster—after all, he'd been raised on the London docks and the high seas, had built his wealth from a handful of copper pennies to the ownership of a successful trade company, and he'd married an earl's daughter and gained a title to boot—the man had always spurned society's tenets. He was a true champion of free will. He had made sure that Becca was educated, taught her a number of skills more common to men and always encouraged her to speak her mind. And all that only made his intention to have her settled as a wife even more difficult for Becca to accept.

She had tried to argue, but in this her father was more unmovable than a stand of oak trees. He was set upon her one day marrying, and not even Becca's mother, who could usually sway her father's opinion, could change that. In the end, Becca had agreed to go more because Barnard's attentions had become tedious than from any sense of contrition. The man simply refused to accept no as an answer.

She wasn't quite sure why she had not told Adam the entire truth about her presence at Kerrick Castle when he'd asked. But she hadn't actually lied. Cecil *was* being a greedy boor. Yet neither had she revealed her true circumstances. She supposed she feared she might see the same disapproval in Adam's eyes that she saw in those of all the other men of *Polite Society*.

He moaned, prompting her to action. She grabbed a water pitcher and a fresh shift, then tore the soft muslin into strips. Getting back onto the mattress, Becca made sure the bed's drapes were drawn before she peeled the dirty shirt and soiled dressing from Adam's body.

She winced. A nasty slash, at least five inches in length, marred his side directly below his ribs where the skin was a dreadful purplish black.

"Look what playing soldier did to you this time, you dimwit," she scolded softly. "Where have you been? What have you been doing?" she asked, expecting no answer.

Gently wiping the crusted blood from his wound, she found a half-dozen torn stitches. Her fingers drifted over several old scars, each a silent testimony to the hard life he'd led. "Reckless and inconsiderate, that's what you are. A dunderheaded boor. You vanish for months without a word, then drop into my

19

lap, bruised and broken, expecting me to piece you back together."

For some odd reason, although she knew Adam couldn't hear a word she spoke, her lecture made the task of attending to his side more palatable. Thankful now that he had passed out, she secured the loosened threads as best she could, then wrapped him with new bandages.

Prepared to offer a bit more of her mind, she heard the bedroom door creak open. Sweet mercy, she'd almost forgotten she wasn't alone in the house. She stuck her head through the bed's closed drapes, then pulled them tight around her body just as her maid peered inside the chamber.

"Pardon me, m'lady. I didn't mean to wake you. I was just going about me duties."

"Never mind, Molly. I have a beastly headache this morning. Simply fetch some laudanum and tea."

A noise came from behind the drapes. Becca plastered her hand against her forehead and moaned most dramatically, hoping to mask Adam's restless whimper.

Remembering how little she'd eaten the night before, and the long day ahead of her, she added, "A biscuit or two or three would be lovely." Deciding that when Adam woke, he would likely be hungry as well, she added, "And a few slices of cheese might be nice, along with one of those lovely kidney pies Cook baked yesterday. And ham. You needn't worry about me. Simply leave them inside the door. I believe I'll spend the day in bed."

"Shall I fetch your aunt?"

"Heavens, no," Becca gasped. Her aunt was the last person she wanted to see right now. *What a coil!* Though she had a heart of gold, Aunt Jeanette was a

20

practiced gossip. And though most people either considered her eccentric like her brother or dismissed her as a woman of fluff, the truth was that she was wily as a fox. If she was notified of her niece's illness, she'd likely sit beside Becca the entire day and chatter. And though the tidbits Jeanette knew about the other London matrons were always fascinating, now seemed hardly the time to hear them. "I mean," Becca added weakly, "I'll be fine. My aunt need not worry herself."

The maid scrunched her brows and disappeared from the room to do as she'd been bidden. After she returned to deliver the requested items, then left, Becca bolted the door. Carrying her bounty to the table beside the bed, she crawled over Adam onto the mattress. He tossed fitfully beneath the cover. She spooned a portion of laudanum through his lips, then dabbed his brow with a damp cloth.

He had definitely lost weight—not that she really cared one way or another, except maybe as a friend cared.

She gently bathed his face, his broad chest, his arms and hands, his slender fingers and callused palms, scolding herself for her boldness in lingering over particularly fascinating body parts that rippled under her tender ministrations. Yet she continued until he calmed and at last slept peacefully.

She would stay awake now, keep guard. Yawning, she lay her head on the pillow next to his, contemplating all the questions she intended to ask the moment he woke. She fell asleep thinking she was glad he was alive.

He'd died and gone to hell after all.

He'd survived the French, his rabid captors, two

21

weeks hidden in a room no bigger than a closet, the rough crossing to England, only to die in his own damned bed. That was the only rationale for the unbearable heat, this oppressive sensation of smothering. The scent of fresh flowers teased his nostrils, which struck him as odd since he felt sure dead men couldn't smell anything. He clutched at his chest and encountered the soft swell of what seemed to be a woman's breast.

Impossible.

Willing his eyes open, he found himself buried beneath a mountain of covers with Becca draped across him like another soft woolen blanket. The last twenty-four hours rushed through his mind. On its heels came relief. Becca hadn't called for reinforcements. Sighing over the unexpected turn of events—her presence in his castle, his bedroom!—he removed his hand from what felt to be a very nice breast and shifted its owner's head to the curve of his shoulder.

He studied her, the woman Fate had cast directly into his path, a woman he was going to have to trust. When she slept, she appeared almost angelic. He snorted at the idiocy of that thought. Becca Wyncomb was anything but that.

In his absence, she had undisputably blossomed into a tempting armful. Chestnut-colored brows and long lashes framed eyes he knew to be chocolate brown, expressive, intelligent and usually laced with either mischief or laughter. Her nose turned up charmingly at the tip. Her lips, a coral pink against alabaster skin, parted sweetly in an unintentional invitation he knew he'd never accept.

He lifted a golden curl to his nose, inhaling the scent of some flowery concoction and soap. How

22

long had it been since he'd held a woman, appreciated the fragrance of her hair, the silkiness of her
skin? It seemed a lifetime ago.

He'd never imagined that Becca would be the first
woman in his bed on his return to England. Even
disregarding their last encounter, which had been so
difficult, this was the daughter of his guardian and
not a woman he should be lusting after.

When highwaymen attacked his parents' carriage,
Adam had been thirteen. He'd been nearly a man by
some folk's standards, though, God, he hadn't felt
like one. He'd laid there in the mud, tied to the carriage, unable to do a thing as his father and mother
were viciously slain for a few gold coins and scraps
of jewelry.

Though he'd been terrified, no one witnessed a single tear, then or at the funeral. Signs of weakness or
any emotional displays were unacceptable for Kerrick men. And, like his ancestors before him, the day
his father died Adam became the Earl of Kerrick—
with all the character and responsibilities the title
entailed. That was why this lust he suddenly felt, this
overwhelming emotion, was so wrong.

Worse, he didn't think he'd have managed those
early years without Edward, Becca's father. The man
had simply appointed himself as Adam's guardian,
expecting nothing in return except the joy of helping
the son of an old and trusted friend. Becca had been
about four years old. He couldn't help thinking how
much things had changed since then.

Before leaving for France, he had gone to Wyncomb Manor to say good-bye and settle his affairs.
During the wee hours of the morning, Becca had
crept into his bedroom, clad in a scrap of cream silk
obviously borrowed from her mother and nearly

transparent when she stood by the fire. She'd bared her heart and soul and proposed to him, and he'd near swallowed his tongue.

Once he came to his senses, he'd sent her away, perhaps more brusquely than necessary, but certainly as honor demanded. By God, she'd only been fifteen, almost sixteen, at the time. Though she'd been of legally marriageable age, she'd only been a young girl on the verge of womanhood. She hadn't been ready to make such a decision.

And although he, being the only heir to the Kerrick line, should have married before he left for war, the truth was, no matter how arrogant the supposition, Adam had never considered the possibility that he might die. So he had felt no need to hurry his wedding vows. His life was like the compartments of his desk, each drawer a task or a responsibility to be dealt with at a designated time. Marriage belonged in one of the latter compartments.

In bed next to him now, Becca began to stir, murmuring in her sleep. She rubbed against him like a contented cat, gave a wonderfully feminine purr and tipped her chin so that when her eyes opened, her dream-filled gaze met his. Without thinking, Adam smiled. "Good evening," he said.

In one tick of the clock, the blissful moment vanished. Becca crawled to her knees and leapt from the bed. Her legs tangled in her nightshift and sent her tumbling to the floor. "What were you doing?" she asked breathlessly from where she sat on her lovely derrière.

"Nothing," Adam answered innocently. He peeked at her from behind the curtains. She would probably not appreciate his earlier assessment of her breasts.

"You, on the other hand, were trying to suffocate me."

"I was hiding you. And don't you think to sleep again without some sort of explanation of where you've been, or I will wake the entire household and announce your resurrection." She stood and tied open the drapes on the bed. "Are you all right?"

His side still ached—the cracked ribs would take weeks to fully heal—but at least the stabbing pain had lessened. He had no fever and was famished, sure signs he was feeling better. His stomach grumbled.

Becca frowned. "I suppose you're hungry."

"*Moi?* I haven't eaten anything truly edible in months but, if there isn't enough, you go ahead. I am, as always, a gentleman." He laughed.

She skirted the bed, snatched the silver dinner tray from the table and deposited it on Adam's lap. Bolstered by the satin pillows, he managed to lift himself to a sitting position. He examined the clean wrapping around his wound. "Thank you."

"I couldn't very well let you bleed to death in this chamber," she explained snippishly. "I'd never be able to answer the questions people asked. And even more importantly, my father would never forgive me if I let you die."

A grin tugged at Adam's lips, but he rubbed the impulse away with his hand. Obviously she was still harboring ill feelings toward him and would likely crack the teapot on his head if he said anything more. Yet he found he couldn't stop himself. "I imagine you were yelling at me while I slept: 'What are you doing going and getting yourself hurt—and why am I supposed to fix you up?'"

"Of course I wasn't. Besides being a waste of time,

25

such behavior would be childish. In case you haven't noticed, I've matured in your absence."

"Oh, I've noticed, Becca." And he had. Most definitely. Possessed by a bit of the devil, a sudden urge to rile her, he added, "I near held that maturity in my very hands."

Her eyes rounded and her nostrils flared. His chuckle stopped the sermon she was surely about to deliver. Instead, she clenched her teeth and smiled, then offered him a cup of tea.

"Here. It's cold, but at least it's wet."

He sipped the drink and grimaced. "I see you still use cream and sugar to excess." He set the cup on the tray and swung his feet to the floor, cautiously standing to test the stability of his legs. Satisfied he'd not drop in a heap, he lumbered toward the far corner of the room.

"Where do you think you're going?"

"We are locked in this room together. I surmise that while I slept you saw to your personal needs. If I remain in bed, I shall wet myself like a tot."

"You mean . . . you plan to . . . while I'm standing here?" She scanned the four corners of the room for any possible escape. "This is absolutely unspeakable."

"If I remember correctly, you once hid in your father's lodge with an entire hunting party. I know for a fact you must have seen and heard all manner of things that night."

"That's different. I was only eight."

"Hmmm." Shrugging his shoulder, he proceeded to the garderobe. Behind him, he heard her grumble and mutter and stomp about, a tempestuous and youthful bundle of femininity still incapable of masking her emotions. When he strode back into the room, she was whistling some ribald sea chantey he'd heard her father sing once.

He scratched the beard on his face, then brushed his hair from his eyes. "You don't, by any chance, think I could have a bath?"

Facing him, Becca folded her arms beneath her breasts and gave him a fierce glare.

"I take that to be no." Adam settled himself back on the bed, leaned against the pillows and attacked the cheese on the dinner salver.

"What are you doing?" she asked.

"Give me a moment." Shoving a piece of ham into his mouth, he closed his eyes and relished the heavenly taste. He sipped the tea once, shuddering, then downed the rest anyway. Proceeding to the bread, he chewed slowly, savoring every fresh bite.

Becca stood rooted to the floor, licking her lips as she watched him eat. Adam shook his head. "Please sit down and eat, too, lest I feel like a complete cad. This is more than I can possibly eat—and twice as much as I've had in months. We can raid the pantry tonight if we need more."

"Which brings us to an important point of discussion," Becca said. She balanced on the edge of the mattress, tightening the belt of her woolen robe and reaching for a berry scone. "What are you going to do? I cannot hide you indefinitely. And, for that matter, I expect some sort of explanation."

Becca was entitled to the truth; Adam accepted that. The problem was, he knew so little himself. And he'd be damned if he'd jeopardize her life. He needed more information and time to think. He poured another cup of tea, sipped slowly and watched her over the rim of the cup. Odds were, she still possessed a stubborn streak equal to that of any mule. Partnered

27

with her innate curiosity, her spontaneity and sense of adventure, she'd likely place herself in danger in no time at all.

"Well?" she asked.

Her tongue slipped out to snare a crumb at the corner of her lips. He imagined removing the morsel of food himself, then furthering his explorations of that delightful mouth. Bloody hell. What was the matter with him? He forced his wayward thoughts from her mouth and back to the business at hand. "What made you think I was dead?"

"My father received word two months ago."

"From whom?"

"I don't know, and I refuse to answer another question unless you do the same."

"That's not a good idea."

"That's not what I meant to say. I will not—"

A sharp rapping on the bedroom door stopped her short. "Open this door immediately, young lady."

Becca's eyes widened. "Just a moment, Aunt Jeanette." She turned to Adam. "My aunt," she whispered. Gathering up the teacup and plate, she set them on the table, then glared at him. "Why are you just standing there? *Hide.*"

Chapter Three

Adam slid soundlessly from the bed. He tiptoed toward the wardrobe, stopping to grab his leather satchel.

"Where are you going?" Becca hissed. "Go back through whatever secret way you came."

"There is not enough time. I'm not sure it will open again."

"Who are you talking to?" Jeanette asked impatiently through the closed door.

"Just myself," Becca answered, scampering behind Adam, helping him to gather his worn boots and tattered shirt. She took one sniff of the stench clinging to his jacket, then ran to the window and, regardless of his astonished expression, pitched the offensive garment out. When he scowled and crawled into the room's tiny closet, she tossed his belongings into his arms and slammed the door in his face. Then she kicked the rags beneath the bed and covered the bloodied water in her pitcher with a towel. Satisfied, she skipped across the room, inhaled a deep breath, pasted a listless expression on her face and opened the door.

Her aunt hovered in the doorway, dressed in a bright yellow gown layered with row after row of lace that added bulk to her already sizable frame. Red sausage curls framed a face with cherubic dimpled cheeks and twinkling hazel eyes. "Do come in, Auntie," Becca said.

"Molly said you were ill. Why was the door locked?"

"I haven't the foggiest notion." Becca twisted the knob several times while Jeanette displayed her infamous don't-try-to-trick-me look. Her aunt was not an easy woman to fool. "Strange."

"Indeed." Jeanette pressed her hand to Becca's forehead. "You have no fever, and Cook said you ate little last night. Exactly what ails you?"

Sudden inspiration struck. The cook had taken to her bed two days earlier with a bellyache. Becca would simply imitate the symptoms. She wrapped her arms around her stomach and inched back to bed. "It's nothing to worry about."

"Hmmm." Reaching the bed first, Jeanette drew back the covers. A scrap of linen fell to the floor. She bent to retrieve it, then stood, one of Adam's bloody bandages in her hand. Her face became a portrait of understanding and compassion. "Why didn't you simply tell me, child? Your mother never mentioned that your monthlies troubled you. 'Tis nothing to be embarrassed about."

"My what?" Becca squeaked.

"Don't be shy. I *do* have two daughters of my own."

Sitting lightly on the edge of the mattress, Becca wanted to crawl beneath the covers and hide indefinitely. Surely her face was the same color as a crimson sunset. Granted, her aunt's false assumption was a gift, a logical answer to the soiled rag, but blast it, Becca would have preferred a stomachache. Nothing more, nothing less. Adam was likely having a jolly old chuckle over this. If he said one word, uttered one single syllable, she would not be responsible for her actions. She had to remove him from her chamber. And soon. Dropping her head to her chest, she moaned.

"You poor dear. I now understand completely. Why didn't you say something? Being a woman can sometimes be so difficult." Her aunt plumped the pillows behind Becca's back, her mouth running faster than a sinner from a priest. "The pains lessen after you have a child. Until then, you must tolerate a woman's pain. Before I gave birth to Trevor, I took to my bed on a regular basis. Many women see this as one of those rare times that she can refrain from her wifely duties. Hard to believe, but there are women who prefer husbands to take a mistress. Take Lady Wakesfield, the silly whit. She actually *hired* her husband's first mistress. After that, when the man handled the task without a problem, she had the audacity to whine. Served her right, in my estimation. Thank heavens Raymond was more considerate. Otherwise, I'd have had to shoot him. Nevertheless—"

"Aunt Jeanette, please. I have a headache."

Her aunt's smiling face became pouty. "I was only trying to help. It will not be long before such information matters to you. After all, you are going to London to find a husband. The marital bed can be

31

frightening, but you've only to ask, and I shall explain everything in great detail."

Sweet Shakespeare! However had the discussion gone from a woman's monthlies to the marriage bed? Her aunt was being her usual talkative self and couldn't be blamed. And her behavior did stem from concern. Still, the last thing Becca wanted to hear at that moment was this particular lesson, especially since Adam hid only a few feet away, among her gowns, her shifts and her nightclothes, with his ear likely pressed to the door listening to every humiliating word. "I appreciate your kindness, Auntie, truly. I simply wish to rest."

"Shall I read to you?"

"No, thank you."

"Shall we play poker?"

"Not tonight."

Halfway to the door, Jeanette asked, "Shall I check on you before I go to bed?"

Becca yawned. "I intend to go right to sleep."

The bedroom door finally closed and the sound of the woman's pattering feet drifted away. Becca bolted the lock, stomped to the wardrobe and yanked open the door.

As Adam crawled from the cramped space, he knocked his head. A fitting punishment, thought Becca, for his causing her to suffer the mortification of the last few minutes. With a scowl meant to quell any pithy remarks he might make, she fisted her hands on her hips. "Do you now understand why you cannot stay here?"

"Yes, indeed. Your presence does complicate matters."

"*My* presence?" The beast. The censure in his voice

made it clear that he thought this mess was all her fault.

"Yes, your presence. It was unexpected. Someone watched the estate for a full week. Other than Weathers and two other servants, the castle was vacant." He dragged his hand through his hair. "Exactly how many people are here?"

Only because he suddenly sounded so weary and had not mentioned Aunt Jeanette's little visit, she answered. "I only arrived three days ago. My maid, my aunt, the new cook, your old butler, the groom and stable boy and ten other servants are also in residence." She gave him a meaningful look. "You sound awful. Come back to bed."

Crossing to the window, he braced one arm overhead and stared into the early evening sky. Golden streaks mixed with shades of red and purple burned across the horizon. "I'd forgotten how beautiful the view was, how much I loved this place. There was many a day I thought never to see it again. Where are my clothes?"

"In the attic." She couldn't remember a time when she'd heard such melancholy in his voice. He had been always so bloody self-assured, a veritable statue of strength who relied solely on his own abilities, almost too much so. Knowing pity was the last thing he'd want, Becca ordered, "I shall be furious if I need to re-stitch your side."

He turned to her. Pain, frustration and perhaps even regret shone in his eyes before he masked his emotions. "What are people saying about me, Becca?"

She paused before answering. "That you are the Leopard, a spy for the French . . . that you sold your soul to Napoleon for money or power. You disappeared before Waterloo, and because of that over half your company of soldiers was killed on their last mission. I even heard one person say you had married a female spy and were living in Italy. One night I heard you owned an entire island in the West Indies."

Other than a slight tick in his left cheek, Adam's face gave Becca no sign if any of the rumors were true. Looking intently at him, she saw a flare of fury ignite in his eyes. She tried to reassure him. "For what it is worth, Father believes everything to be malicious rumors spread by idiots. But he has talked with people in the War Department several times. They say the evidence is irrefutable."

"And you? Do you think I'm guilty of treason?"

"Don't be a bigger idiot than those spreading the rumors. You are incapable of betraying your precious king and country. You could never sell England's secrets. You're too bloody honorable. I, of all people, should know."

"Becca . . ." His voice held a note of apology.

She raised her hand. "This is not the time to discuss the foolish ranting of a young girl fresh from the nursery who thought herself in love."

"I never said you were foolish."

"You didn't have to. But never fear: I am well over my childish infatuation. That said, you obviously need my help. Yet I will not lift a finger unless you tell me where you have been and what you have been doing. I believe I am entitled to that much."

Pacing the room, Adam touched various objects as if he were reacquainting himself with his previous life. "For some unknown reason, I was smashed on the head and carted off to a nasty makeshift prison housing a dozen or so other fellows, mostly French.

They could tell me nothing. After a month or so, I heard a rumor that Napoleon had abdicated, yet still I was not freed. Days became weeks, weeks became months. God, I thought I'd die from boredom and frustration."

"Were they horribly cruel to you?"

"Other than an occasional beating due to some impertinence of mine, my keepers pretty much left me alone. Until six weeks ago, and I decided the sudden attention I was getting did not bode well. I took advantage of the growing and obvious chaos and confusion amongst the jailers: I traded identities with a dead man and as he was buried I walked out the door as a French peasant."

"Is that when you were injured?"

"No. I owe my cracked ribs to a sailor in Cherbourg who objected to my borrowing his purse."

"Stealing? *You?*"

"Do you want to hear the details or not?" When she placed a single finger to her lips, he continued. "I had no money and wasn't sure whom I could trust. I finally reached the coast, sent a message to a friend and with his help made my way here, thinking to heal my wounds in the solitude of my own home. I intend to find out who and why. You being at Kerrick is an unexpected complication."

His blatant displeasure at her presence cut her to the quick. "Pardon me for fouling up your plans," she said, trying to sound lighthearted, but it came out petulant.

His strong fingers gripped her chin, tipped her head. "I'm not displeased to see you, Becca. I merely wish the circumstances were different. If I'm going to clear my name, I must have access to this castle. And I need to discover a way to move about London without notice. Now I must worry about keeping you safe as well." He yawned, a huge, bearlike grumble.

"I am not a defenseless mutton head. I can help."

"No doubt," he said dryly. "Allow me a night to think. I'll find a logical solution, but I need time."

Veering toward the bed, he opened the velvet panels nearest the fireplace. Becca stood rooted to the floor, her mouth gaping. Was he planning on sleeping in the same bed as she? He answered her with an amused look that sent shivers tripping down to her toes. "Are you going to try and smother me again?"

More disturbed than she cared to let him know, she adopted a prim tone. "I think not. With the use of the ottoman, I will be most comfortable sleeping in the chair by the fireplace."

His expression grew serious. "In a chair? Come now, Becca. I can't stomach the thought of you sleeping there. I would never dishonor you."

"As if I'd let you. And don't think for a moment that you have answered all my questions. I will allow you to sleep, though." Admonishing herself for the fluttering in her stomach caused by the intensity of his eyes, Becca gave an elegant snort, grabbed a blanket and two pillows and settled herself in the soft leather chair by the hearth. Closing her eyes, she listened to the rustling of the covers, the creaking of the wood and the heavy sigh that escaped Adam's lips. She pictured him sprawled on the bed, one arm thrown over his head, his bare chest rising and falling with every breath. The urge she felt to go to him shocked her.

She was lonely. That was all. Once she returned to her parents in London, all these irrational, ridiculous impulses regarding Adam Hawksmore would dissipate like early-morning fog.

"By the way, Becca," Adam's laughing voice drifted into her ears. "I do hope you're feeling better. If and when you're ready, as an old friend, I'll be more than happy to offer *my* advice about the marriage bed."

Her pillow sailed from her hands before she even realized she'd thrown it, bouncing off the drapes around the bed. His rumbling laugh echoed out. "By the stars, Becca, it is good to be home."

"Adam, why would someone do this to you? It simply makes no sense at all."

"The Leopard was a spy for the French. There were rumors that he was about to be exposed. Since I have been accused of being him, I surmise someone wanted to shift suspicion from himself to me. I happened to be in the wrong place at the wrong time."

Entirely enclosed within the velvet draperies of the bed, a small brass lamp her only light, Becca concentrated on Adam's answer. She tried her best to ignore the fact that he sat in a tub of hot water a mere five feet away, naked, scrubbing with her lilac-scented soap those glorious muscles she'd caressed the day before. It was simply too much. She stared at the abandoned embroidery in her lap, the outline of the small yellow butterfly no more defined than it was a half-hour ago. "But you must have an idea of who?"

"I've a theory or two."

Getting Adam to tell her anything was like prying open a clam with her bare hands. She'd been trying to get the whole story for the last thirty minutes and, having received only half answers, she was still confused. "And?" she prompted.

"I need more facts. Ahhh, Becca," he murmured. "You are a miracle worker. This bath feels heavenly."

"Flattery will not redirect my train of thought. I want to know all of what happened. Elsewise, how can I help you? Three days before you were going to face Napoleon at Waterloo, you went to visit an acquaintance—I shan't ask whom, though I can only imagine—at a small inn. Right?"

Adam sighed heavily, then groaned what she surmised was a yes.

"There you encountered two friends."

"Not exactly friends. I knew Lord Seavers at Oxford. We bought our commissions in the army about the same time and served in the same regiment. Lord Oswin was more of an acquaintance. Since he worked with the ambassadors, I had only heard of and never seen him. Until that night."

"So you have deduced that one of these two men are responsible for kidnapping you? Why?"

"As Napoleon was pressing toward Brussels for a final assault against us, the duchess of Richmond hosted one final soiree for the officers and the upper crust of society. Even Wellington would be there. I was planning to attend, but at the last minute I changed my mind. Returning to my lodging, I saw Seavers at the Red Goose Inn. He said he'd taken a few days' leave, and at the time I had no reason to think he was lying.

"Then I saw Oswin, and his behavior seemed most odd. He never really explained why he wasn't at Lady Richmond's ball. He was as surprised to see me as I was to see him, and he was downright rude. Like Seavers, he was meeting a woman."

"There seemed to be a lot of that going on," Becca snapped, somehow sure that Adam, too, had gone to meet a woman, and wondering why she cared. He was certainly free to do as he pleased. "I still don't see why you think one of these two men abducted you."

"Because it is the most reasonable conclusion I can muster. They were the only two men I talked with that night, other than my companion; I knew no one else at that inn. And the man I met there—my companion in arms and friend—is now dead. I must assume he was killed to help set me up. After all, I stepped out for a breath of fresh air, was knocked out cold, and awoke imprisoned the very next day. Now, nine months later, I'm accused of being a traitor!"

A lengthy silence descended as Becca considered all Adam had revealed. Outside, water sloshed and dripped. Becca pictured Adam dipping low in the copper tub to rinse the soap from his body. She squeezed her eyelids shut, in hopes the action might erase the unbidden image in her mind: Adam rising from the suds much like Neptune rising from the sea, magnificent and powerful, water sluicing down his bare chest. The small, confining area in which she sat suddenly seemed unbearably warm.

Quickly, she opened her eyes. She should never have taken pity on the man this morning. But having a bath had seemed such a harmless request since she often bathed in the morning herself. And the stench on his body and clothes had been quite dreadful. But now? Goodness, she was beginning to have heart palpitations. This was dangerous for other reasons than she'd expected.

"You really must hurry," she said. "We assumed a great risk asking for that tub of water. If you hadn't smelled so horribly, well . . . Aunt Jeanette expects me downstairs shortly."

"I'm almost finished." His subsequent groan of delight, much like Becca's own when she immersed herself in a tub full of bubbles, echoed through the chamber. Her heart seemed to flip three or four times, which amazed and irritated her all the more. "Have you thought of a plan yet?" she asked. She waited for him to elaborate, but when she realized he wasn't going to, she offered, "I have one."

Deathly annoying silence.

She guessed that if she could see him, his face would bear a patronizing expression conveying skepticism. *Men*. Why was it so difficult for them to believe women were capable of more than embroidery, serving tea and bearing children? She yanked a loose thread from the hem of her day gown. "Unless you have a plan, at least listen to what I have to say."

"All right," he answered hesitantly.

"I thought about this much of the night. You could play the part of a poet, traveling in the area and set upon by brigands." Her enthusiasm grew when he did not stop her right away. "Francis Cobbald shall be your name. Injured, and seeking sanctuary, you shall appear on our doorstep. I, being the generous soul that I am, shall allow you to stay."

"What twaddle. I am capable of playing at many things, but poetry? I'm not a man of words, but a soldier better suited to the sword, to devising tactical plans and strategies."

She crawled closer to the curtains, prepared to argue, but as the heavy drape parted, the retort on the tip of her tongue slipped down her throat and lodged in her chest.

Wrapped in the pink robe she'd given him, his legs

bare beneath its white ruffled hem, stood Adam—a large oak tree dressed in a fancy slipcover. Becca's lips twitched.

Wagging a finger in her face, he said, "Say one word and I swear, I'll wear nothing but a towel in short order."

The memory of his bare chest, stomach and narrow hips popped into her mind, causing her cheeks to heat. She doubted he'd actually resort to such despicable behavior but, unwilling to test her theory, she snapped her mouth shut and waited.

There was something about the way he stood, an innate confidence bordering on arrogance, a suppressed power and something else she couldn't quite name, that touched her soul. He certainly was a man comfortable with himself no matter the circumstance, one accustomed to being in charge.

The muscles of Adam's back rippled beneath the stretched satin robe as he dragged a chair to the sunny spot beneath the window to sit. Becca tried to force her eyes to his but couldn't help them straying to his bare knees and calves. His legs were dotted with ebony hairs, matching those on his chest. For some absurd reason, Becca found herself thinking of her favorite dessert: candied almonds, glazed to a delicious golden brown. That was when Adam cleared his throat.

Mercy. Had she been staring? Most definitely, she had been. But she wouldn't apologize for her curiosity. Aside from those of her father and the stable boy, she'd never seen a man's bare leg. Of course she was intrigued.

Focusing on a seagull soaring outside the window, she pretended nothing had happened. "But the guise of a poet is perfect. No one would ever expect it of you, and according to an acquaintance of mine, there is a new star among the poets who—along with his companion—are staying in the village. His name is Percy Bysshe Shelley. You can say you came to sing his praises. Perhaps we shall even invite the man to tea. This way you can recover here at the castle and you shall have access to everything you need. If we hurry in our plans, you—Francis Cobbald—can arrive this afternoon in time for tea."

"Let's not be hasty," Adam said, looking skeptical.

"Pardon my saying, but we do not have an endless amount of time at our disposal. . . . Well?" Becca asked defensively. "You think you can come up with a better solution?"

"My experience in such matters does outweigh yours."

"Because you're a man?"

Massaging his right temple, he said in a somewhat beleaguered fashion, "Because I'm a soldier."

Becca clasped her hands in her lap. "All right, then, Captain. Since you are such a master tactician, tell me *your* idea. One that removes you from my bedchamber, gives you anonymity, a reason to be at Kerrick Castle in the first place and a suitable disguise for London."

Chapter Four

"Certainly." Adam paced back and forth before the window, his hands behind his back, trying his damnedest to maintain a facade of cool dignity, a difficult task considering he wore a woman's robe. And not just any robe, but a ridiculously feminine garment with embroidered flowers, no less. And lace. Becca's delicate scent clung to the fabric and enveloped his body like a perfumed cloud. She'd given him this feminine garment, and now she planned to make him a poet? What rubbish!

He, better than anyone, knew he needed a plan. He had laid in bed much of the night trying to find a plausible excuse for his sudden appearance at Kerrick Castle, but he'd spent more time listening to Becca make delightful mewling noises while she slept. Twice, he'd left his bed to watch her sleep, propped uncomfortably in his chair. The oddest desire to hold her in his arms, to coddle and protect her, had warred with his good sense.

Surely the reaction was the result of gratitude for the proclamation of love she had made before he left England. While in France, he'd spent many a cold, lonely night cherishing that memory.

It was ironic: he'd refused to marry Becca so long ago because she was too young and he himself hadn't known whether or not he'd have a future. Now, here he was again, in much the same position. But this time she was a grown woman, and now that he was attracted to her, he had even less to offer.

Circling the room, he forced his thoughts back to the problem at hand. *Thunder and turf.* Him, a poet? One of those sniveling fops who spouted philosophy and reform but was rarely man enough to take any action? Someone who wrote odes to bumblebees, sonnets to the moon, epics to dead people and verse after verse about love, spinning idyllic dreams for young girls and old maids to cling to? Adam preferred books on the great military battles in history, a study of Genghis Khan or "Black Dick," Francis Hastings, or any great men of strategy—those works were reading of substance and merit.

Becca was right about one thing—people would never suspect the Earl of Kerrick of such flummery.

Fingering a black marble egg on the mantel by the fire, he considered the difficulties before him. Becca's presence was an obstacle he had to overcome, one way or another. She had never listened and rarely obeyed rules. And she was distracting, something he couldn't afford at the moment. Yet, she was already here and unwilling to be dismissed.

The egg wobbled from side to side as it slid from his fingers. Why the devil hadn't Becca stayed home?

He crossed to the bed. "Explain this one more time. Why are you here?"

"Good grief. Father sent me here to ready the house for the new owner—be it the king, your cousin or heaven knows whom."

"Why *you?*"

"My father felt I was the appropriate person. Does the reason matter?"

"I suppose not." He paced again, pondering the answer she'd given him three times already. For some reason, something about her story—maybe it was the manner in which she spoke—struck him as odd. She wasn't telling him everything. He'd stake his life on it.

"Well," she prodded, "what do you think of my plan? It doesn't sound like you've come up with anything better."

He hated to admit it, but she was right. Her scheme might work. Weathers, his old butler, would have to be included. After all, he had practically raised Adam from a pup and nothing could fool him. He was a sly old dog, one Adam could count on to the bitter end. If they could create a convincing disguise for him, Becca's plan would grant him everything he needed. The specifics for the trip to London could be decided later. He sighed. "Your idea has merit."

"I know I am a *mere* woman, but—" Her mouth fell slack. "It does?"

"In a general manner of speaking. There are details that must be worked out, such as my appearance."

Scrambling from the bed, she withdrew a small jar from her pocket. "I have the perfect solution for that! With your hair as long as it is and with your beard, no one will recognize you. We can dye both red."

Staring at him, Becca nibbled on her lower lip in

a provocative manner that had him thinking thoughts far from hair dye and disguises. He tightened the belt about his waist.

"I suppose we could give you a potbelly like Sir Humphreys, or perhaps a scar?"

With a baleful expression, he asked, "And how am I to get that? Slit my own throat while I'm shaving?"

"Don't be silly." She smiled wickedly. "I'd be more than happy to see to the task. Do you trust Weathers?"

"With my life."

"I thought so. I'll be right back. Lock the door."

In her excitement, she practically ran for the bedroom door. "Becca," he ordered as forcefully as possible, considering he had to whisper. "Sit down."

She froze, tipped her chin in the air, then waltzed back to the chair by the fire to plop down in an obvious snit. Adam watched, annoyed. If she was angry, it was too damn bad. He would make the decisions, give the orders, and she would obey. Assuming the tone of authority he often used with his soldiers, he said, "I expect you to listen carefully. What we embark on is not a day of shopping on Bond Street. This will be dangerous. I need you to promise a few things. First off, once Weathers is involved, if anything should happen, I expect you to deny any knowledge of who I really am."

"I see no problem. Right now I wish I'd never met that person."

He knew she muttered more to herself than to him. She hated orders, always found a way to go against them if they didn't suit her fancy. But this time, the stakes of the game were too high. She needed to learn to follow instructions, and she needed to exercise caution.

Clearing his throat, he added, "Never use my real name unless we are completely alone. Do not question people in this household regarding my affairs. *I* shall ask the questions I want answered. Remember, you and Francis Cobbald are complete strangers and it is crucial you always act accordingly lest we alert someone to the truth. We have no idea if anyone is watching the estate. Once I arrive, you will keep me informed as to your whereabouts at all times. . . ."

He continued instructing her for another five minutes until he was satisfied that she understood who was in charge.

"Are you finished?" she asked sweetly when he fell silent.

"Yes."

"I have something to say." Pushing herself up from the chair, she tossed her braid over her shoulder and glared at him. "Go ahead and lecture me if you think it's necessary. But whether you wish it or not, you need my help. You won't be able to ignore or avoid me, nor will I bow to your every edict. *I* expect to be kept informed of your every movement, too. I am not just a pawn in this game. Much has changed since you left three years ago."

She rose majestically and sailed to the door, her shoulders squared. Pausing a moment, her hand on the doorknob, she added, "And do not presume that I am the same lovestruck girl who would before have allowed you to rule her life without question. As I said, much has changed."

Before he could utter another word, he was facing a slammed door that shimmied on its hinges. Bloody hell, what had he done? He had just formed an alliance with a tempestuous, headstrong vixen. One who was certain to open up a whole new world of danger for him.

As Becca descended the winding staircase in search of Weathers, the painted faces of Adam's ancestors loomed beside her on the pale gold wall, listening silently to her complaints.

"How dare he sail back into my life and issue orders as if he were my commanding officer, my superior, my husband or even my father?" Becca snorted in a most unladylike way, one that always earned her a maternal lecture on proper manners. Well, her mother wasn't here.

"The brass-faced bully," she muttered to the white-haired man hoisting a sword in the air in a nearby painting. "He abandoned all rights to order me about three years ago when he refused my undying devotion and my virginity."

Even after all this time, the shame and humiliation she'd felt still chilled her blood. She'd been such a fool, declaring herself like that. The saving grace in the entire debacle was that Adam had left the country the morning after.

She stole three more steps and stared at a portrait of a man so identical to Adam, she imagined it must be his father.

"Thank goodness I came to my senses," she said to herself.

In Adam's absence, two events had changed her way of thinking. First, she'd watched her three best friends marry, and the three young women she'd known, whom had all shared dreams of white knights and adventure and craved love and excitement, had vanished like wisps of smoke, replaced by meek, obedient mice. They seemed to forget that they were capable of intelligent thought. Worst of all, when Millicent's husband, Lord Graves, determined that Becca was a negative influence on his new wife, the lifelong friendship had ended with a polite note.

Secondly, Becca had discovered the writings of Mary Wollstonecraft. Mary, too, believed that women were capable of intelligent thought and had been severely limited by men's prejudice.

Proceeding another few steps, Becca halted before the painting of a red-haired beauty with sapphire eyes like Adam's. Maybe this woman could understand Becca's dilemma. "Had I married Adam, my life would have been much the same as my friends'. He simply doesn't possess an egalitarian bone in his body. He's a tyrant, autocratic and dictatorial, with a rule for everything."

As an afterthought, in case the woman in the picture disapproved of her ramblings, Becca added amicably, "Don't misunderstand me. I like Adam. He's intelligent, certainly handsome, and when he's not offering a lecture or brooding, he can be charming. I even enjoy his company. I simply refuse to become any man's tenant for life. I might as well become a cocker spaniel." She moved on.

The woman in the next painting had such a severe countenance that Becca wondered if she had ever laughed in her entire life. Which reminded Becca of Adam's problem. "Granted, it is his life, his future, hanging in the balance, but I have ideas too. Good ones. He misjudges me horribly if he thinks I will sit idly by, simply because there might be some danger."

Lost in her musings, she practically toppled poor Weathers as he climbed the stairs. A stack of papers on the silver salver he held tumbled to the floor.

"Dear me, Weathers. Are you all right?"

Nodding, he pushed his wire glasses back on his nose and bent to retrieve the daily post. Becca dropped to her knees as well and tugged on the red collar of his perfectly pressed livery. He raised his bald head, which gleamed like the brightly polished buttons on his jacket.

"I must speak with you," she whispered, glancing over her shoulder.

He gazed down the hallway as she had done, then looked back to her. His brown eyes filled with questions and his broad forehead furrowed with wrinkles. "Yes, miss."

"Can you keep a secret?"

Nodding once again, he rose to his full height of five-foot-two and extended his arm. She clasped his slender hand, wrinkled from age, and guided him toward her bedroom. There, rapping on the door three times, feeling quite mysterious, she enjoyed the sensation immensely. When Adam failed to answer, she pressed her mouth to the door and whispered, "Open the door. It's me."

If Weathers found her behavior odd, which he most likely did, he kept his opinion to himself. As the lock clicked and the knob turned, he did, however, expectantly watch the door. She shoved him inside.

Adam stood to the side of one chair with his feet braced apart and his hands laced behind his back. Dressed in Becca's pink velvet rode, he still managed to appear in total command.

Weathers stood immobile, his face a frozen mask of disbelief. "Master Adam?"

If Becca ever doubted the wisdom of including Weathers in this plan, or the man's loyalty, her reservations vanished with the one solitary tear that slid down the butler's cheek.

Weathers, always stoic and mindful of his position, gathered his wits and straightened his spine. "If I may say, my lord, it is time you returned home."

Grinning like a beggar with a new copper penny, Adam said, "I quite agree. I've missed you, too."

"And you are abysmally thin," the butler complained.

Crossing to him, Adam vigorously slapped Weathers on the back. "A problem I hope to correct under your expert supervision. But first there are things to discuss."

Adam moved to the fireplace and leaned one elbow on the mantel. There he calmly explained where he'd been, how he'd arrived and the plan for him to play a traveling poet.

Weathers remained rooted to the bedroom floor, a stunned expression on his face. Every now and then his lips twitched as if he might smile—a grand feat since like Adam, Weathers rarely smiled—but then the butler would catch himself.

Becca sat in the same chair she'd slept in, watching, listening and waiting expectantly for either man to include her. The least they could do was credit her with such a brilliant idea in the first place. At last, when they even started to discuss Adam's wardrobe without consulting her, she cleared her throat.

Adam kept talking. "We shall worry about the rest of my apparel later, but I need clothes for today, an outfit a poet might wear. Can you fetch something from the attic?"

"A minor task, my lord. With a few adjustments to some clothes left by your cousin during his last visit, they should be just the thing. Cecil even left a cane. That might prove a handy accessory."

"Good. After I dress I'll take the secret stairway

51

down to the beach. I can climb the cliffs and circle around through the woods to the north. Shouldn't take me long."

"How do you plan to climb the cliffs?" Becca asked, feeling more and more uninvolved and not liking it one bit. "Have you forgotten your stitches?"

"There is a hidden, fairly accessible path a mile down the beach," Adam explained. "I'll be careful."

"Why not use the servants' stairs? You could sneak out through the kitchen and move back around to the front."

"We best take no risk of being seen. The path will take no time at all."

As Adam then went onto detail his arrival at Kerrick Castle, Becca drummed her fingers on the arm of the chair. She tapped her right toe in agitation.

"If I might make a suggestion, my lord," Weathers said, "you should likely alter the manner in which you walk and talk. A bit of a swish, perhaps. Like Lord Everly. He also has that annoying habit of blinking his eyes. Or you could slouch."

Grinning, Adam said, "I remember. Very good, Weathers."

"And metaphors, my lord. I should think they might be useful. Some sort of flowery, nonsensical way of speaking."

"That shall take a bit of work, but I suppose the effort would be beneficial. Now, about my disguise . . ."

"*Excuse me.*" Becca spoke more sharply than she intended. "I might have an idea or two."

Adam raised a solitary brow in a silent question. Weathers looked appalled by the suggestion. She ignored them both. "What of your luggage?"

"It will have been stolen by the thieves."

"And just how will you explain that your injury is already stitched?"

"Weathers will be the only one allowed to tend to me. He'll lie."

Adam seemed to possess all the answers, making Becca feel useless and unappreciated. It was ridiculous, she knew; nevertheless, it was how she felt. Surely there was some significant detail they hadn't considered.

Crossing to her side, Adam clasped her hand in his. His expression softened as he spoke. "Becca, I am not discounting your assistance. You have been a tremendous help. But now Weathers must see to my needs. I depend on you to help me downstairs."

Drat the man for understanding. He'd always possessed the uncanny ability to know how she felt before she herself did. And blast him for making her think he cared about those feelings. With every ounce of dignity she possessed, she removed herself from her chair. "It is obvious that you do not need or want me here at the moment. I will make myself useful and find Aunt Jeannette before she decides to visit again."

"That's a very good idea."

She tipped her chin. "No last-minute rules on my behavior?"

The corner of his lips pulled slightly upward into what she feared might become a grin. He reconsidered when she scowled. Instead he said simply, "I trust you."

She ignored the swell of pride those three words caused. The man was simply trying to appease her injured sensibilities. "Hmph. Until we meet again, Mr. Cobbald."

Chapter Five

Sunlight from a rare bright day streamed through the lace curtains. Becca used that as her excuse to perch on the window seat and peer outside every five minutes, wondering all the while where Adam was. She'd left her room three hours before, and Weathers, too, had emerged, but Adam had yet to make his appearance. *No time at all, the man had said. Hah! Careful? Indeed.* The stubborn man was probably lying in some ditch, bleeding to death. He had ten minutes to appear at the door or she was going after him. Shifting her legs beneath her gown, she pressed her nose to the glass.

Aunt Jeanette closed the book on her lap with a thud. "By the swells, your fidgeting is driving me to distraction. Come play cards or something. Are you sure you're feeling all right? You've been acting strangely all afternoon."

Becca blew the curls from her forehead with an expansive sigh. Reluctantly joining her aunt at a small mahogany table, she fingered the deck of cards. "I'm merely bored."

"In that case, ruminate over the actions that secured your presence here in the first place. Write your father a letter. Perhaps he'll let us come home."

Not bloody likely, Becca thought. This time her father was so furious with her that even her mother, who usually managed to sway her father's mind, had been unable to calm him. Thankfully, Becca would travel to London soon. Until then, time would pass quickly enough.

Especially with Adam here.

The cards slipped from her fingers and scattered on the table. Why the deuce had she thought of something as ridiculous as that? Sheer unequivocal boredom was, had to be, could only be, the logical reason for such an irrational thought. Surely she didn't harbor any lingering affection for Adam Hawksmore.

Granted, he had been the first man she ever loved. . . . Thought she loved, she amended quickly. And he had been the first man to ever kiss her. It was unsurprising that her heart carried a tender memory of the way he'd held her, as if she were a priceless heirloom; the way his mouth, those delightful lips, had melded with hers. Even though the kiss had ended as quickly as it had begun, it had haunted her for days, weeks, months. But if she now was experiencing a bit of excitement over his return, surely it was because she considered him a friend, or a member of the family. They'd spent holidays together, for goodness sakes.

Before she drove herself crazy with her own private debate, a commotion in the foyer had her leaping from her chair. She immediately sat back down and waited for Weathers to make his announcement.

She didn't wait but five seconds. The butler appeared in the doorway, a perfectly blank expression pasted on his face.

"Excuse me, miss. We have a visitor. A Francis Cobbald. He wishes to speak with you."

Becca repeated the name out loud several times as though searching her memory for any familiarity. Shrugging her shoulders, she glanced at Jeanette. "What do you say, Auntie? Are we at home?"

"Might as well be," the older woman muttered. "Perhaps this fellow can offer the distraction you seem to desperately need."

Clearing her throat and her mind, Becca said, "Show him in, Weathers."

Wearing a pained expression and a hideous puce-colored jacket with lace cuffs, Adam hobbled into the salon, leaning heavily on a brass-handled cane. He wore a ridiculously tied cravat as well, which made Becca marvel that he could even breathe. The rest of the clothes, which hung loosely due to his loss of weight, were mussed and torn. His beard had been neatly trimmed. A long white streak was painted in his hair, which fell unbound to his shoulders. A black patch covered his left eye, which she admitted was a stroke of genius. The patch, coupled with the hair coloring, added an air of distinction and mystery. Odd, but her gaze strayed directly to his mouth of all things. She shook her head to clear her mind.

"Good afternoon, sir," Becca said, most formally.

"Pardon the intrusion, ladies." Facing the two women who now controlled his home, Adam exe-

cuted a bow as Weathers had instructed with what
he hoped was a sufficient flourish of his wrist. "I fear
I was assaulted by brigands and seek a brief respite,
a safe haven in which to regain my equilibrium and
calm my nerves." He shuddered, rapidly blinking his
eyes. "A nastier gathering of wastrels have I ever
seen. Vicious, brutish men, with absolutely no re-
deeming qualities."

"Thieves? Here?" Becca's aunt clasped her hand to
her ample breast. "What is this world coming to? Are
you wounded?"

Dabbing his brow with a linen handkerchief, he
heaved an enormous sigh. "Only my pride, my dear
lady."

"Need we summon the doctor?" asked Becca, her
expression more of a frown now than the compassion he'd first witnessed. What had he done? He'd
barely arrived and she was scowling at him.

No, he didn't need the doctor, but he actually
looked forward to crawling back into bed. As Becca
had predicted, he had torn a stitch or two during the
climb. Nevertheless he needed this opportunity to as-
certain the difficulties, if any, that Becca's relative
might present.

The woman's hair was flame red and set into an
elaborate stack of curls on the top of her head. Her
cheeks were full with a rosy tint. Judging from her
waistline, she enjoyed all her meals. Watching her eat
a berry scone like a mouse nibbling on a piece of
cheese, Adam doubted she'd be a problem.

He glanced toward the chaise with longing. "If
only I could rest my weary bones. The ordeal was so
terribly unsettling."

"If you're certain you don't need a doctor . . ."
Jeanette said. Her voice was full of compassion. "Do

sit down. As you can see, we've just started tea."

"You are too kind. But then, I knew the moment I saw you that you possessed a heart of gold, brighter than the burning sun. You have the face of an angel, my lady."

The words were difficult for him to spit out, but they were effective. Jeanette guffawed like a tavern maid while Adam crossed the room, half limping, half gliding. The limp came quite naturally, since he'd twisted his ankle climbing up the blasted cliff. He was more thankful than ever now for the cane. The climb had been more of a strain than he imagined, but he'd succeeded despite his fall. That alone made him less angry at his misstep.

Easing his body into his favorite chair, Adam refrained from stroking its dark, smooth surface. "Does a woman as lovely as you have a name?" he asked Becca's aunt.

Laughing again, her nose twitching like a rabbit's, Jeanette answered, "Thacker. And this is my niece, Lady Rebecca Marche."

Adam returned Becca's nod with one of his own, then blinked and sighed for effect. Her eyes, now twinkling with humor, widened as he gently tugged on the lace at his wrists. "This house was a gift from the Gods, a balm to soothe my worried soul. I feared I'd perish in the wilderness," he admitted.

Jeanette poured tea into the cup Weathers had promptly delivered. "Whatever happened?"

"It was horrible." Adam crossed his legs at the ankles, placed one hand on his knee, and waved the handkerchief in the air with the other. If anyone from his company saw him at the moment, they'd laugh him right out of the military. Nevertheless, the disguise seemed to be working. He remembered

Weathers's suggestion on metaphors. He should probably make a few to cement his identity. "Like big black—" He paused and thought. Big black what?

"Crows, perhaps," Becca finished.

He grinned. Perhaps this wouldn't be so difficult after all. "Precisely. Big black crows, swooping down to invade and attack like the vultures that feed on the rotting, putrid flesh of the battlefield. Buzzards—"

Becca cleared her throat.

Adam noted, better late than never, that Lady Thacker's mouth hung open. The bit about the rotting flesh had been likely more descriptive than necessary, even for a woman he personally knew to have picked the pockets of many rich fools who dared the London docks and sailed the seas with her brother and his crew. "Pardon me, ladies," he apologized. "Nevertheless, the thieves stole everything. My purse, my horse, even my bags." He sighed. "Simply horrible. I only just managed to persuade then to let me live."

"Dreadful," Jeanette said. "We must inform the sheriff, for all the good it will do. Not much happens in Lynmouth that warrants his attention, but according to the servants the man spends most of his time in the local tavern. Do you live nearby?"

Adam accepted the cup from Weathers, who hovered close at hand. His servant had likely seen the fresh blood on his coat and wasn't leaving his side. Sipping the tea, he studied the older woman. "No, madam. I hail from up north, the Lake District."

"You are a long way from home, young man."

"Indeed I am. I traveled all this way to visit Master Shelley, the poet, in hopes of meeting the man before he left for Switzerland."

"Dear me." Jeanette cast a glance toward Becca. "Another poet."

"I beg your pardon?" Adam asked, wondering what she meant.

"Never mind," Becca added a bit too quickly.

Pasting a smile on his face, he speculated on the morsel of information. It was too tempting to ignore. What was Becca hiding? "Do you write poetry yourself, my lady?"

"I've dabbled."

"Perhaps you would be willing to share your poems with me."

"Only if you are willing to share yours."

Challenge shone in her eyes. A spot of color highlighted her cheeks. She clearly felt uncomfortable, which made Adam all the more curious. Unfortunately, the longer he sat, the more the pain in his side grew, and he really didn't have the energy to concentrate on churning out anymore flowery language or—heaven forbid—metaphors. It was time to move onward. " 'Twould be an interesting exchange, I am sure. Perhaps another time. The sugar, please." Standing with his arm extended, he purposely swayed a bit and dabbed his forehead.

Becca gasped. "You're bleeding."

"By the moon and the stars, I am," Adam admitted.

"Weathers," Jeanette cried, her voice filled with alarm. "Send for the doctor."

The butler immediately moved to Adam's side. "Perhaps, madam, I should see to his wounds first, then decide if the doctor should be summoned."

Jeanette hesitated as she considered the suggestion. "I suppose. It's true that there are plenty of rooms here in which he might recuperate."

"We could use the blue chamber, Auntie." Becca

leaned closer to her aunt so that Adam barely heard her whisper, "I doubt he has any money left."

"Very well," Jeanette agreed. "I see little harm in his staying."

"A saint and an angel," Adam praised, only slightly annoyed that he had to connive to gain admittance to his own estate.

Jeanette waved her hand in the air. "You are a scamp, Mr. Cobbald. Can you make it up the stairs?"

"I believe so."

Leaning on Weathers, Adam climbed the stairs to the upper level. Jeanette followed at his heels, mumbling. Becca raced before them, tossing an I-told-you-so glare over her shoulder. He imagined she'd express her opinion about his freshly garnered injuries the moment they were alone. Molly was summoned and rags and hot water were brought, while Becca hovered beside the bed with her arms crossed, clearly planning to stay. Her aunt had other ideas.

"Come along, Becca. Let Weathers tend to the gentleman."

"What if they need something?"

"Weathers will let us know. This is no place for a young lady." Jeanette was already halfway to the door. "Until tomorrow Mr. Cobbald. I imagine that you could use a rest, so I will have dinner brought up. We will see you when you are feeling rested. Perhaps then you can share a bit of your poetry with us."

Good lord, Adam thought. He hoped not. Pasting a smile on his face, he blinked his eyes at them one last time for good measure. "Splendid. I look forward to such a time."

Reluctantly following her aunt, Becca suddenly grinned. "One of your poems? Now that, sir, is some-

61

thing even I shall find pleasure in hearing."

The instant the door slammed, Adam frowned. He rested his hands behind his head. "Weathers, my man, it appears I am home. Again. Now, how the devil am I to write a bloody poem?"

Chapter Six

After a fitful night, Becca descended the staircase toward the breakfast room. This morning, rather than converse with paintings of Adam's ancestors, she kept her mouth closed. She could never reveal the past few nights' scandalous dreams, about Adam of all people, with anyone. Even still, in broad daylight, her skin tingled as she remembered her mind's wanton images.

She should never have read that book, had happened upon it quite by mistake, in fact, secreted away in a corner of Adam's library. The scarlet binding, along with tiny, intriguing oriental markings, had captured her attention immediately. The incredible, and she decided highly implausible, drawings of men and women had near sent her into a swoon. Drat her curiosity! The images were now foremost on her mind. As was Adam.

After two days, Aunt Jeanette and the servants had seemingly accepted Adam as Francis Cobbald. Clean wrappings now protected his injury, he was well fed and on the way to a full recovery. Everything was going according to their plan.

Everything except the wicked notions that kept intruding upon her peace of mind. She was here to make decisions about her future. Adam's presence was not helping that task in the least.

Heaving a sigh, she waltzed into the breakfast room, only to find it deserted, the dining table cleared. No apple tarts, coddled eggs or ham remained. Not even a scrap of cheese. She found herself wondering why, she hadn't slept that late!

She searched the salon, the great hall and the library. Adam and her aunt were nowhere about. In fact, the few servants at Kerrick Hall were conspicuously absent as well. At last, the one lone maid she found replacing wicks in the brass wall lamps provided Adam's location. Retracing her footsteps, Becca veered toward the back of the house to a room she'd only entered once. As she neared, she heard her aunt's familiar squeal and applause.

Inching closer, Becca peeked around the mahogany molding. For the second time in two days it was sunny, as if the sea and land celebrated Adam's return. The heavy velvet drapes had been drawn, and sun shone through the sheer white curtains. Hundreds of swords, sabers, rifles and breastplates, an endless array of weapons, lined three walls, the sheer number of them staggering to her imagination. A small black drape covered with playing cards hung on the far and otherwise bare wall marred by scratches, slashes and gouges of all shapes and sizes. Two burgundy leather chairs and a low table were nestled beside the enormous stone fireplace. A decanter, several glasses, a small tea service and a basket of bread covered the table's top. There were four mahogany cabinets lining one wall, and the oak floor was empty of any covering.

Servants lined the doorway, and Becca's aunt sat on the edge of her chair, a box of chocolates in her lap, her eyes glowing with enthusiasm. "Please. I promise not to ask again."

Adam stood beside one of the cabinets, a patient look on his face. "This is the last time."

Yawning behind her hand, wondering what he'd done that Aunt Jeanette found so highly entertaining, Becca entered the room. This was Adam's private domain. Her expectant glance, one learned from her mother, sent the servants back to their duties.

"Come in. Come in," Jeanette said cheerfully. "Mr. Cobbald's about to give another demonstration."

Becca smiled sweetly at the source of her insomnia. "Good morning, *Mr. Cobbald.*"

"And the fairest of fair mornings to you, Lady Rebecca."

Adam was wearing the same set of clothing he'd arrived in, though it was obviously freshly pressed. He appeared alert and rested, but when he smiled at her his eyes betrayed annoyance. She couldn't fathom why. She was the one who hadn't slept all night. Settling herself in the chair beside her aunt, she asked, "Have you both eaten breakfast?"

"Ages ago," answered Jeanette. "Like myself, Mr. Cobbald happens to be an early riser. And we've had such fun. You'll never guess what he can do."

Becca tended to sleep late, while Jeanette woke early, then napped in the afternoon. Perhaps Adam was annoyed because he'd hoped to reacquaint himself with his house and had been denied the opportunity. "I'm glad he was able to keep you company."

"Your aunt is a brilliant sunflower on an otherwise dreary morning," Adam added in his newly acquired complimentary manner. "We've discussed all manner of things."

Becca didn't bother to mention that the sun shone brightly and his metaphor made no sense at all. She poured herself a cup of cocoa with extra cream. Wishing for a bit of cheese and a scone, she eyed her aunt's candies and asked, "Such as?"

"He'll tell you in a moment," Jeanette said. "Show her your trick."

"I'm sure your niece deplores such silly displays."

Jeanette dropped her head and fashioned her lips into an artful pout. "But you promised."

Becca's aunt had the tenacity of a terrier. Realizing it was easier to comply with her request than argue, Adam nodded. He stomped to the wall where the black felt hung, yanked a small silver dagger from the king of spades, glanced at Jeanette and asked, "Which one?"

"The ace of hearts," she answered, barely containing the thrill in her voice.

Becca tapped her finger against her lips and watched expectantly. One moment Adam was casually sauntering toward them, the next he was spinning on his heels and his dagger was sailing through the air. It landed with a thud in the center of the red heart.

Jeanette clapped her hands together. "Isn't that marvelous? I caught the rascal this morning. That's the fourth time and he has yet to miss."

Becca barely nodded as she recovered from the shock of what she'd just seen. The speed, the agility, the accuracy, were . . . well absolutely staggering. Her next thought was one of dismay. What the devil was the fool man thinking? He was supposed to be a poet, not a bloody assassin. And he'd winced. Surely such activity couldn't be good for his ribs. "A surprising skill for a man of artistic temperament," she said with a hint of warning directed solely toward Adam.

"An old habit from my misspent days as a brutish youth. As I explained to your aunt when she espied me this morning, I discovered this room quite by accident. Curiosity coupled with temptation and all was lost. I hope you don't mind."

"Not at all. 'Tis a pity you had no knife when you were attacked by thieves."

"Indeed. However, I like to think that over the years, I have learned skills of diplomacy . . . that, shall we say, the verse is mightier than the sword."

"A noble thought with which I heartily agree. Weapons, fighting and such are so tiresome," Becca said. Unsure why she felt like pricking Adam's patience but satisfied when he frowned, she asked, "What other tidbits did the two of you discuss?"

"The English weather, British pirates, the coming of spring, berry versus raisin scones and your upcoming season." Adam paused, the innocuous act of tugging on the lace at his wrist contradictory to a sudden predatory gleam in his eyes. "And your affection for poets."

Even though he smiled, the hard edge to his voice suggested something else altogether. A sinking feeling settled in her stomach. "Poets?"

"No need to play coy, Lady Rebecca. Your aunt told me all about your friend."

Becca gulped her drink, scalding her tongue. She

knew her aunt possessed a mouth looser than that of any seamstress on Bond Street, and she prayed that Jeanette hadn't revealed all the particulars of the affair with Barnard. Her private life was none of Adam's business; Becca had purposely avoided the subject. Adam would likely offer a lecture equal to the one she'd already heard from her father.

"My 'friend'?"

"Barnard Leighton, my dear," Jeanette cheerfully clarified. "I was curious if Mr. Cobbald and young Leighton knew one another. They possess—"

"Aunt Jeanette," interrupted Becca, "I'm sure Mr. Cobbald has better things to concern himself with."

Leaning against the mantel, his legs crossed at the ankles, Adam twirled another, smaller dagger in his fingers with amazing dexterity. "Nonsense. All poets interest me. My decision to become a purveyor of words struck me rather recently, yet Leighton's name is vaguely familiar. Dare we hope he might visit?"

Jeanette coughed, choking on a chocolate candy. "Oh, dear, I hope not. Since my brother charged me with his daughter's care, he would rant and rave in an endless tirade about my inadequacies as a chaperone if such were to happen. And his lectures are so tedious."

Adam kept his gaze fixed on Becca. "Your father dislikes poets?"

Unfortunately, Jeanette mistook Becca's dumbfounded silence for the opportunity to elaborate. "Not all poets. And while Edward can be rather pigheaded about many things, in this case I agree with him. A girl should experience one season. To elope is unacceptable."

Becca gasped as her teacup tottered in her hands.

"Elope?" Adam asked, his eyes narrowing suspiciously.

"I knew this tale would interest you," Jeanette said, leaning toward Adam, "being a romantic sort and all."

Becca groaned. With a simple look, a single word, Adam had the uncanny ability to make her feel like the foolish young girl who had proposed marriage to him over three years ago. She should never have left her room this morning. Better yet, she should have shot Adam when she'd had the chance. She certainly wouldn't give him the satisfaction of thinking she still harbored any feelings toward him—even if she had to be less than truthful about Barnard. No matter how difficult, she remained silent and affected fascination with the embers glowing in the fireplace.

Jeanette, on the other hand, plunged ahead like a youth who had just discovered her older brother behind the stable with the upstairs maid. "If you knew Becca's father, you would appreciate the tale so much more. He's such a blusterbuss. I doubt I'd ever seen Edward that particular shade of red before, and trust me, he has had ample opportunity to express his ire. Anyway, Barnard hired a coach, thinking to steal Becca away in the middle of a party. Unfortunately, while Becca was offering a grand speech to the revelers, Barnard grabbed Lady Silverhill. She's fifty-four and as contrary as a rabid dog. Needless to say, the plan went awry. So here we are, keeping the lovers apart and all, biding our time until we travel to London. Her father thinks that will help, but I see it as a pointless task if true love is involved. Isn't that how you poets feel, Mr. Cobbald?"

Adam plastered a serene expression on his face, one that hopefully concealed his increasing agitation. This first day out of bed had begun with Jeanette's unexpected interruption. Now, the revelation that Becca had a beau was oddly annoying. To discover that she might have eloped was truly aggravating.

"Some poets debate the existence of true love," he began. "But love found, or love lost, poets are an imaginative lot, often avoiding the harsh realities of life by steeping their decisions in fantasy. It is possible that he would follow her to London. Is this fellow successful as a poet?"

"Like you," Becca answered, "he is early in his career."

Waving her hand in the air with a chocolate balanced between two fingers, Jeanette piped up, "The boy is the third son of a baron."

"I see." Indeed, Adam did. The chap was likely broke, surely depending upon a small family stipend and wasting his time on poetry. "How did you and Barnard meet?"

"He lives near my home. We met years ago," Becca said. Becca's hands were fisted in her lap. She likely imagined his neck trapped between them.

Adam had spent a great deal of time at the Wyncomb estate, had met many of the neighbors, yet the Leighton name was totally unfamiliar to him.

"Neighbors. How sweet," Adam cooed. "Like tender budding blooms growing together, a *child-hood* romance."

"Not at all. Though I once experienced *such* an infatuation and learned my lesson. I assure you, Barnard and I mean more to one another than I ever thought possible."

Weathers stepped into the room. "Pardon me, Lady Thacker, but Cook requires your presence."

Clucking like a mother hen, clearly disappointed by the interruption, Jeanette placed her candy on the nearby table and stood. "As delightful as all this has been, duty calls. Becca dear, you might show Francis the rest of the house so the poor fellow won't have to wander about aimlessly. And Mister Cobbald, though you are injured and likely incapable of much harm, and since I have no intention of following you two around like a guard dog, I expect you to treat my niece with the utmost respect. Otherwise my brother, a temperamental sort, will hunt you down and castrate you. And let me remind you that Weathers shall not let you out of his sight." Obviously satisfied with her warning, the old lady waltzed from the room, humming.

Adam waited until Jeanette cleared the corner, then sauntered across the room to lock the door. Oddly peeved, he snatched the ridiculous black patch from his face. "At least now I understand your choice of disguises."

"One has nothing to do with the other. And my personal affairs are no business of yours."

She had a point. He'd given up all rights to Becca three years ago. Still, illogical as it was, the idea that Becca fancied herself in love with another man was annoying as hell. In fact, the possibility was downright unacceptable—not that Adam had any claim to her. He wasn't even sure he wanted one. Even if he were interested, he couldn't court her. Not with an uncertain future looming before him.

"What were you doing in here?" She interrupted his thoughts, obviously hoping to sidestep the discussion of Barnard. "You realize you could have ruined our plan?"

"I'm not worried about your aunt. I came in here

71

to test how my ribs were healing, never thinking Lady Thacker would find me." He gave her a look. "Tell me, Becca, did you really try to elope?"

A seabird's shrill cry from outside the window broke the silence. At last, Becca stood and wandered toward the sunlight. "No," she began. "Although Barnard and I discussed the possibility of running away together, he misinterpreted my meaning. I do not plan to marry." She glanced over at Adam. "Father is set on my having a season, though. He refuses to accept my decision not to wed. So I will go to London, dance the dance, then return to Lincolnshire. But whether I remain a spinster, write my own poems or live with Barnard, I will decide."

Adam's hands gripped the back of his chair in horror. "Not marry? You would be this man's mistress?"

"Don't be a dolt."

"Then you *do* plan on marrying the chap?" he asked, growing more confused.

"Not necessarily."

Adam's starched cravat suddenly seemed too constrictive. He didn't dare touch it since the blasted thing had taken Weathers ten minutes to knot, so he circled the room, scanning his family's treasury of weapons. He stopped before one cabinet, grabbed several daggers and a match, then lit three candles perched on top of another cabinet. "Pardon me. I seem to have misplaced my parlor skills while fighting in France, but when I left, if a man and a woman lived together out of wedlock, it meant only one thing. If you will not be his mistress, what would you call it?"

"An arrangement. A man *owns* a mistress. With an arrangement, neither party controls the other. I have chosen freedom from society's strictures, independence from rules created by men to dominate women. And Barnard agrees with me."

"No doubt. He wins no matter how you look at it. He'll be enjoying the milk without having to buy the cow. No wonder your father wants you to go to London."

He launched three knives in rapid succession. They sliced through the air, extinguishing the candles one by one, then piercing the already nicked wall with solid thumps. Accepting the feat for what it was, a hard-won skill learned from hours of practice, he ignored both the pain in his ribs and Becca's stunned gasp. He wasn't sure which had shocked her more: his blunt comment or his skill with knives.

Becca finally found her breath and said, "You sound just like my father. I realize most people marry for convenience or status, and some women, like my mother, happen to marry for love. But contrary to what men think, marriage is not the solution to *all* women. We have minds. We are capable of work. And some of us want to."

Granted, he was trying to stay calm, but, in his absence, this fool girl had truly lost her mind. "You intend to work? Good God, this is unbelievable."

"Whether I choose to work or not, marry and birth a dozen children or not, sit at home and embroider all day *or not*, the choice should be mine—not the dictate of my father, the church or society. I refuse to become some man's tenant for life."

He was thoroughly confused now. "You don't like men?"

She stomped her foot in frustration. "You're missing the point altogether. If you can't abide the company of the person you must spend your days and nights with, what good is money, stability or a bloody title? Why must a woman abandon her rights and hand them to her husband along with her virginity and her holdings?"

This girl was truly off her chump. Adam had thought her more levelheaded. Her opinion, idealistic as it was, was that of a young girl—one who knew little about the financial complexities of supporting a family and feared marriage as the unknown, not realizing she would gain the benefit of security and support.

Adam advanced to the wall and pulled the three daggers free. "Considering the fact that you proposed marriage to me before I left France, I find this change of heart rather sudden and unexpected. How did you come to these realizations?"

Becca studied the walls, the weapons, the fire and finally leveled her gaze at Adam. "Thanks to Barnard, I recently discovered the brilliant teachings of Mary Wollstonecraft. She wrote extensively about the liberation of women, and I can honestly say her opinions make sense."

He snorted. "The woman was a fanatic, a bloody anarchist."

"Because she threatens your precious male code?" Throwing her arms in the air, Becca stuttered a moment, snapped her lips shut, then finally found the words she sought. "Typical. The minute a man thinks his ego, his private domain, is in jeopardy, he faults a woman's common sense. And I once thought you more open-minded than most men. I was so wrong."

"The fact remains that you would give this man your virtue without any commitment whatsoever, and you excuse it away as freedom of choice without any consideration to the consequences."

"That is precisely what men have done for hundreds of years. They expect a virtuous woman on their wedding night, yet they themselves expend their passions whenever they choose. They want a passionate bedmate but keep young girls ignorant of all that lovemaking entails."

All of Adam's muscles clenched. It was probably a good thing this Barnard chap was miles away. Otherwise Adam might have had to punch him in the nose simply on principle. "So you *would* share this man's bed?"

"Sweet mercy! I swear you are being purposely obtuse. Whether or not I share Barnard's bed is not the point. A man and a woman should *fulfill* one another."

Slamming the daggers down on the cabinet, he stomped to her side. "What the devil does that mean?"

"I doubt a man like you can understand. Since we have been thrown together, for the sake of goodwill lest you misunderstand me completely, I will try to explain. A man and a woman should function with *commonality* and *respect* for one another on a *higher plane* other than *desire*, one that nurtures deeper emotions and sentiment."

Adam felt adrift in a sea of female logic with no lifeboat in sight.

Clearly this was the perfect example of the ageless struggle between men and women, why men retired to their studies with newspapers and a glass of sherry while women went off to do whatever it was they did. This type of unsettling conversation was the reason women would never be allowed in a gentleman's club, or given the vote. They were simply too damn emotional. Too irrational.

Furious, he trapped her between his body and the

windowsill. "Have you made love with him?"

Her mouth fell open again. Her eyes rounded. Granted, his question was rude, but it was suddenly imperative that he know the answer, and he doubted there was a tactful way to ask. "Well? Have you?"

"Your assumption shows how little you really know me. And it proves that you haven't listened to a word I've said. True love transcends physical pleasure."

"Has he kissed you?"

Her cheeks flamed to the same red color as the ribbon on her dress. "That is none of your business."

"For some inexplicable reason, I'm feeling quite irritated over this entire situation, and I've yet to meet Barnard. As for this higher plane rubbish, if a man refuses to take you into his arms and taste you, kiss you senseless, then he's a fool."

"Or a gentleman concerned with a lady's sensibilities."

Adam snorted. "Becca you are not some demure flower in need of pruning and tending. Passion burns in your blood. You'll never be content with some philosophical gibberish."

"You don't really know me any longer."

"I think I do." He leaned closer, his fingers tracing the slender column of her neck. Her pulse beat rapidly beneath his hand. She wasn't as immune to him or his words as she wanted to believe.

But neither was he to her. His body hardened like an oak beam the minute he allowed his mind to drift, wondering how she'd react if he kissed her, whether he'd taste chocolate on her lips. Tiny green flecks danced in her golden eyes, and he inhaled the sweet scent of lilacs that clung to her skin. It would be so easy to lose the memory of the last few months in her arms. Certainly one kiss couldn't hurt. He brushed his thumb over her lower lip again and again, slowly, as he spoke.

"Indeed, your poet friend and I are as different as flock and herd. If I were in love with you, if I desired you, if I intended to elope with you, mere words would never be enough. I'd make sure you understood what I expected in our relationship as husband and wife, man and woman." His other hand drifted along the edge of her bodice in a slow, sensual pattern, lightly skimming her flesh. His gaze slid from her eyes to her mouth, then to her breasts. "I would need to touch every delicious inch of you. That tiny mole behind your left ear. The tender pulse point on your wrist. The soft flesh of your thighs. I'd make sure you realized that passion runs deep within your soul."

"This discussion is inappropriate," Becca stammered. And if the discussion wasn't, the indecent images from that oriental picturebook coupled with Adam's words certainly were. An unbidden thrill cascaded through her body. *Damn.* She would be more cautious in her choice of reading material in the future. Glancing from side to side in hope of possible escape, she found none. Besides, she wasn't so sure she wanted to flee.

"Inappropriate? You just claimed to scorn society's rules, to frown on the virtue of innocence. Remember?" He allowed her time to withdraw, but when she didn't Adam slowly lowered his head. He gently pressed his lips to hers.

When he pressed his body closer, Becca felt all the many differences between men and women's bodies. Undeniable, overwhelming desire flared deep within her.

"Open your mouth for me," he whispered. Using his tongue and teeth to seduce, tease and torment, he unleashed the passionate beast trapped within Becca. At first, her tongue darted out timidly against his, but she grew bolder, more playful, like a curious child exploring a new toy.

When he slanted his mouth over hers and deepened the kiss, the undeniable urge to crawl into his arms drowned all reason. Succumbing to the impulse, Becca wrapped her arms around his neck and pressed closer still. No matter how tightly she bound herself to him it wasn't enough. She felt feverish. Her heart hammered against her chest. Her breasts ached.

Adam must have sensed her dilemma, for he inched his hand upward to cup her breast. Welcoming his caress, her nipple tightened against his palm. He continued to kiss her. Thoroughly. With deep, mind-dulling, persuasive kisses. A wondrous throbbing crept from her belly to settle in the secret place between her thighs. The fire that began to burn within her threatened to engulf them both.

Then Adam stopped and pulled back. He glanced toward her, and she felt how swollen her lips were from the passion of their kiss. She felt dazed, and almost didn't notice the smug look that crossed his face.

"Well, Becca," Adam said, "I'd say you're not as averse to physical pleasure as you might think. Do Leighton's kisses heat you as mine do?"

"Who?" she asked.

He smiled patiently. "Your beau."

Her mind snapped back. "Oh." She stumbled to the side and placed a chair between them like a chastity belt. "The fact that my body reacts to yours means nothing. What good is physical pleasure if the mind and soul are not fed as well?"

Adjusting his jacket across his chest, Adam said, "Damn good, if you ask me. That was passion, Becca. Pure and true."

She exhaled, slowly regaining her senses, more afraid than anything that Adam might misinterpret her reaction to his touch. Heaven knew she herself was tempted to do so; her heart hammered ferociously.

"All right," she said. "I admit it. I obviously find you attractive. But you and I are completely unsuitable for one another and have no future. You cannot simply go about kissing me to prove your points. Now, we must forget this foolishness."

Adam, drat the man, seemed wholly unaffected by the intimacy they'd just shared. He sauntered to her side and extended his arm. "As you wish. Truce. *I* shall not kiss *you*. Now come along. There are papers I need to find."

Suspicious of this sudden compliance in a man who'd always been argumentative with her, she stood firm. "I mean it, Adam. No kissing."

"As do I, Becca," he solemnly pledged.

Why didn't she believe him? Then again, perhaps she was the one who needed to make such a promise. To herself. She would not kiss Adam Hawksmore again. Certainly no good could come of it.

Chapter Seven

He looked like a bloody toad.

That was the singular thought whirling through Adam's mind as he stood frozen before his bedroom mirror, staring in mute horror at his reflected image. He wore a pair of chartreuse trousers with a matching coat, a paisley vest and a hideous yellow cravat tied into a ridiculous knot. He hated green. He hated paisley even more. Hell, he hated to wear any colors other than black, brown or, occasionally, burgundy.

Surely this outfit was some sort of vengeance on Becca's part.

Three days had passed since their session in the library and her absurd edict on kissing. Since then, to his brewing consternation, she'd managed to avoid being alone with him. She slept late, tended to her daily duties, then shadowed her aunt like an apparition. At night they played chess or poker, always in Lady Thacker's company. He felt a trifle abandoned and disappointed that Becca refused to spend time alone with him. It was an odd and uncommon sensation for him.

Hence, he re-established a daily schedule, the pattern he had tried to follow for as long as he could remember, and spent his days reacquainting himself with his home—a grand thing after being absent for so long. Trivial tasks such as reviewing estate ledgers brought him great satisfaction. Sherry drunk from a crystal glass, fresh rolls steeped in melted butter, clean linens on his bed and hot baths seemed like gifts from the gods. He read, exercised as best he could and walked the cliffs above the pounding surf. He visited his stable, appreciating the fine collection of horses. Yet his danger was everpresent in his thoughts as he reexamined that final night at the Red Goose Inn. And the whole time he did his best to perfect the tedious act of a poet.

Weathers had gathered some of Adam's old clothes from the attic. Combined with his cousin's leftovers and Becca's alterations, his new wardrobe miraculously appeared near the orchard in his "stolen" suitcase. Jeanette had accepted his presence with unexpected ease, offering occasional reminders of what Edward would do if he misbehaved. Adam had his home, his clothes, and his wounds were healing nicely. He should have been thrilled. Elated.

But stuff and nonsense, today he was unhappy. He'd already finished his daily projects, and a nasty thunderstorm threatened, eliminating all hope for any outside diversion. That being the case, he sought the one person who could entertain him.

Squinting in the doorway to his library, wishing he could blame the sight he saw on his damn eye patch, Adam found her. Amazed, he watched as Becca balanced on a rickety ladder that, in his opinion, leaned precariously against the room's wooden bookshelves. Her hair was hidden beneath a ridiculous white mobcap with only a few blond ringlets visible. A dark smudge touched her left cheek, making him wonder what she'd been up to, and her dress was wrapped between her legs, showing a good deal of her shapely ankles and dark blue stockings. She clutched a feather duster in one hand, but her full attention was focused on a book that lay open on the top rung. My God, if the Persian rug shifted an inch, or if she leaned too far to one side, she would tumble to the floor and break her lovely neck.

Glancing from side to side to see if they were alone, Adam snapped, "Rebecca Marche. What are you thinking?"

Startled, she lurched to one side, which practically toppled the wooden support. Her book sailed to the floor with a resounding thud. Regaining her balance, she glared at Adam. "Are you out of your mind? I nearly fell."

He sauntered to her side and, mindful of his side, braced the ladder. "You could accomplish that just by climbing up there. What are you doing?"

"In case you've forgotten, I'm supposed to be readying the estate for your successor."

"Why do you think I have servants in my employ?"

"There are not enough people left to do everything unless you wish to hire more staff, but then we'd have even more curious servants milling about."

He frowned at that thought.

"Besides, I was bored to tears," she admitted.

The fact that she had been bored eased any worries he had about seeking her company. Nevertheless, to find her cleaning his house evoked the strangest, most discomfiting notions. A *wife* ran a man's home, saw to his personal needs.

"Certainly there are other tasks you could perform," he complained. "Less rigorous duties."

She turned about and sat on the top rung of the ladder. Her eyes twinkled with merriment, likely some joke at his expense. "I've dusted before. And I'll have you know I've even made a bed."

"Not in my home." Bending to retrieve the book she'd dropped, he suffered another shock—one that set his brow to a high arch, his eyes wide and his manhood to stirring. "*Lysistrata?* Hardly appropriate reading material for a young woman."

"I was dusting."

"I can see that. Page fifty-two is particularly tidy. In case you've forgotten, it's the part that relates to a man's phallus."

Her cheeks blossomed to a lovely pink. "You will not make me feel guilty for expanding my intellectual horizons."

"Is that what you call it? Perhaps because you know you shouldn't be reading such literature."

She crossed her arms beneath her breasts. "Likely so, but that is precisely what I meant about women's lack of rights. Why can't we read what we choose? Why must everything be some grand secret?" She pointed an accusing finger in his direction. "Because men shelter us for fear we might actually learn something that might challenge their superiority, that's why."

"You gleaned all that from this one book? Amazing."

She shook her head. "Stop being contrary or I'm

likely to throw the book *at* you. I will not allow you to ruin my day. What do you want?"

"I want you to come down from there before you hurt yourself."

Apparently resigned to the fact that he'd not leave her alone, she stepped carefully from the ladder. Reaching the last step, she leaned right and the ladder tipped left. Becca gripped the post to stop her fall, but her feet hit the floor hard. "Ouch."

"Let me see," Adam said, worried. Taking her hand in his, he examined it. "It is only a splinter." He pinched the small sliver of wood free and tucked her finger into his mouth. There he suckled it, trying to soothe her.

She tasted so . . . female. He tried to think of a poetic comparison, but the only word that came to mind was "delicious." He suckled harder. Her small gasp shot his errant thoughts into more dangerous territory; he considered other delightful body parts he'd enjoy sampling. Every nerve in his body, already on alert, shifted into full readiness.

When he lifted his gaze, Becca was staring at her finger trapped inside his mouth, mesmerized. Golden flecks danced in her dark brown eyes. Odd; he'd never noticed those flecks before, or her incredibly long lashes. Her mouth parted with another breathy gasp that did nothing to ease the growing ache in his groin.

In self-defense, lest he forget any and all gentlemanly behavior or his intended explorations of the castle, he practically spit her finger from his mouth. He stepped a safe distance away, his hands locked behind his back. "If you intend for me to obey that nonsense about kissing, I suggest you bank the fires in your eyes. A man can only take so much."

"I beg your pardon?" she asked, obviously confused.

For all her declarations on womanly rights, she had no idea what he meant. She was such an innocent, which roused his masculine inclinations more even than the thought of her reading *Lysistrata*. Passion laced with innocence was one of the greatest aphrodisiacs, and Becca possessed both. Given the heat in her eyes and the fire in his body, he could bear no additional temptations. He skirted the room, pausing occasionally to scan the titles of the books he owned, half of which he'd never had time to read. All the while, he willed his baser urges under control. It was no small feat.

"Adam, whatever is the matter?"

He paused, unsure what to say. He certainly couldn't admit to the struggle he was having controlling his desire. At last, he decided to say, "If you must know, I'm bored as well. I cannot remember the last time I wasn't responsible for or looking after someone or something. I'm not quite sure what to do with myself." When she grinned and extended the feather duster in his direction, he laughed. "That is not what I had in mind. Come."

"If you hadn't noticed, I was preoccupied."

Always eager for a challenge, and knowing Becca's weakness for mystery, he whispered, "You'll like what I'm about to do far better."

"What?"

He shrugged. "A bit of exploring. You'll have to trust me." She stood perfectly still, her mind whirling with possibilities and questions, he was sure. She stared at his mouth. Reading her thoughts, he said, "Yes, I remember. No kissing." Because he anticipated the afternoon with renewed interest and truly wanted her company, he placed his hand over his chest in a solemn pledge. "I promise."

Becca's subsequent decision to abandon her duties took all of three seconds, which pleased Adam immensely.

He kept an appropriate distance between them, in case any servants lingered in the hall. Also, he feared that if he got too close he might change his mind and drag her into a corner somewhere to meld his lips with hers or test his theory on how the tiny spot behind her right shoulder might taste. He led the way through the manor, up the stairs and past the portraits of his ancestors. In order to avoid the napping Jeanette, they crept past the bedrooms, up another flight of stairs to the third floor where Adam finally stopped before a large tapestry. "Ready?" he asked.

"For what?" She glanced around skeptically.

Pulling a key from his pocket, he lifted the edge of weaving and unlocked an old wooden door, which opened to a narrow set of stairs.

"Where does it lead?" she asked.

"My secret hiding place. Watch your head." He grabbed a candle from the hallway, clasped Becca's hand and led the way, stopping to light the small torches in iron sconces every ten feet as they climbed the stairs. At the top, Adam stopped, opened another door, then stepped into a circular room no more than ten feet across. A bank of windows with beveled glass and iron bars circled the room, providing a magnificent view of the sea and endless horizon. Clean brocade pillows, obviously provided by Weathers in anticipation of Adam's visit, lay on top of four stone benches built into the tower wall.

As Adam lit more candles, Becca skipped to the nearest window, pressing her forehead against the cold pane of glass. A flash of lightning burst across the heavens. When thunder reverberated off the stone walls, she leapt backward into Adam, alternately gasping, then giggling. "This room is marvelous. It is incredible. Fantastic."

" 'Tis only a tower."

Turning toward Adam, Becca cocked her head to the side. He was dreadfully serious. Did he truly see nothing more than a room made of stone and glass? Certainly, if he was going to behave as a poet, he had best start thinking like one. "Look outside. What do you see?"

"Rain," he answered dryly.

"Try to be more specific, even descriptive, however difficult that might be."

"There is no need for sarcasm." He peered through the window, squinted, then shrugged. "A bloody nasty thunderstorm. I've seen many. What do you see?"

Circling the room, going from window to window, Becca watched lightning dance across the heavens. "I see the ancient hand of Mother Nature, her great gales of wind a voice from the heavens, reminding us mortal men how truly powerless we are."

"You see all that?"

His voice held a vulnerability she knew most people would never recognize. And he didn't even realize it. Becca's heart twinged ever so slightly for this man whose emotions were hidden like buried treasure at the bottom of the sea, just waiting for someone to discover it. "Oh, Adam, as a poet you are in a coil, aren't you? Don't you see there is more to life than what can be touched or explained by books and science? Like the magic that comes from one's soul."

"Ah," he said with a sardonic smile. "*That* must be

the problem. You see, I've been told before that I lack a soul. Actually, I have always dealt with fact rather than fantasy, reality versus whimsy, probability rather than possibility. It's how I was taught to think."

"But how were you taught to feel?"

His arm halted in midair, his candle's flame flickering as wind escaped through small fissures in the window glass. "I beg your pardon?"

"The question is not so difficult. What of your emotions? Surely your mother and father taught you about love and sorrow, pain and joy, anger and patience."

He continued to light the remaining candles. "Of course they taught me. And I've learned more since. Wallowing in sorrow solves nothing. Anger leads to hasty and illogical decisions. Patience is necessary when working with green troops. No man ever died from pain. All in all, emotions negate a leader's authority and judgment. They fog the mind, hinder sound thinking and discipline. Quite simply, they are better suited to women."

A hundred different arguments lay on her tongue, rebuttals to his cold-hearted analysis, but she forced her mouth shut. How could one argue with a way of life? Becca wasn't sure, and needed time to consider the best tactic. She certainly wasn't about to give up. Adam needed her help. He needed her, desperately, and his words only made it more evident.

Crossing to a window, she knelt on a red velvet pillow on the stone ledge and peered downward. "I had no idea we climbed so high. Where are we?"

"The east tower. This is one of the parts of the original building that my great-grandfather kept when he rebuilt Kerrick Castle." He sat down beside her.

"We didn't climb very high. The view is deceiving because we're directly over the cliffs."

Grinning, she asked, "What was this room used for?"

Three small alcoves contained wooden and tin boxes. He bent to the side and retrieved a sturdy wooden box. When he opened the lid, he pulled a brass spyglass from inside. "Originally when the castle was built, men kept watch for raiders. When the threat of war ended, someone began sitting here on stormy nights with candles and lamps, signaling ships and watching for those that might founder on the rocks. It's also been rumored that smugglers once signaled one another from such posts."

Her grin grew lopsided. "Are you telling me that the honorable line of Kerricks had a smuggler in their midst?"

He waggled his brows. "Family history can be fascinating, can it not?" Raising the spyglass, he offered it to her. "Have a look."

Offering directions on how to use the narrow tube, Adam hovered near her shoulder. The heat of his body melted through her linen dress to her bare skin. His familiar and pleasant scent, like nutmeg of all things, teased her nostrils and reminded her of spiced apples. She found it difficult to equate Adam Hawksmore with such a delicacy, but the thought came nonetheless. Forcing her mind from such foolishness, she focused on the black clouds roiling on the horizon, the merciless waves pounding the shore. Lightning flashed again, and she winced.

Adam chuckled.

She meant to shoot him her most withering glare, but catching a glimpse through the spyglass, she cried excitedly, "Look, a ship!"

He followed the direction of her finger to the hulking shadow in the sea, the small lantern on the ship's forward bow barely visible through the rain and mist. "So it is."

"Do you think she'll founder?"

"No. He's far enough out. These shores are treacherous for experienced seamen on a clear day, and they know to stay away. Only a fool would dare this shoreline in a storm."

She watched the ship, tossed as it was by the raging weather outside. Nearby Adam scoured for, found and pulled a tin box from another shelf. Curious, she returned the spyglass to its wooden box and glanced over his shoulder as he sat back down. About twenty-five miniature wooden soldiers lay in the tin box's bottom. Snatching one, she studied the figure curiously. The tiny man was nicked at the neck. She looked back into the box.

Each miniature was separate and unique. One soldier carried a sword and a shield. One poor fellow was without an arm. She found them all oddly delightful. "Were these yours?"

Adam lifted a particular piece in his hand and nodded. "You see, this room was my own personal war room." He extended to her what he'd picked up, a wooden horse. "These were my personal army. I played with them for hours on end."

"Did you *make* them?"

"A few. My father gave me my first set on my seventh birthday, when he told me it was time to start thinking of more manly professions. I began carving them right after that. Over the years, with the help of a friend, I added to my collection. I believe that one without the arm was Mac's handiwork."

"Mac?"

"Yes. An honest man and a good friend."

Becca pulled several more soldiers and horses from the box, examining the different pieces. "They're like a chess set."

"Yes," he said, nodding. "There are many similarities between chess and war."

Setting a one-legged horse down, she tucked her legs beneath her dress. "Adam, did you ever think to do something different than soldiery?"

Obviously taking time to consider her question, he grabbed a woolen blanket from another alcove and draped it across her shoulders, allowing his hands to linger at the nape of her neck. A burst of fire seemed to radiate from his fingers through the blanket, her dress and into her skin.

He stood with his foot on the bench, his elbow braced on his knee, his chin tucked in his hand. His other hand gripped one of the iron bars of the window. His gaze seemed to travel back a hundred years. "My ancestors have protected kings and country, starting with my great-great-grandfather, who saved dear Queen Anne's life from an assassin. He became her faithful servant until she relinquished the throne. She rewarded his valor with this land. Hence he became the first earl and set the standard for all Kerricks to follow."

"But didn't you ever dream of being a painter or an explorer? Maybe an artist?" He looked so utterly baffled, she added, "I don't know what exactly, but anything other than a soldier?"

"My future was ordained the day I was born. I knew I would serve my king and country as my ancestors had."

Silent for a moment, Becca thought about his family. Honor and pride were obviously essential to the line. "I don't understand why men must fight. . . . Or why women allow, even support, it."

"We rarely have any choice," Adam answered. He studied Becca's face in the candlelight. Sweet mercy, she was beautiful. Her eyes shimmered with confusion, and he could see that she'd spoken more to herself than to him.

He moved to another window and stared out, the west wing of the castle barely visible through the rain. "I doubt we fully understand ourselves, often. There are many reasons, though—freedom, power, money, greed, truth. For me, it's simpler, as it has always been for my family. We swore fealty to the king and loyalty to our country. We do what we must."

"Why, then, don't women go traipsing off to war? Surely we're capable of loyalty and such."

He chuckled at the absurdity of the notion of women at war. "Maybe because you're smarter than the lot of us men." When she frowned, he crossed to her side and sat down. The inclination to hold her hand seized him. He folded his arms across his chest. "Truth be told, men need women to stay home, to give birth, then raise their sons so the world will have more soldiers. Some man somewhere will always want what the other has for some reason or another, and there will always be those who rise to oppose it. War will always be."

As if Mother Nature attested to the truth of his statement, thunder erupted outside, shaking the tower. The storm was upon them. Becca edged closer to Adam, sighed, then rested her cheek against the iron bar of the window grate. "I don't think I could stand to watch my son ride away and know I might never see him again. Or my husband."

"I hope to think that you would honor their decision and stand proudly by their side. Everyone dies, Becca, one way or another."

"I prefer a more peaceful death, thank you very much."

"Whether thrown from a horse or struck by a carriage, death is, without doubt, a fact of life. Men seem to have grander notions of how they want to die than women."

"You've actually considered how you might die? Oh, Adam, that's morbid."

"When you face danger day after day, you're forced to think of it. And, if given a choice, I'd much rather die with my boots on in the midst of a battle than be struck down by a phaeton. I suppose there's only one other way I might prefer to go."

"I can't believe we're having this discussion, but I'll ask anyway. How?"

He tipped her chin toward his face. "In my bed, after making love with a beautiful woman."

Becca's lips parted with a sigh, those same lips that had kept him awake night after night. Her tongue slid from her mouth to wet her lower lip in an instinctual invitation he doubted she knew she extended.

They were alone. No one would disturb them. How easy would it be to peel that serviceable blue linen dress from her shoulder inch by inch, to sample her breasts, her collarbone, the tender spot on her wrist? Lust surged through his veins. His sex hardened like the ruddy iron bar over the windows. The urge to pull her into his arms nearly blinded him to reason. But one taste would not be enough.

She swallowed, then shivered.

If they didn't leave immediately, he doubted he'd be able to control himself. Clearing his throat, he managed to spit out, "You're chilled. One last thing and we'll go."

Becca was barely able to nod at his words. Unsolicited cravings settled in her stomach and lower still, heady illogical sensations. Sweet daffodils, she'd wanted Adam to kiss her, actually imagined his lips on hers, his tongue in her mouth. She'd practically lapped him up like a bowl of cream. And she'd been the one who had issued a lecture on him kissing her. Heaven forbid, she was turning into a wanton.

A sudden realization that Adam might, after all these years, still mean something to her emotionally, that he could possibly break her heart again, ended any and all romantic musings. She forced herself to calm down. This moment of insanity was due to the drama of their surroundings.

Curiosity was another plausible reason. She had been reading that book that talked all about men, women and lust. That had to account for some of her current frame of mind. It certainly wasn't simply Adam himself. But then again, this was the first time in her life that she felt she truly understood him.

None of this changed the fact that they were still at cross-purposes with one another, though. No. She couldn't have, wouldn't have, feelings for this man. They were untenable. She wanted freedom and adventure. Adam wanted peace and solitude. He believed in structure—so much so that he even followed a bloody schedule each day. Becca wanted to be first in a man's heart, not runner-up to power, honor or pride. And that was what Adam wanted.

Why were these realizations so perplexing?

She watched him through hooded eyelids as he lifted the bottom from the small box that contained the soldiers and pulled out two small blue velvet bags. Their contents jingled as he set them on the bench. Becca's brow rose in speculation, thrilled to have a diversion to turn her mind from the mass of black hair that fell to Adam's shoulders, the broad shoulders that filled the jacket he wore. Sweet mercy, she had to stop this silly woolgathering.

She opened one bag and gasped. "How much gold is in here?"

"Enough to pay my expenses and then some. Information costs a pretty penny, and even a poet needs money. Come."

Standing, Becca peered through the glass, the rain and gray skies, one last time. A small skiff fought the waves and inched toward shore. "A boat is coming to shore. It must have been put off that larger craft."

He snatched the spyglass and cursed vividly. "What the deuce is that blockhead doing?" Stashing the gold in his coat pocket, he grabbed her hand and bounded down the stairs, slowly enough that he wouldn't trip, but quickly enough to signal urgency. They extinguished the torches in the stairway as they descended.

"What is the matter?" she asked. "Where are we going?"

"You'll find out soon enough. Only one man is arrogant enough to dare these waters during a storm, and he better have a damn good reason." Adam led her back the way they came, stopping at the door to the master bedroom—the chamber Becca now inhabited. He entered without a second thought and stomped to the wooden cabinet that hid the secret stairway down the cliff.

"Adam," she gasped. "What is wrong with you?"

"I believe we're about to have company."

"You're joking," she said, but he didn't answer.

95

"Someone else knows about the secret entrance you used to get here? Who?" She walked to her window to stare toward the edge of the cliff. "Ah. The man in the boat." She stood on her toes, straining to see through the rain, wishing she could actually see the beach below. "Is he a friend?" In the next breath, she said, "Of course he is, silly me. How else would he know about the secret passage." Turning to Adam, she said, "Well? Are you going to answer me?"

"You seem to be doing a fine job of answering yourself," he muttered. Taking and lighting a candle, he twisted the door to the passage's old lock and slid the heavy barrier open.

Cold air danced into the room, swirling around Becca's ankles. She peered over Adam's shoulder as he sheltered the flame of his candle with his hand. Sure enough, from the passage there came the muffled sound of footsteps, and the dim glow of a light appeared. Adam leaned against the wall beside her, his ankles crossed, an expectant expression on his face.

Becca watched the top of the stairs with anticipation. A figure appeared, carrying a lantern, and in its glow the first thing she saw was a head of auburn curls tucked beneath a dark knit cap. Broad shoulders followed. When the man saw Adam and Becca waiting, he stepped up onto the landing wearing a cocky grin and a soaking-wet greatcoat. Standing only an inch or so shorter than Adam, he was clean-shaven, with a ruddy complexion and moss-colored eyes that twinkled with merriment. His clothing proved he was a sailor, but why he was here at Kerrick Castle remained a mystery.

Adam pushed away from the wall with a snort. "So, Mac, did you miss me so much that you risked your miserable hide to share a brandy and a few tales?"

"Miss your ugly face?" his friend asked with a grin. "Never. But I do have a hankering for that drink." Stepping closer, the man glanced from Becca back to Adam. "And here I was feeling sorry for you. You didn't waste any time, now did you? And such a lovely wench. Where did you find her?"

"It's not what you think," Adam grumbled, knowing his friend had to be freezing. He ushered everyone into the bedroom, closed up the passage and replaced the bookshelves before it. Then he moved to stoke the fire. "Before you say anything else you might regret, allow me to present Lady Rebecca Marche, daughter of the Earl of Wyncomb."

Mac's brows rose. He dragged his coat from his shoulders and his hat from his head, then tossed the sodden garments to Adam. "As in *the* Lady Rebecca?" When Adam nodded, Mac grinned at her. "Blow me down. I didn't expect to find *you* here. I didn't expect to find anyone except Adam."

"That's rather obvious," Becca retorted. She'd clearly been put off by the man's assumptions.

Draping Mac's soaked garments by the fire, Adam stirred the coals one last time. "Since I saw the *Fleeting Star* sail away, I assume you're here for a few days. Why?"

Mac shot a questioning glance at Becca. "I have news."

"It's all right. She knows all of it."

Extending his arms toward the flames, Mac's expression grew serious. "After I dropped you here, I returned to Portsmouth, visiting a few taverns to do business. Someone's been asking questions about a passenger from France in ports along the coast. The description of the man he was looking for sounded a lot like you."

Adam cursed. Why? Who was after him? What did they want? Furious with his own ignorance, he clamped his fingers over the top of a nearby chair and forced himself to calm down. Nodding, he steadied his voice enough to ask, "How long will you be staying?"

Becca, silent until now, slid closer to him. "He just informed you that someone is searching for you. What if they're watching this estate? Aren't you worried?"

"Worrying will not alter the situation," Adam snapped. "At least we know we must double our efforts toward secrecy."

Becca gave him a pained look. "I will never understand you. How can you stay so bloody imperturbable? Someone wants you *dead*." She threw her hands in the air.

Adam was bemused by her impassioned reaction. After all, it wasn't she who was being sought. A typical female response, he decided at last. Characteristic of the gender, to give in to her emotions. Women would never possess—or understand, even— the discipline required to deal with danger and death day after day. In order to maintain one's sanity and the ability to lead, restraint was mandatory. That understanding was what had kept Adam alive for so long. But Becca was different.

"If I thought a tantrum could alter my circumstance, I'd pitch a fit equal to one of King George's," he said at last, dragging a hand through his hair. "I am totally, utterly aware of the danger of my situation. Trust me in that. But first, before we do anything about my anonymous enemy, we must decide what to do with Mac."

Chapter Eight

"No need to fret, Weathers. If I shoot anyone, it will be Lady Rebecca."

The butler took in Adam's stony expression and shrugged his shoulders in silent apology. He offered a pair of polished black boots with bright silver buckles. "She seems to think these garments appropriate, my lord."

"Terrifying, isn't it? However, I've accepted this role and, if it means saving my hide, I will play the part as best I can." Adam glared into the mirror before him. If such a thing were possible, he disliked this outfit even more than his previous ensembles, and more than he had a few minutes ago. The offensive trousers were vermilion, for heaven's sake, and so tight, Adam doubted he'd be able to sit without permanent damage to his privates. The cravat alone, a drab umber, had taken Weathers a good ten minutes to knot. Worse, an excessive amount of green piping decorated the gold waistcoat. "By the saber, do all poets dress like idiots?"

"I am sorry to say, sir, that my knowledge equals yours in this matter. We shall have a better idea after today."

Adam practically growled. Inviting Percy Shelley, some new profound poet, and his companion to dinner had been another of Becca's ideas. It wasn't altogether bad. The evening would provide Adam with the opportunity to study the man, to learn more about a poet's life and make the necessary adjustments to his own disguise for the eventual trip to London.

But though even Mac thought this plan a grand idea, truth bc told, Adam would have rather faced the French cavalry than this blasted poet. At least on the battlefield Adam knew what was expected of him. Cursing, he stomped to a chair and tugged one boot over his calf.

There came a knock at the door just before Becca bustled into the room, followed by Mac. Becca managed two steps before she noticed Adam. Stopping abruptly, she slapped a hand over her mouth, but not before an odd gurgle sounding suspiciously like a laugh emerged.

He stood, his arms crossed. "Typically one waits for a response to their knock before they enter a gentleman's quarters. What if I'd been undressed or bathing?"

Weathers's expression mirrored Adam's disapproval.

Becca's lips, ones he had begun to fantasize about, curled as she continued to stare in silence. The blasted female wasn't paying his words the least bit of attention. She was too busy trying to contain her laughter.

Mac, quite comfortable in his role—they'd introduced him to Becca's aunt as a schoolmate of Adam's—wasn't as obliging. Gnawing on a cigar, he burst into laughter.

Wagging his finger in the air, Adam snarled, "Say one word and I'll find a way to exact revenge. Wait and see." He yanked his other boot on. "What were you thinking, Becca? Yesterday I resembled an amphibian, and today I look like the bloody Spanish flag."

"More like a Christmas treat. If only your disposition was as sweet. Your outfit is certainly colorful. You look—" she pursed her lips together when Adam frowned—"umm. Perfect."

"For a masquerade or a farce?" Mac asked gleefully as he leaned against the mantel.

Adam marched to his dresser. Weathers followed in order to add the final piece to the costume, a red ribbon to confine Adam's hair. "I've seen dandies at Ascot dressed better. No sane man would dare wear something like this."

Mac blew a ring of smoke in the air. "You forget Beau Brummell. Though he fled for greener pastures, men still emulate his fashions."

Adam frowned. "As I said, no *sane* man." He turned to Becca. "Are you sure you know what you're doing?"

This time Becca did laugh. "Mind you, I've only met a few poets, but each possesses his own personal style. Trust me. You are trying to create a disguise. No one would ever suspect that the Earl of Kerrick would dress in such a manner." She turned to Mac for support. "Would they?"

"She has a point, my friend."

Adam snorted. He'd had similar thoughts himself, which was the single consolation to his attire and his continued performance as Francis Cobbald. "On that we agree."

Becca smiled. "By the way, I came to tell you I think I saw their carriage." She gave Adam an excited look. "I've heard wonderful things about Shelley. The fact that he agreed to come is marvelous."

"In all likelihood, he wants a free meal," Mac interjected.

Adam chuckled, pleased to have another man on his side of the fence.

"Shame on you both."

"You're the one who told us he has little money," Adam corrected.

"I should never have said anything. That's only a rumor I heard from one of the maids. I'm sure he's coming tonight because he is eager to share his poetry with someone who enjoys intellectual thought. I doubt there are many people in the village who appreciate his talents. Besides, I'm anxious to meet his companion. You have no idea how exciting this is for me." Crossing to Adam, she adjusted his cravat so that the lace trim drooped slightly to the right. Weathers hovered nearby, sulking over her interference, but she continued to play blithely with the linen until satisfied. Done, she smiled. Weathers scowled.

"Mary and Percy have loved one another for the longest time," Becca continued. Pulling a small velvet box from her dress pocket, she set it on the dresser and opened it. "But Percy is bound to another by marriage. They have thrown caution to the wind and vowed to be together. Granted, his wife,

Harriet, must feel rather abandoned. But it's all so very sad and yet romantic, it surely provides great inspiration for his poems."

Shaking his head, Adam tapped his finger to her nose. "Mind yourself. You have been listening to more than just a little gossip."

Frowning, Becca said, "Gossip is based on speculation. This information is based on fact. Mary believes, as her mother did, that marriage is simply society's rule meant to trap women into slavery."

"What the devil is she talking about?" Mac asked.

"You're better off not knowing," Adam answered. "Trust me."

Becca gave him a dirty look. "Nonsense. I'm sure your friend would be fascinated with the concept of an independent female. I will eagerly elaborate later. When we have more time." She jabbed Adam in the arm. "And stop acting as though I were sending you to your room without supper. You're simply contrary because you're afraid you'll do poorly. Think of this afternoon as training. Eventually you must appear in London as Francis Cobbald."

Adam refrained from response. Instead he watched as Becca found a silver pin shaped like a peacock and added the jewelry to his lapel.

"Don't be nervous," Becca said with a laugh. "We don't expect you to be perfect on your first outing. This is merely a way for you to observe and improve your impersonation of the literary minded. Goodness knows you can use the help."

Just as quickly, Adam removed the pin and set the offensive object back on the dresser. He wasn't wearing a damn bird on his coat. "My performance has not been *that* bad."

Shrugging, Becca looked doubtful. "That remains

to be seen. If we were performing for someone who knew you, other than Weathers and my aunt, of course, that would be even better. It would be a true test of this plan. Now, if you're ready, we had best go down. Our guests should be here shortly."

Mac excused himself with a wink and a promise to rejoin them later. Adam, resigned to the task ahead, slid his annoying eyepatch into place and followed a chattering Becca out the door. Her exuberance contrasted with his reluctance. Weathers followed at a discreet distance. When they were halfway down the hallway, a raucous disturbance erupted from below.

Hurrying to the stairs, the trio stared in stunned silence. The well-laid plans for the afternoon collapsed like a burning building. Edward, Earl of Wyncomb, and his wife, Lady Miriam, stood in the foyer, surrounded by several bags, along with a sodden, overgrown hound Adam recognized all too well and a bustling group of servants. Becca's parents had come for a visit.

Groaning, Becca ducked back behind the corner. "This cannot be happening. What are we going to do?"

"Have dinner with them, I imagine," Adam said.

She buried her head in her hand. "Do be serious. Father was angry with me to begin with. He'll be bloody furious that I've allowed a strange man to stay here . . . And if you tell him the truth, he'll be angry that I didn't notify him of your return immediately."

"It's too late for me to pretend to leave," Adam said. "And *they're* certainly not leaving. You wanted a test for Mr. Cobbald with someone who knows me? This is the perfect opportunity. If we succeed tonight, we can tell your father the truth in the morning. With any luck, he'll be so surprised, he'll forget to be angry . . . and he won't have me arrested." He studied her face, recognizing the signs of panic. "You told me to trust you. Now I'm asking you to do the same."

"What about Jasper?" Becca hissed. "Father brought your bloody dog with him."

Once again, Adam peeked around the corner. His old foxhound was investigating every possible inch of the marble floor that his restraining strap allowed, his tail wagging wildly from side to side. Jasper could be a problem. "Three years have passed. Perhaps he won't remember me." When Becca's eyes filled with skepticism, he added, "Maybe not. But I promise to think of something. Go on, go down there before your father comes in search of you."

Nodding her head, accepting the inevitable with an admirable resolve, Becca squared her shoulders and skipped down the stairs, a cheerful smile brightening her face. From the welcome she called out, she seemed thrilled at her parents' sudden visit.

Lord Wyncomb shook the rain from his coat, a puddle of water forming on the marble floor at his feet. Looking much the same as Adam remembered him, Edward was still built like a prize pugilist; he had enormous shoulders and a barrel chest. Those muscled arms, capable of breaking a man in two, enveloped his daughter in a bearlike embrace.

Adam couldn't hear a word Becca spoke, but her lips moved frantically and her arms flapped like a seabird's wings. Next, she hugged her mother. Seeing Weathers and Adam peeking around the corner, she discreetly shooed them back out of sight.

The devil with that, thought Adam. Edward knew

him as well as any person. He wished he could confide in the old man, hated to deceive him, but if he could fool Lord Wyncomb, he could fool anyone. And while Jasper was an unexpected complication, one he couldn't avoid, he would simply have to deal with the dog. It was now or never.

"Just a moment, sir," Weathers said as he started from his hiding place. The butler scurried, as much as he was capable of scurrying for his fifty-five years, toward the bedrooms and returned with a small crystal bottle. "For the dog," he added. With an apologetic expression on his face, he proceeded to dump the contents on Adam's pant leg.

The overpowering scent of roses filled the hallway. Adam leapt backward. "Thunderall, enough! I smell like a cheap whore." He lifted his head to the heavens in silent prayer. Dear God, he was going to need every bit of help. Sucking in a deep breath, he stepped onto the upper landing.

"Metaphors, your lordship," whispered Weathers, his voice wavering with distress. "Slouch and blink. And talk through your nose. A bit of submissiveness might not hurt either." As an afterthought he added, "Try sneezing, too, sir."

Nodding curtly, Adam descended the stairs in a half glide, half prance. All activity in the foyer ceased.

Edward shot Adam a piercing glare. Raising his gray brows, he bellowed, "Who the devil are you and what are you doing here?"

"Father," Becca interjected, "I can explain."

"Bloody right, you will."

"Edward, do watch your language." Miriam Marche Wyncomb spoke with patient authority as she drew her gloves from her hands. "Your daughter has learned enough of your bad habits. And do calm down. We have only just arrived."

"In the nick of time, it would seem," Edward muttered.

By this time, Adam had successfully maneuvered the stairs to stand a mere foot from Becca's father. He twirled his hand several times, allowing the lace at his wrist to circle and cascade downward. Bowing from the waist, he introduced himself. "Francis Cobbald, at your service, my lord."

Edward sniffed the air several times, cast a stony glare at Adam, then at his daughter. His snarl quite matched Jasper's. "Is that right?"

"Do ignore my husband, Mr. Cobbald. We've had a frightfully long trip and he detests surprises. Always has and likely always will. Especially when they pertain to his daughter."

A crude seaman's chantey, something about mermaids, mermen and strategically placed seashells, came floating down the stairs. By God, he'd forgotten all about Mac. Adam whirled about just as his friend reached the landing, holding a cigar in one hand, a brandy in the other.

Edward stacked his hands on his hips. "And just who the hell are you?"

Obviously taken aback by the nobleman's ire, Mac glanced over his shoulder, as if he hoped someone else might answer that particular question. Realizing he was on his own, he stuck the cigar between his teeth, scratched his ear and strode down the stairs as if he owned the house. Marching directly to Edward, Mac thrust out his hand in welcome.

Lord Wyncomb managed to contain himself enough to shake it. He nodded at Adam. "Are you with this fellow?"

"No, sir. Macdonald Archer at your service."

"Odd. Everyone seems to be at my service and yet I don't know who the deuce anyone is."

Leaning against the oak banister, Mac studied the tip of his cigar. "I could say the same for you, guv."

Edward's eyes narrowed to small darts, deadly points fixated on Mac. Accustomed to dealing with angry, powerful men, and one of the best poker players Adam knew, Mac held his ground without so much as a blink. He took a slow drag of his cigar. "If you must know, I'm a friend of Adam Hawksmore, the late Earl of Kerrick."

"I know who the earl is," Edward stated indignantly.

"And you are?"

"Lord Edward Marche, Earl of Wyncomb. The person who happens to be handling Lord Kerrick's private affairs as a favor for him, and the father of this young lady." He studied Mac for the longest time, then glanced at Adam. At last, he settled his gaze on his daughter. "You have some explaining to do."

Becca's mother stepped to her husband's side. "Darling, please. May we move to a room other than the foyer? There will be a dozen or so questions, and I for one would like a warm fire, a comfortable chair, hot tea and privacy."

Mac slapped Edward on the shoulder. "A capital idea."

"I'll fetch the tea." Weathers, who had silently joined the gathering, hurried toward the kitchen as if sustenance might alter the outcome of events over the next half hour.

Miriam extended her arm toward her husband. Edward hesitated, then marched forward, his wife's hand on one arm, the dog tugging at the other.

Mac followed. As he passed, he took one sniff of Adam and winced. Giving his friend a quick glance, he winked once, then swaggered in Edward's footsteps. Adam wasn't sure whether to shoot Mac or himself.

Becca crept over to Adam and whispered, "What are we going to do?"

"Have some tea. We can't possibly retreat. Mac seems to be handling your father, and we knew Francis Cobbald would meet your parents sooner or later."

"I'd rather it have been later."

"Becca!" Her father's roar echoed off the tapestry-covered stone walls.

Shaking her head, she called down the hallway in answer. "Coming, Father." She turned back to Adam. "Perhaps we should simply tell him the truth."

"No. I am unwilling to trust anyone at the moment, even your father. I need more time to think matters through."

"You trusted me."

"I had no choice, did I?"

She stared at him incredulously. "You actually think my father would gain by your death?" When Adam offered no denial, she leaned her nose near his. "How dare you? My father loves you. He can be manipulative and contrary, but he would never hurt you."

Adam refused to stand in the hallway and argue with Becca. He proceeded toward the salon. Over his shoulder, he agreed, "Not intentionally. Are you coming?"

"Wait a moment." Becca tugged on his elbow. "What does that mean?"

"Only that your father is just like you: Impulsive.

Maybe even more so. Once he hears my tale, there's no telling what he'll do. I don't need a loose cannon running about England trying to prove my innocence. He's likely to simply shoot Seavers or Oswin on principle. Now come on. Our prolonged absence will only fuel his curiosity. I want you to march into that room, speak as little as possible and let me handle this. This afternoon was to be a test for Mr. Cobbald. So will it be. The only difference is that now I shall perform for them all, Mr. Shelley, Mac, your aunt, your parents and my own damn dog."

"Mr. Shelley or Jasper can't banish me to Scotland for the rest of my life."

Adam halted between two suits of armor belonging to an old deceased ancestor and turned to look her over. Becca looked guilty of any number of things. Fretting and nervousness would not help this performance. He needed to divert her worries. Cocking his lips to one side, he ran his finger across her furrowed brow and down her cheek, stopping beneath her chin. He rubbed his finger across her lips. "Admit it. You're worried about me as well, aren't you, darling?"

She opened her mouth in a gasp, then snapped it shut with a delightful little growl similar to the one she'd made when he'd kissed her. Spinning about, she sailed toward the salon. "Not a whit, you lummox. It's your neck, not mine. I can plead temporary insanity. And by the way, you stink."

Chapter Nine

Edward huffed as he paraded back and forth before the fireplace, his hands clasped behind his back. He looked the same as he always had. A gray bushy mustache lined his upper lip, and it flared with each breath, reminding Adam of the painting of the fire-breathing dragon above the mantel. Adam forced himself not to smile. Most of the time, unless truly provoked, Edward's bellow and sharp tongue were only bluster. For all intents and purposes, he was a predictable man. Adam was counting on that predictability to see him successfully through this evening.

Miriam Marche was every inch the lady, a petite woman with delicate features, wholly the opposite of her daughter. She reminded Adam of china teacups and lace doilies, while Becca made him picture thunderstorms, passion and rumpled bedsheets. Miriam possessed a quiet demeanor coupled with an inner strength that often fooled people. Becca wore her emotions on her sleeves. Miriam directed every one—including her husband—with soft words and gentle patience. Becca, quite simply, demanded one listen to her.

Mac leaned against the wall beside the liquor cabinet. He seemed content to let Edward speak first. Typical, thought Adam. Like himself, Mac was one to patiently study his adversaries. That skill alone had kept Mac out of Newgate prison any number of times.

Sitting beside her mother on a satin chaise, Becca nervously twirled a long peach ribbon from her dress around her finger. "What a lovely surprise. I didn't expect to see either of you until London."

Miriam patted her daughter's hand. "I know, my dear. You've only been gone a week, but your father thought you might be lonely."

Edward snorted into his brandy. "It appears she managed to find company after all."

"Father, don't become quarrelsome until you hear me out."

"Did you hear?" he asked his wife. "She called me quarrelsome. Humph. Why the devil would I be quarrelsome? After all, I traveled two days over the worst roads in England in a nasty storm to keep my daughter company for fear she might perish of boredom only to discover strange visitors in residence." He ended his sentence with a piercing glare toward Adam. "Bored, my—"

"Edward," warned Miriam.

Weathers rushed into the salon carrying a salver laden with tea and pastries, his cheeks flushed. Sweat dotted his brow. Obviously worried, it appeared Weathers had run all the way from the

112

kitchen. Adam wasn't sure whether to feel insulted by his butler's lack of faith or pleased by his show of loyalty. When they exchanged glances, relief shone in Weathers's old gray eyes, and Adam settled upon being pleased.

Edward refused a raisin scone and stomped over to the liquor cabinet to pour himself another drink. He shot a questioning glance toward Mac, then marched back to the center of the room. Adam knew Edward's tactics. It was all about pretense and illusion—drawing the enemy out of his defense and smashing him.

Adam decided the best strategy to take was the offensive early. Thankfully, Becca honored his wishes and remained silent. He set his glass on the table beside him and folded one hand beneath his chin. "You have no idea, my lord, the scope of my gratitude. Conversing with your lovely daughter is a paltry price to pay for her overwhelming generosity." He tipped his head to one side, sending her a resolute smile. "She has been a tender rosebud on a thorny bush."

Edward's brows scrunched together along his forehead and his eyes narrowed dangerously. Jasper lifted his nose in the air. Tugging against his leather leash, his tail thumping and spraying droplets of water in the air, the dog inched toward Adam. Edward seized the hound, while Adam seized Weathers's advice and sneezed.

"Do something about that dog," Miriam said. "Why you brought him is beyond me."

A single command from Edward brought Jasper to heel. The hound sat, whined once, stood back up, whined a second time, then plopped to the floor and laid his muzzle on his front paws. Adam swore the dog looked like it might cry.

"Where the devil is my sister?" asked Edward. Next to him, Jasper whined and watched Adam.

Lady Thacker strolled into the room on the heels of Lord Wyncomb's question, her arms extended in greeting. "Dear brother, how are you?"

While Edward's gaze never wavered from Adam, he accepted his sister's embrace. "I sent you along to chaperone my daughter. Instead I find a household of strangers in residence. Have you lost your mind?"

Tittering as she waved her hand, Jeanette plucked a fruit pastry from the tea tray and joined Miriam on the chaise. "You should be grateful I'm here, you old goat."

Edward sputtered several times. "Old goat? Why, I . . ."

"Behave," Miriam ordered, shaking her head in amusement. "Both of you. Edward, where are your manners? Sit down and be quiet. Give Jeanette and the young men a chance to explain." She turned to Adam. "Mr. Cobbald, you may go first."

Adam looked from Edward to Miriam, who sipped her tea, a contented smile on her face. The woman might fool most people, but he knew her mind absorbed every detail.

Blinking a half-dozen times or so, he related the wild tale of being accosted by brigands, then of his arrival, adding an abundance of sighs and swirls of the wrist for good measure. He searched for a metaphor for the event, but aside from the black crows, which Becca had already told him were not the least bit appropriate, all efforts were in vain. Noticing Jasper inching toward him on his belly, Adam sneezed.

"Why are you in these parts?" asked Edward.

Becca glanced at Adam, and he noted panic in her eyes before she turned back to her teacup.

"Mr. Cobbald is a poet," Jeanette enthusiastically offered between bites.

"A *what?*" Edward's thunderous question was likely heard in the village two miles away. He glared at Becca. "I specifically told you to stay away from men like that Barnard chap! I made my opinion abundantly clear. Didn't I, Miriam?"

"Yes, dear, you did. Quite loudly, too, if I remember correctly."

"It's not as if I *invited* Mr. Cobbald here," Becca began.

"Truly, your lordship," Adam interjected, raising his voice to a breathy squeal, "your daughter saved my life. My wounds are healing nicely and I should be able to leave in a day or two."

"Good," was all the man said.

Miriam shook her head. "Mr. Cobbald, my husband loves his daughter a great deal, and you must admit, one cannot be too careful with a young lady's reputation."

"I understand perfectly." For a metaphor, he opted to stay with what seemed to be, with his own dousing in perfume, the floral theme of the night. "A rose such as Lady Rebecca must be sheltered from all manner of . . ." He paused. What did one shelter a rose against? He stared at Becca and blurted the first thing that came to mind. "Blight."

Becca, who had been watching and waiting expectantly, frowned. Weathers gasped and Mac coughed into his brandy. Jasper climbed to his feet and howled. Rather than drown himself in the nearest brandy bottle, Adam blinked a few more times for good measure.

"Jasper, sit," Edward ordered before he turned back to Adam. "What is wrong with your eye?"

Adam flinched. "A childhood malady, sir." His eyelid twitched. Damn. Now he couldn't seem to stop blinking. He cleared his throat and coughed. "Anyway, your daughter offered me a safe haven. So here I am."

Wyncomb rubbed his mustache as he turned and studied Mac. "And you?"

Mac sauntered toward the blustery earl. Stopping, he knelt and scratched behind Adam's dog's ear, and Jasper rolled to his side, his hind leg twitching back and forth. "Adam and I grew up together. I recently returned to England and sought out my old friend only to learn of his demise. Sorry state of affairs, if you ask me. Unfortunately, I discovered his absence after my transport left. It returns in two days." He stood and leaned an elbow insolently on the mantel. "Lady Thacker offered me shelter until then."

"Damn good thing a packet of thieves didn't stop by for a visit." Tapping his finger against his upper lip, Edward asked, "Where's your home?"

"Here. There. I captain my own ship."

"I meant who are your parents?"

"My mother was a fine young woman who spent her life scrubbing up after fancy gents in order to keep tuppence in her pocket." Mac crossed his arms over his chest. "Tell me, sir, do you have a problem with bastards?"

"Then I'd have a problem with myself," Edward said matter-of-factly, mirroring the other man. They looked like two bulldogs squared off over a bone. "A bastard's one thing, young man. A temperamental bastard's another. You've a familiarity about you, that's all."

Mac had certainly succeeded in shifting Edward's attention from Adam. Now he waited for Mac's answer, unsure of Edward's purpose. If there was one subject his friend detested it was that of his lineage. Born with absolutely no knowledge of who his father might be, Mac avoided the subject like a virgin avoided a priest's lecture on the marriage bed, and he became quite irritable when pressed about the issue. Thankfully a servant appeared in the doorway.

"Lady Rebecca, your company has arrived."

All at once, Shelley's visit seemed propitious. A boon. With luck, aside from providing the opportunity to study an honest-to-goodness poet, it meant Lord Wyncomb's inquisition just might be postponed, allowing Adam time to gather his wits and plan his next step.

"What company?" Becca's father asked, disgruntled by the interruption.

Plastering a cheerful smile on her face, Becca said, "How forgetful of me? Mr. Percy Shelley and his friend are here for dinner."

"Shelley?" Wyncomb asked. "Why is that name familiar?"

Mac, ensuring the afternoon was going to be even more interesting than anyone ever contemplated, supplied the answer. "This must be your lucky day, sir. Shelley is another poet."

"Did God wage war against Napoleon? No. Because God does not exist." Shelley leaned against the mantel of the fireplace. "Over the years, the church has filled its coffers with the dead souls of many young men—all in the name of God."

The poet spoke with passion, Adam would admit that much. It was a shame he was so bloody misguided.

Adam reclined in his chair, his head cocked in

feigned agreement. In truth, he had a mind to punch the man in his delicate lily-white face. Surely his teeth would pain him later for all the clenching he'd done the last hour. He glanced over at Lord Wyncomb.

Thus far, seated in an overstuffed chair beside his wife, Edward had done a fine job of defending England's position on politics and war. His vociferous rebuttals had provided no end to Adam's enjoyment, though at the moment the man did appear rather apoplectic.

Becca, on the other hand, reverently clung to every word Shelley uttered. That was, of course, when she wasn't whispering with the man's companion, one Miss Godwin, on the settee. Heaven only knew what nonsense they discussed.

Mac, coveting his corner by the brandy, entertained Jasper while Jeanette contented herself with a box of chocolates.

With a graceful swoop of his arm, Shelley dragged his fingers through his long, bushy locks, adding an even wilder appearance to his already rumpled look. "Man makes conscious choices. He wages war in the name of right and wrong when, in fact, his goal is to further his own nefarious plans—to gain property or wealth, or simply to play at being a hero."

"In other words," Adam interrupted with a serenity he did not feel, "you believe that our very countrymen sailed to France, trudged through mud, rain, blood and death to return home to entertain a room full of gossipmongers and sluggards? To brag about their exploits?"

Shelley stroked his palm against the starched collar that lay open at his throat, a style Adam envied, considering the restrictive cravat he wore. The visitor's informality alone was a relief in sight for the excruciating evening. Adam intended to remove his own horrific neckwear as soon as possible.

"Precisely my point, Mr. Cobbald. Those poor souls, misguided as they were, manipulated by society, burdened with a ridiculous code of honor, did not know any better. Like lost sheep in the meadow, they followed the easiest path, guided by their ancestors before them."

It was as if Shelley were referring directly to the Kerrick legacy. And Adam did not like it one bit. Yes, most definitely, the man's appearance would be vastly improved with a blackened eye alongside a bloodied nose. Adam grinned at the image. Becca must have seen and correctly interpreted his thoughts, because she cleared her throat and shot a warning glare in his direction.

Had Miriam not been seated next to her husband, keeping him down, Shelley would have been sprawled across the Aubusson rug by now. He slapped his hand on the arm of the settee. "Enough. I have never heard such a ridiculous mountain of misinformation and sedition in my entire life."

Jasper, content with Mac's attention up until now, leapt to his feet and barked as if he agreed with every word Edward bellowed.

Bristling, Shelley straightened his slumped shoulders. He glanced from Adam to Miss Godwin, then back to Edward. "I mean no offense, sir. Every man is entitled to his opinion."

"Not in this house," Edward snapped. "Mr. Archer, keep that dog quiet."

"By all means, sir." From his spot in the corner, Mac settled the dog with a few soft words. Jasper spun in a circle three times, then plopped to the floor, his head on Mac's boot.

Clasping her hand over Edward's clenched palm, Lady Wyncomb smiled politely. "Gentlemen, please. Unfortunately, men with strong opinions often leave little room for any middle ground, therefore some topics are best left unexplored. Perhaps another subject? Miss Godwin, tell us about yourself."

While Adam looked unsure this discussion would be any better, Becca was thrilled. She practically sat on top of Miss Godwin.

"Do tell," she enthused, barely containing her excitement. Surely Miss Godwin had a multitude of information and personal insight to share. Dressed in a simple gray linen dress with a pale and thoughtful face, she was everything Becca expected: young, intelligent, sincere and absolutely besotted with Shelley. "Shall you continue your mother's writings?"

"I've always been given more to flights of imagination," Miss Godwin explained. "I plan to finish my first novella soon, but since the birth of my son, I have had little time to write."

"I didn't realize," Becca's mother said in a most maternal fashion. "Will your husband join you soon?"

Shelley affectionately squeezed Miss Godwin's shoulder. "I am William's father."

The color drained from Miriam's face. "Oh. I had no idea. Your names—"

"Are not the same," Miss Godwin interjected without the least bit of embarrassment. "We know. Percy and I have had little choice in the matter. Quite unintentionally, we conceived an ardent passion for one another, yet his wife refuses to dissolve their marriage."

"Isn't that marvelous? Miss Godwin is the daughter of Mary Wollstonecraft," Becca quickly added, thinking her mother looked like she was about to faint. "Naturally her beliefs are of a less traditional point of view."

"I should have known," Becca's father snorted, with a disapproving scowl at her.

Miriam mustered another breathy "Oh my." Jeanette nibbled a berry scone, watching the scene with relish. Adam and Mac shared one of those secret male glances that made women wish for an object to throw.

"Exactly," Mary agreed with a genteel, soft-spoken voice. "I wholeheartedly believe in the importance of the advancement and education of women, though I cannot claim to be as bold in my writings as my mother. I choose to live my life more by example."

"Obviously," Edward muttered.

"Father, be quiet," Becca whispered, knowing she would likely hear of this all tomorrow. But she wanted to know more. Much more. "Go on, Miss Godwin."

"My mother felt marriage was an institution created solely for the benefit of men."

"So very true," Becca added with deep conviction.

"She said it best when she wrote that in our society, 'a woman is the toy of a man, his rattle, and it must jingle in his ears whenever, dismissing reason, he chooses to be amused.' "

"I remember that passage well," Becca said. "It was one of my personal favorites."

Miss Godwin cast a starry-eyed gaze toward Shelley, who lounged indolently against the side of the chair. "The legal document involved in wedlock sends the message that the man owns the woman. If love and respect bound two people together, rather than a scrap of paper, perhaps there would be far more happy marriages among Polite Society."

How many times had Becca said the very same thing to her parents? She wanted to stand up and cheer for all liberated women, or applaud at the very least. Unfortunately, given the sneer on her father's face and the frown on Adam's, she'd never again see the outside of her bedroom. Even Mac had the audacity to snort. And Becca couldn't remember ever seeing that trout-fished expression on her mother before.

Miriam snapped her mouth shut and her gaze swept about the room. No doubt she was searching for a way to extricate everyone from what she considered an unsuitable topic. Her eyes fell upon Adam. "Mr. Cobbald, why don't you share a poem with us."

Edward groaned. "Must we?"

"Ignore my brother, Mr. Cobbald," Jeanette piped up. "He's never mastered the art of diplomacy. I'd say a poem is just what we need."

"Thank you, but no." Adam wasn't about to offer himself up as the sacrificial lamb. "Perhaps Mr. Shelley. He's been at this poetry business much longer than I."

"Don't be shy," Shelley encouraged as he sat on the other side of the room. He was fortunate that Adam's arms couldn't reach that far to strangle him.

Determined to calm the fireworks one way or another, Miriam ordered, "Yes, Mr. Cobbald, you will share one of your poems with us. *Now*. We can hear from Mr. Shelley when you are finished."

Hell's bells. Adam had no desire to draw attention to himself. Unfortunately, Miriam had a gleam in her eye that meant trouble for anyone who dared argue.

There was no hope for it. Adam left the security of his winged chair and stood beside the window. He braced his feet apart as if he were preparing to address his troops, then shuffled them back together to balance his weight on one leg. It was a more effeminate pose, he supposed, and he was creating a persona.

"Oh," Adam squealed, perhaps a bit higher than necessary. " 'How this spring of love resembleth . . . the uncertain glory of an April day! Which now shows all the beauty of the sun . . . and by-and-by a cloud takes all away.' "

Shelley chuckled, a warm but ineffectual laugh. "Not Shakespeare, man. Something original."

All eyes were glued to Adam. Even Jasper whined in interest and tugged at his restraint. By Adam's estimation, Shelley truly deserved two black eyes. Inhaling a deep breath, he sought a notable subject. Something inspirational.

Jasper howled.

"A dog," he blurted. "Friend to one and all." Adam grinned at Becca, quite pleased that he'd managed to compose one entire line. He ignored Mac's rude chortle, which the man unsuccessfully hid behind his hand.

"Loving creatures, born to hunt, they love their masters, even a . . ." He crossed to the window, searching for a word that rhymed. "Runt," he cried. "Man's best friend indeed. For surely that is what they are."

Silence reigned. Utter, disheartening silence.

It wasn't that bad, he thought despairingly.

Finally, Shelley uncrossed his legs. "If I may be so bold, Mr. Cobbald, you might try a touch more imagery. And perhaps a more relevant subject. For example—" He gathered a faraway, dreamlike look on his face. " 'And the spring arose on the garden fair, like the spirit of Love felt everywhere.' " The poet clasped his hands to his chest dramatically. " 'And each flower and herb on Earth's dark breast, rose from this its wintry nest.' " His expression became most serious. "Give it another go, Mr. Cobbald."

Adam wanted to go, all right. Directly upstairs. He stared at the painting of a ship being ripped apart in a wild storm on the far side of the room and wished he were on board. Better to drown and end his suffering than compose another bloody poem.

Imagery? Hell. He raised his voice a few notches. He blinked. He sighed. He remembered the afternoon with Becca in the east tower. He wasn't above plagiarizing. And he'd seen any number of plays. Surely he could enunciate in the same odd manner as Shelley, too.

"Effulgent shards of lightning explode across the starlit heavens." He violently waved his arm in the air. "The ancient sword of Mother Nature. The pounding rain, her fist that strikes the ground, blows flowers 'round and 'round. She wields her power as thunder on the land." His voice gathered strength and pitch in what he considered the most effective manner. The clap of his hands at the end seemed a stroke of genius.

Instead of applause, however, Jasper whimpered once, staring long and hard at Adam, then buried his head in his paws and moaned a very houndlike prayer. Adam almost joined him. He was saved, however.

"Dinner is served," Weathers announced most precipitously.

The entire room seemed to sigh with relief.

Hell, I wasn't that bad!

Chapter Ten

Pleading exhaustion, Lady Thacker excused herself the moment dinner concluded and the guests departed. Adam intended to do the same. He was so relieved the evening was over, he practically wept with joy. He wanted the privacy of his room, time to regroup, a stiff drink and a shirt without a bloody collar that choked the very breath from him. Wasting no time, he bade everyone good night and turned toward the stairs, hoping Mac and Becca would follow. They needed to discuss how they were going to break the truth to Edward come morning.

His progress was stopped by Edward, who, grabbing Adam's elbow, beamed at him with an overly wide smile. "If you don't mind, I'd like to share a brandy in the library before we retire."

As Mac tried to sneak past unnoticed, Edward added, "You, too, young man."

Ushering his wife before him, Lord Wyncomb led them to the library and closed the mahogany doors, the click of their locks an ominous sound in the otherwise silent room. His audience had only just settled in their chairs when he rounded on his daughter, stalked across the wooden floor and calmly asked, "Do I look like a fool?" The odd, wolflike smile never left his face.

Becca's eyes rounded. "Of course not, Father."

"Perhaps I suffer from old age like your Uncle Albert?"

"Don't be silly," his wife offered. "You'll die from a fit of temper long before that."

His nostrils flared as he asked, "A candidate for Bedlam?"

Miriam and Becca both answered with a resounding "No."

Adam remained silent, content to watch and determine Edward's course. After all, a skilled player never revealed his cards until the entire hand had been dealt.

The older man stomped toward the desk in the middle of the room, circled once, twice, then stopped directly in front of Adam on the third go-round. "If not me, then you." He crossed his arms over his chest and bellowed, "What in the name of Neptune do you think you're doing?"

Startled from her seat, his wife stood. "Edward! Do not accost our guests. I swear you have lost your mind."

"You think so? Humph!" He arched one brow, glaring first at Mac, then Becca, and finally settling his full wrath on Adam. "Have I lost my mind, *Mr. Cobbald?*"

The ruse was up. Adam knew it. To continue the

charade would be an insult to both of them. Accepting the inevitable, he slowly stood and slid the patch from his eye.

Miriam stared at him in shock. As recognition dawned, she melted back into her seat like a glob of butter. "Adam?" she asked weakly.

"Yes, madam."

Edward stepped even closer, and although Adam stood several inches taller, the older man was a good deal angrier. He stuck his nose within an inch of Adam's face. "By God, son, I ought to have you whipped."

Mac took two steps, his hand tucked inside his jacket for the gun Adam knew he kept there. Waving his friend back, Adam stood with the rigidity of a military man greeting his superior officer; his feet braced shoulder-width apart, his hands clasped behind his back, his gaze focused forward. "I understand, sir. How did you know?"

"Certainly not because you saw fit to tell me. Thank goodness for Jasper. That dog has not done that odd praying trick you taught him since the day you left. After that, I simply put two and two together. Do you realize there is a price on your fool head?"

"Obviously, sir, you will do what you must. I would, however, like the opportunity to explain before you turn me over to the authorities."

"The authorities? And here I thought you an intelligent lad. Why the hell would I do that? You're innocent, aren't you?"

"As a matter of—"

"Yes or no?"

"Yes."

"Damn straight. Bloody nonsense, if you ask me.

The minute I heard that drivel I knew there had to be another answer. Bloody bureaucrats. We leave for London tomorrow. You can meet with Lord Archibald at the War Department and clear up this misunderstanding."

Adam finally allowed his gaze to meet Edward's. "That's impossible."

"Poppycock! You said you were innocent."

"Yes, sir."

"Quit addressing me like a damned superior officer, or have you forgotten *my* name as well?"

"Perhaps, dear," Miriam said, recovering from her shock and becoming the voice of reason her husband sometimes needed, "if you quit badgering Adam, he could explain."

"I'm not badgering him," Edward snapped. When she matched his stony glare with one of her own, he sat in a chair like a petulant schoolboy, angry over the decision but smart enough not to argue with the teacher. "I'm just glad to see the boy, that's all." As if he had just remembered her presence and her duplicity, Edward glared at his daughter. "And don't think I've forgotten your actions in this idiotic farce. Lying to your father. It's a damn shame."

Clearing his throat, Adam said, "I forced her, Edward."

"And she agreed?" Edward asked with a raised brow. "Hah! I can barely coerce her to agree on the color of the sky. Have sons, Adam. They'll honor their father right and proper."

Shaking her head, Becca shared one of those I've-heard-this-all-before-looks with her mother, who patted her hand in support. Her father snorted in disgust. "See? Already they're forming an alliance. How's a man to keep a household?"

Miriam smiled sweetly. "Exactly as you do. With love and, every now and then, a bit of patience."

"And to clarify," Becca added along with a pointed glare at Adam, "I knew very well what I was doing when I agreed to keep his identity a secret."

"Why didn't you write of this . . . or to me at all since you arrived? You are my daughter. I was beginning to think someone had kidnapped you." Glaring back at Adam, he asked, "And what's your excuse?"

"On the Continent I had no means to communicate, but even had I, I doubt I would have written. Once I arrived here, I thought it best to let the situation develop slowly. It was a matter of trust."

"As I said, I ought to have you whipped," Edward muttered. His fingers drummed on the arm of the chair.

"Enough," Miriam warned. "You and I both know you have no intention of beating Adam, so stop making idle threats."

Grinding his teeth, his back as stiff as a stick, Edward clasped his arms across his chest.

Adam yanked the pin from his cravat and loosened the confining fabric from his neck. Crossing to the bar, he shared a conspiratorial glance with Mac and poured himself a whiskey.

"An old man could die with the waiting. Are you going to disrobe, or are you going to tell us where the hell you've been?"

Adam tried to find any reason that Edward might be dangerous, but all logic defied the possibility. He had only one choice: to trust Edward completely, tell him all there was to know and keep the man from running amok once in London. With that decision, Adam felt a huge weight lift from his shoulders. He kept his position beside Mac. "I imagine you'd like me to start at the beginning?"

"Now there's an idea," Edward said sarcastically, obviously still upset at being played for a fool. He listened as Adam explained his situation, interjecting a question only now and then. When Adam finished, he slapped his hands together. "By Jove, I knew you were innocent. We need a plan."

Becca wasn't about to be left out. "If you haven't noticed, we *have* a plan. Adam is going to London disguised as a poet. I intend to act as his sponsor. He can begin his investigation once we're there."

Scanning Adam from head to toe, her father sneered. "I wasn't sure if he was a poet or one of those high-falutin' dandies who can't tell where they end and the horse's ass begins."

Lending his support, Mac interjected, "His poetry does needs a bit of work."

Edward snorted.

Adam cleared his throat. "If I could—"

"What about Aunt Jeanette?" asking Becca. "What are we going to tell her?"

"She can visit our brother for a few weeks," Edward said.

"Perhaps she should come." Miriam folded her hands in her lap. "Amazing as it seems, she does manage to gain entrance to practically any parlor in London. She could be a great help."

"Fine," her husband grumbled. "But remember, she spreads gossip faster than a leper spreads disease. Keep Adam's identity a secret from her. What about Cecil? That no good jackanapes will do anything he can to snare that inheritance. He'll have to be dealt with."

"May I say something?" Adam asked, but suddenly

everyone was talking at once. This was exactly what he had feared: total and complete chaos. No one seemed to remember that he even stood in the same room. He pounded his fist on a table several times, sending into a jig the seven small porcelain musicians that stood upon it. "Wait a bloody minute!"

There were those brows again, arching high on Edward's forehead. Adam didn't even wince. He knew the old man's tactics. "Save your scowls for someone who doesn't know you."

"You have a problem with what we've discussed?" Edward asked.

"It's my neck heading to the gallows. I might have something to contribute to these discussions. Exactly what new plans do you have in mind?"

"Well, lad, your disguise is a good one. I can't fault you and Becca on that—no one who ever knew you would ever expect you to look like this. But wear a costume like that and every man, woman and child will watch your every move."

"We did the best we could," Becca grumbled.

"Of course, darling," her mother readily agreed. "He paints an interesting picture, but your father has a point. Perhaps you should keep the patch and the dyed hair, but you must tone down the dress. He'll draw less notice that way."

Adam knew the final decision was his. Everyone watched him expectantly, a myriad of expressions on their face. "The devil take it," he said. "What do I have to lose?"

"That's my boy." Edward grinned.

"We have a more immediate problem," Mac added from his corner of the room. "Someone has been asking questions about Adam along this coast. We don't know precisely why. I caught a glimpse of the fellow, but he disappeared before I had a chance to chat with him."

Stroking his mustache, Edward crossed to the window and back. Suddenly his eyes twinkled with mischief. "There's no hope for it, Adam. We're simply going to have to kill you."

"I beg your pardon?" Mac asked sharply.

"You did say someone was asking questions about Adam," Lord Wyncomb said. Mac nodded. "In that case, let's give them a funeral, complete with witnesses—something to prove that Adam is truly dead. No one will dare question me. Maybe, just maybe, we can buy some precious time. Then we'll go to London."

"One small problem," Adam interjected. "If Lady Thacker and the staff think I'm Mr. Cobbald, how do you intend for me to be Adam Kerrick at the same time?"

Grinning wolfishly at Mac, Edward said, "I wasn't exactly thinking of you, but someone who could pass as you in gloomy surroundings."

As if scripted, all heads turned to Mac at the same time.

His brows drew together as his lips flattened to a straight line. "Oh, bloody hell."

Chapter Eleven

"Be still," Adam snapped as Mac scratched his throat for the fourth time.

"Easy for you to say. You're not the one having his face dusted with white powder while your arse freezes on a slab of stone. Damn unnatural if you ask me."

"What is?"

Mac waved his hand in the air. "This. The way you titled folk die. I don't think I'd enjoy the idea of my dead relatives sleeping below stairs while I snored above. It's not natural. Bury me at sea and leave it at that."

Adam glanced about the family tomb. Stone coffins housing his ancestors were stacked three high along two walls. They bore names, dates of births and deaths and some illustrious memories—like his Great-Uncle Harold: "a sword worthy of one hundred men. Nearby, four iron sconces held small torches. Their flames danced like fiery apparitions as cold air wafted through the dimly lit chamber. The stone dais, graven with cherubs and Latin words of honor, occupied the center. What could he say, the room was what it was. A tomb. "I can't say I'd prefer being dinner for some fish."

"What fish?" Becca asked.

She hovered in the arched doorway, dressed in a dark-colored dress. A shawl covered her curls and shoulders. Her gaze darted from wall to wall, as if she expected Uncle Harold or Aunt Margaret to rise from the dead. Adam thought he even detected a slight hitch in her voice.

"Come on in and I'll introduce you to my relatives." Adam dabbed more powder on Mac's neck. "Why are you whispering, anyway?"

"Because I feel like it." She shuddered. "It is freezing down here."

"The dead don't mind the cold," Adam laughed.

"I do," muttered Mac.

"The sun is shining brightly outside. Why couldn't we hold this gathering in the upstairs salon with plenty of light and sunshine?" She wrinkled her nose. "And fresh air."

"Remember, this whole fiasco is your father's idea. This chamber is cold, dark, damp, musty and thoroughly inhospitable. Need I go on? According to him, the setting is perfect. No one will be inclined to linger."

"Thank the stars for that," Mac added, scratching his chin yet again.

Cautiously, Becca tiptoed forward, her shadow climbing the stone walls and arched ceiling like some giant from a child's fairy tale. She carried a single candle in one hand and a blanket of sorts in the other.

"Don't tell me that you," Adam drawled, "a woman who proclaims herself hungry for adventure, independent and worldly, is afraid of a skeleton or two."

Rolling to his side, Mac lay his head on his elbow with one foot crossed over his other leg. His lips curled to one side. He looked every inch the rake Adam knew him to be. "Never fear, my lady, I promise to keep you safe."

"Hah!" snorted Adam, shoving Mac back onto the stone. "You're dead. If she needs any reassurance, I'll be the one to provide it."

"Thank you very much for your generous offer, but if anyone's to comfort me, it will likely be my father. I'll be fine. I'm simply not accustomed to climbing near dead people." Unfolding a blue velvet drape with the Kerrick family crest sewn on the edge, she spread the fabric over Mac's chest. "The magistrate and the vicar have arrived. Father is sharing a brandy with them, and Mother looks every bit the lady who has lost an adopted son. Aunt Jeanette's not quite sure what to do. They'll be down shortly."

Adam grinned. "Time to die, my friend."

Mac practically growled, which provided no end of amusement for Adam. His friend could grouse all he wanted, but the man would do anything to keep Adam safe. They'd saved one another's backsides many times, and in far more dangerous circumstances. Mac knew as well as Adam what lay at stake.

So tonight, Adam Hawksmore, the Earl of Kerrick, would be laid to rest, his death the result of a tragic accident. *Good riddance. The man had been a traitor.* No one would question, or so they hoped, Edward's judgment on the matter.

The plan was simple, as the better ones usually were. Disguise, distract and direct. Only one question remained unanswered: Were the players capable of their roles? "All right, my friend, give it a try."

Mac laid back, crossed his hands over his chest and closed his eyes. Black shoe polish hid his red curls, and he wore Adam's finest military dress. He stilled his breathing until it appeared almost nonexistent. With the dim lighting and a touch of luck, this just might work, Adam mused. "You look good dead."

"Stuff it," Mac muttered.

Becca fussed with Mac's jacket. "You must remember to breathe slowly. No matter what."

"Not a problem. With this collar, I'm lucky I can breathe at all."

"I understand completely," Adam added, suddenly inclined to tug on the elaborate cravat at his own neck. His decision to abandon the fancy cravats like Shelley had been vehemently vetoed by Weathers and Rebecca, but he could always just decide on his own. "Just be careful."

Grinning for the first time, Mac said, "Not to worry. The local magistrate cares more for his liquor than his job. Why do you think he's never caught me? And the vicar is too old to tell a dog from a cat. Coupled with a few brandies in their bellies and these charming surroundings, they'll be eager to identify me as you and hurry on their way." Mac winked at Becca. "Can a dead man get a kiss?"

"I think not," Adam snapped. He knew Mac was only teasing but, nonetheless, the suggestion was irksome.

"I wasn't asking *you*."

"You're incorrigible," Becca answered, her voice

finally freed of nervousness. "Now be quiet." Laughing at Mac's forlorn expression, she made several last adjustments to his costume.

"Remember your part, sweet lady. If anyone comes close to this battered body of mine, feel free to drape yourself over my broken bones and weep in sorrow."

Becca best not drape herself too closely, Adam thought. As a matter of fact, she seemed to be lingering at the task of straightening Mac's clothes far longer than was necessary. Adam pulled her hand away. "I'll take care of that." He tugged the drape over his friend's body.

Mac grinned again. "Jealous?"

Adam's brow rose. "Of you? Not on your life. You forget; I know your wicked ways. I'm simply protecting an innocent from the likes of your scurvy hide."

Mac chuckled. "If you say so, my friend. If you say so. It reminds me of the time we stopped at that tavern near Reading. There was that delightful wench, a brunette, I think. If I recall, we both—"

"Oh, shut up and die."

"I think I'd like to hear this tale," Becca said, a teasing lilt in her voice.

"No, you wouldn't," Adam snapped.

Like the midshipman's warning bell, Edward's voice echoed down the stairway, ending their teasing. Mac winked and lay his head on the small red velvet pillow just as footsteps pattered on the stone floor. Becca settled beside Mac, a white handkerchief as her single prop. Adam drifted to the far corner, the darkest and most unobtrusive part of the chamber, and waited. After all, he couldn't miss his very own funeral.

Edward came first, followed by Darwin Patterson, the local magistrate, and the latter's jowls were still as round as they had been the day Adam left for France. Jeanette and Miriam appeared next, arm in arm, the vicar on their heels. All gathered around the doorway as if they waited for some sign.

Stepping aside, Wyncomb faced Patterson. "Do whatever it is you need to do," he said, his tone matter-of-fact.

Patterson swung about, but, as he did, he noticed Adam. "Who are you?" he asked.

Adam dipped into a deep bow. "Francis Cobbald."

"And who is that, exactly?"

Edward moved beside Patterson. "If you must know, he's a bloody poet my daughter intends to sponsor in London." Shaking his head, he added, "Makes a father wonder where he's gone wrong."

Becca lay her head beside Mac's shoulder and sobbed like a foghorn. Patterson inspected Adam one more time, then turned back to Edward. "What's the matter with the girl?"

"If you must know," Miriam answered softly, "Lord Kerrick was her first love. They had even discussed marriage. She's been inconsolable. Certainly you understand. I'm not sure she'll ever forgive her father."

"Be quiet, Miriam. That's none of the man's business. Besides, Hawksmore was a spy." Edward slapped Patterson's back. "Go on. It's damn cold down here."

As if on cue, Jeanette huddled closer to Miriam. She was playing her part beautifully without an inkling of what was truly transpiring. "Where are the flowers? Shame on you, Edward. The poor boy ought to at least have flowers, traitor or not. My Raymond had hundreds of flowers, bless his soul."

As Jeanette mumbled something about red roses, Becca clutched Mac's arm and sobbed again. In Adam's opinion, she was far closer than she needed to be. He fought the impulse to march forward and remove her hands. Not a smart tactical move, he decided, for a man who was supposed to be dead.

Clearing his throat, Patterson stepped within two feet of the stone dais, leaned to the side and peered over Becca's shoulder. "By golly, it looks like the earl. You say you shot him?"

"Right in the heart," Edward offered proudly, as if he'd bagged a prize boar. "I'm a very good shot." Adam couldn't see his face, but he thought Edward might be grinning. "Bloody shame. Ruined the carpet in the upstairs room. Thought he was a common thief. I suppose it spares England the task of hanging the lad."

"That's absolutely horrid." Becca sniffed, stifling her cries in the handkerchief she held to her face.

The vicar, his old bones hunched over, shuffled over next to Patterson. Due to his shorter height, he peeked around Becca's other side and hiccuped. "Yes, that looks like the earl all right."

"What do you think I told you both?" Edward snapped. "Now that we all agree on this man's identity, perhaps we could have a few words." He watched the vicar expectantly.

Now this would be interesting, Adam thought. The vicar had watched him grow from babe to man and had accepted Adam's past generous donations to the parish with glee. Surely he'd have a wealth of praise to share.

The vicar smacked his lips several times, rubbed his hand over his face and hiccuped once again.

"May the blessed Lord take pity on this poor, misguided soul. Amen." He turned away. "Now, I think I could use another brandy, if you don't mind."

That's it? Adam wanted to shout. Irrational as it was, he wanted a tale of valor or, at the very least, a few kind words. Damn if he'd allow the vicar to say prayers over his dead body ever again.

Becca sobbed several more times, her shoulders shaking as she did. Miriam dabbed her cheeks with her own handkerchief while Jeanette continued to rail at her brother for his inconsiderate nature. See if she brought flowers to his funeral!

Obviously delighted to have the affair over and done with, Lord Wyncomb slapped his hands together to assemble everyone at the door.

Rubbing his jaw, Patterson stopped before Adam. "Did you know the earl?"

"I never had the pleasure. Until he was dead, of course."

"Of course," Patterson answered dubiously. "Why did you come today?"

It appeared the magistrate was going to do his job after all. Undaunted, Adam pulled a small snuffbox from his pocket. "I rarely have the opportunity to attend the closure of someone's life. They say life is death and death is life, and in death we find glorious life. Of course we have to live first."

As intended, Patterson was thoroughly confused. He shook his head, tucked his tongue in his cheek and crossed to Edward. "I see what you mean, sir."

"Are we finished, then?" Edward asked.

No one answered, which Wyncomb took to be a yes. He ushered the group up the stairs. As planned, Becca refused to follow, which added fuel to her father's grumbling about a daughter's disobedience.

The vicar simply asked if he might have another brandy before he took to the road.

Adam and Becca remained silent until the voices drifted into the distance, finally disappearing altogether. He crossed to Mac and punched his friend in the arm. "You did well."

Opening one eye, Mac grinned, opened both and said, "Of course I did. What did you expect?"

When Becca hugged Mac, Adam stacked his hands on his hips. "That's a fine how-do-you-do. All he did was lay there and keep his mouth shut."

Becca tipped her head and bit her lip in the most delightful way. "And what about *my* performance?"

Adam couldn't contain himself any longer. They'd done it. He wasn't sure what the outcome would be, but the tale of his funeral would be common news before midnight tonight. If someone had doubted that he was truly dead, and if they came to Lynmouth asking questions, the facts would speak for themselves. Both he and Mac burst into laughter at the same time, which prompted Becca to giggle even as she hushed them both.

"Stay here until I come back." She skipped to the door, pivoted and said, "This was such fun. London will be even more exciting." With that, she disappeared up the steps.

Mac slapped Adam on the back. "I'm almost sorry I can't go with you."

"The game there will only grow more dangerous. And with this company of players, I should likely go mad while trying to control their efforts to aid my cause. As it is, it will be like herding frogs. Damn difficult."

"You'll find the scoundrel responsible and clear your name. Of that I have no doubt." Mac nodded toward the doorway. "But when I said I wanted to come, I was talking about seeing you with Lady Rebecca. You can't take your eyes off her. Besides invoking your protective instincts, she tests that precious control of yours. She's the perfect countess for you."

"Hah! We're as different as fish and fowl. Granted, I find her attractive, but I'm not sure I'm up to the task. She would require a great deal of effort, guidance and a firm hand."

Mac snorted. "Guidance and a firm hand, my arse. Now I *know* I must come to London after I finish my business along the coast."

Chapter Twelve

"Under no circumstances are you to use my given name."

Becca showed Adam her back. He was being positively tyrannical, his lecture growing more tedious with each spoken word. Goodness, he'd harped at her since early morn. Ignoring his newest tirade, she climbed the brick steps that led to Lord and Lady Grayson's front door, passing a dozen tiny Chinese paper lanterns indicative of Lady Grayson's new passion in decor. Over her shoulder, she cheerfully said, "I believe you've already reminded me of that particular rule six times today."

To think when he'd escorted her into the carriage, dressed in black trousers with a burgundy waistcoat, white lace at the wrists and a simple striped cravat, she'd thought him quite dashing. His hair fell loosely about his shoulders, his crimped curls slightly tousled, the white streak and eye patch adding an air of mystery and distinction. He'd kissed her hand and looked her over in turn.

She was dressed in a gown that was one of her favorites, pale peach with moss-colored floral accents. His bold gaze had lingered on the bare flesh above her bodice, making her feel like a cream-filled scone. Her heart had actually tumbled all the way into her satin slippers. Then he'd opened his mouth.

Adam leaned both hands on his brass-handled cane. "Do not ask any questions that might seem suspicions. You should appear only concerned with finding a suitor."

"That's the fourth time you've said that particular rule," she complained, waltzing up two more steps. "And as I've told you before, I do not desire or need a suitor. I'm here to help you."

She thought she heard him growl and struggled to contain her smile, but that was impossible. Regardless of what Adam thought, said or did, the Graysons' ball was going to be thrilling. Not because she wanted to act the part of an insipid young debutante, but tonight they would earnestly begin the search for Adam's betrayer.

They'd arrived in London four days earlier after an arduous and soggy five-day trip from the coast. Her father had grumbled most of the time about the abominable road conditions, while her mother embroidered and soothed Edward's impatience. Aunt Jeanette had slept for hours on end, saying she was massing vitality for the next few weeks of activity. Becca and Adam had talked, sometimes debated, on topics ranging from foxhunts to Plato, the Peninsular War to tea with the Prince Regent.

When they arrived at Wyncomb House, notices

were immediately sent announcing their return. As planned, the invitations poured in that very day. Gowns were ordered, additional servants hired, and Jeanette shared tales about Francis Cobbald with her friends. Now, at last, all was ready, Becca thought. If only Adam would relax and have a bit of faith in her abilities.

His hand clamped her elbow, halting her ascent. "Remember our story. Your father and mother are occupied elsewhere tonight. Your supposed tender feelings toward me—me meaning Adam, not Francis, of course—will allow you to ask some questions. Do not probe too deeply. When I—"

Whirling about, Becca slapped her hand to his chest. "Enough, Adam." He raised his brow in that I-told-you-so manner, silently reminding her that she'd just broken his first rule. Between clenched teeth, she spat: "Pardon me, *Mr. Cobbald*, but I believe we have reviewed our roles a good half-dozen times. I am not a blithering idiot."

Adam dropped his chin to his chest and cleared his throat, undoubtedly preparing to explain the necessity for details. She'd heard this lecture three times as well.

"What are you two whispering about?" Lady Thacker asked from a higher step. Smothered in lace, her gown shimmered in the moonlight like a large silver bell, matching the beads woven through the flaming curls piled on top of her head.

"Certainly nothing important," Becca answered as she spun about. She ascended the last few steps to the enormous mahogany door, which was flanked by four servants. "Mr. Cobbald was expressing his nervousness about this evening."

As she halted before the two servants at the door

of the town house, Jeanette waved her fan in the air. "Shame on you, young man. You have nothing to fear. Once Lady Grayson extends her seal of approval, which I'm sure she will do, the Ton will open their doors to you like the people of Troy. Society matrons love the opportunity to flaunt their generosity, some more than others. Lady Grayson falls into the former category. Just be your charming self."

Becca practically bounded through the doorway on her aunt's heels. Granted, the high season had yet to begin, but enough families were in residence, hosting functions, for Adam to begin his investigation. She also admitted that a small part of her, a fragment of pure female romanticism, was excited about the prospect of her first ball. She'd attended smaller affairs back home, country parties with neighbors, but she'd never been allowed to dance more than a quadrille. Here, in London, she intended to waltz.

She envisioned herself circling the ballroom in Adam's arms, his hand wrapped tightly about her waist, their bodies close enough for their breath to mingle.

Caught up, she nearly tumbled over the waterfall of ferns at the entryway. The near-accident returned her to her senses. At the moment, she didn't even like Adam. Regaining her balance, she dismissed her daydream as pure whimsy.

At least three dozen candles perched in silver candelabra lit the long, narrow foyer leading toward the reception line. Assorted Chinese vases were displayed on pedestals in between those candles. Muted conversation hummed all around, filling the air from the twenty-foot domed ceiling gilded in gold to the brilliantly colored rug patterned with dragons and blossoms.

As they approached the host and hostess, Jeanette opened her fan and leaned toward Adam and Becca one last time. "Remember: Lady Grayson, a self-proclaimed benefactor of the arts, is the key to opening all the doors you wish to enter, Mr. Cobbald. Please her and, in turn, she will procure you a bevy of invites any titled lord would envy. Try a bit of flattery. A vain creature, she is particularly fond of her red curls, which according to her are God's gift—though I have it on good record that, unlike me, she uses coloring herbs on a regular basis. Do you hunt?"

"I beg your pardon?" Adam asked, trying to follow the stream of information Jeanette was spewing.

"Lord Grayson has a passion for hunting. The man will ramble for hours if given the opportunity. With one question, you can successfully distract him from any other topic. It irritates the devil out of his wife. She happens to be considerably younger than he and, in return for all the things he does which annoy her, she searches for, shall we say, distractions to irritate him back. Capitalize on that. Now, watch and learn."

With that last bit of advice, she glided toward Lady Grayson and exchanged exuberant smacking kisses in the air along with their introductions. She put one question to Lord Grayson, and within seconds she and the man were ensconced in a conversation as though no one else existed. Like Edward, Jeanette certainly had a talent for manipulation.

Adam puffed up his chest, arrogantly tipped his chin in the air and swaggered forward with the tiniest sway in his hips, in the fashion he'd practiced for two entire days. Dear Lord, he felt ridiculous.

With one toe pointed before him, one hand on his cane, he bowed, adding a flourish of his other hand. He kissed Lady Grayson's fingers, then studied the woman as an artist studies a subject.

She was fair, with a lush figure and bright, assessing eyes, but a vain creature who knew how to make use of her attributes, of that he was sure. And her hair was certainly red.

"What magnificence, my lady. I was prepared to encounter beauty, but given the radiant splendor of your hair, the flame of sunset must surely be weeping this eve. Even the most lush rose must hide her pedals in shame."

What rubbish! Becca thought she just might spew the contents of her stomach on Adam's feet or kick his shins at the very least.

Lady Grayson glanced to her husband, found herself ignored and eyed Adam as if he were a Banbury tart. She tapped the inside of his wrist with her fan, then cooed like a morning dove. "Lady Thacker warned me about you. She says you're a poet?"

"Lady Thacker is generous. Time will tell the tale whether or not I am deserving of such praise, but my heart professes to such an esteemed honor." He lifted one corner of his mouth like the worst of swains, and winked. "As long as there are women like you, inspiration abounds."

Running her tongue over her painted lower lip, Lady Grayson whispered, "You scamp. If there is something you need, do let me know." She leaned closer and with the tip of her fingernail drew an imaginary line over her chin, down her neck and along the edge of her bodice. "In fact, when I finish here, we can become better acquainted. I shall introduce you to some of my friends."

Friends, hah! Lady Grayson wasn't the least bit discreet about her plans for Adam. Becca was prepared to mutter an unflattering observation under her breath when Lady Grayson turned. The woman's expression shifted from one of seduction to haughty superiority. "I understand you intend to sponsor Mr. Cobbald. To be sure, I question the wisdom of such an endeavor for a young girl in her first season . . . especially one seeking a match. Watch yourself. The matrons surely will be."

How dare this woman question her behavior? Becca thought. If Lady Grayson's finger drew her decollétage any lower, her breast would tumble right into Adam's palm. Becca gritted her teeth, squelching the retort on the tip of her tongue. She certainly didn't need to alienate one of the foremost matrons of Polite Society on her first night in London. "I hope to follow your example, madam."

Lady Grayson gave a curt nod, then reluctantly released Adam's hand. "To new and interesting friendships. Until later, Mr. Cobbald."

Adam actually tittered.

The next hour became a blur. Jeanette made countless introductions, providing Adam and Becca with a mountain of information that boggled their minds. True to her word, Lady Grayson captured Adam and sported him on her arm like a new diamond bracelet, while Becca endured the company of several young women who chirped like starlings whenever a male of any shape, size or age breathed in their direction. At the first opportunity she excused herself and hid behind a half-size statue of two half-naked bronze wrestlers. This evening wasn't going at all as she'd envisioned. Just about the time she was feeling abandoned and quite sorry for herself—

which she knew was horribly selfish—she caught
Adam out of the corner of her eye.

"Merciful heavens," he muttered as he slinked over
next to her. "If I must poetically describe one more
woman's feminine assets, I think I just might swallow my tongue and choke to death. I now remember
why I avoided Polite Society all those years."

"How good of you to join me," Becca managed, her
words curt. "Surely there must be some lady you've
yet to meet?"

"I hope not," he groaned. "Those women are merciless. If I survive this adventure, I shall go to church
and pour forth my eternal gratitude. Lady Grayson
expects me to meet her in the library in private to
discuss commissioning a poem about her hair. Hair,
indeed." He shuddered at the thought of the
woman's wandering hands. "Another matron wants
an ode to her eyebrows. By the sword, her bloody
eyebrows."

"How difficult for you."

"Precisely. I told her that despite the obvious inspiration, a humble wordsmith like myself needs
time to create an epic that would do her justice. She
gave me one week." He rubbed the back of his neck.
"Truly, I never thought women to be so—"

"Shallow?"

"Exactly."

"You forget, sir. These are weak women of fashion,
uncommonly proud of their delicacy and sensibilities, functioning by men's rules. I have it on the best
authority that docile creatures with pretty faces,
beautiful clothes and no intelligence are just the
thing this season. Men *expect* this ridiculously insipid behavior."

He defensively splayed a hand in the air. "Spare

me. I haven't the energy to debate the roles of men and women tonight. My head is pounding." When she actually remained silent, he noted the set of her jaw, the scowl on her face. "Are you angry?"

"Me? No. I *love* conversing with women who don't know the difference between Socrates and the *London Times* social page. Aunt Jeanette insists on introducing me to every eligible man in this room regardless of my protests. You and I are partners so to speak, this is my first ball, I have yet to waltz and off you went, having yourself a grand time. That was, of course, after you lectured me for most of the day. What possible reason would I have to be angry? I'm enjoying myself immensely."

Muddling through Becca's speech, somewhat confused as to the reason for her obvious displeasure, he asked incredulously, "You wished to discuss Socrates tonight?"

She snorted.

He tried another tack. "Have you danced at all?"

"No, but not for lack of invitations."

He scratched his chin. "Is this really your first ball?"

"Yes," she snapped.

Ah, there it was, the thorn in her side. But he wasn't sure exactly what to say to that. He was used to dealing with men, not soothing the ruffled feathers of women. His fellow soldiers; the married ones, had complained about their wives' inability to be direct. How was one to overcome such oddness? "I am sorry if you felt abandoned," he tried.

Adam's blasted sincerity made Becca feel like the worst of shrews. He had simply been doing what they had come to do. She thought for a moment, trying to decide how she truly felt, finally admitting that she had hoped tonight would be special. He, of course, had come with an entirely different purpose. "Never mind. Do you see anyone familiar?"

He snagged a glass of champagne, pasted a languid expression on his face, leaned insolently on his cane and scoured the ballroom. If anyone did bother to spy on him, they would see a dandy, seemingly bored with his present company.

"Any number of lords and ladies, most of whom before now I managed to avoid quite nicely. Thankfully, I spent most of my time on the coast or in service to the king. Even if I do encounter them, I feel confident they shan't recognize—" He stopped, suddenly terse. "We're in luck! Both Lords Seavers and Oswin are here tonight. See the man near the orchestra, wearing the navy waistcoat and tan breeches? My height. Blond hair."

In order to have a better view, Becca casually circled the bronze statue.

"That is Lord Benjamin Seavers," Adam went on. "He's an old acquaintance and the captain in France with whom I had final words before my abduction."

The man reminded Becca of a beautiful Greek god. He had classic features that gave the impression of sensitivity and goodness, and he was currently regarding his companions, a trio of gray-haired gentlemen, with amusement. Coupled with the halo of blond curls framing his face and a bright easy smile, the man appeared almost angelic. It was difficult to think him capable of deceit and murder. "He appears quite harmless."

"Rule number one."

"No more rules, I beg of you."

Ignoring her plea, he repeated, "Rule number one. Never trust appearances. A man's character is not

152

written on his face. Most people believe what they are led to, or they never bother to look beyond the surface. Many people never take the time to really know a person. They base their decisions simply on appearances. Take me, for instance. I've been here for better than an hour, and not one person has questioned who or what I am.

"As for Seavers, he possesses a nasty temper and can be quite ruthless. However, he has always behaved honorably in the field. I can't imagine him betraying his country or me. And yet, until proven otherwise, I'm forced to consider his guilt."

Across the room, an older matron, hovering over two young girls, vigorously flapped her fan in Adam's direction. Beaming, he responded with a jaunty wave, then swiftly veered the other way, dragging Becca with him.

Becca cocked her head for another peek. The woman continued to wildly swing her fan in the air. Sweet mercy, the matron's coiffure, towering on top of her head, precariously swayed from side to side with her effort. "Who is that?"

"Do not look," Adam whispered almost desperately, sashaying to a nearby planter that hosted an array of purple and white orchids. "That is Lady Winshim. If you feign the least bit of interest or make direct eye contact for longer than two seconds, we are doomed. In her humble opinion, her two daughters each possess beauty that merits a poem with a minimum of six verses. She is desperate for me to meet the young ladies."

Becca found herself thinking that perhaps she had been too harsh earlier. Adam seemed miserable as well. She leaned over the planter, appreciating the fragrance of the flowers, suddenly enjoying Adam's company even more. "Where is Lord Oswin?"

"East of the dragon ice sculpture, behind the column with the pink floral streamers near the doors to the garden. He seems content to remain on the periphery, but then again, he was never a friendly sort to begin with. His choice to become a diplomat always struck me as odd."

Remembering what Adam had said about appearances, Becca tried to objectively observe Lord Oswin, with watchful eyes trained to see the unexpected, to notice more than the casual observer might. He had angular cheekbones, a narrow strip of a nose and a prominent chin that bespoke a great arrogance. He scowled at a passing servant, checked his timepiece and settled against the wall. *Fierce* was the one word that leapt into her mind. This man was capable of any number of vile things, she was sure.

"Lord Oswin is a definite possibility. Look at the way he scrutinizes everyone as if he were expecting something or someone." Quite pleased with her assessment, she awaited Adam's opinion like an attentive student.

Adam nodded. "Better. But you're still basing your conclusion on what you think you see, not what you actually do. Rule number two. Above all else, seek only the facts when you are watching or listening to someone. Especially when you talk with someone. Their speech will often conceal as much as it reveals."

Granted, Becca thought, what he said made sense. Sort of. "Do you ever rely on premonitions?"

"They can warn you to be aware, alert. But facts must be the sum and substance of any plan or decision."

"Will you talk with Seavers or Oswin tonight?"

"Perhaps. But only if the perfect opportunity arises." His mouth curved into a tight-lipped smile. "Wonder of wonders. There is my dear cousin."

Becca followed the subtle tip of Adam's head. Cecil paraded down the ballroom stairs, his stocky legs trapped in a pair of tight gold breeches. A matching waistcoat stretched across his protruberant belly, its buttons barely holding the garment together. An elaborately knotted cravat climbed his neck all the way to his double chin.

"I see my cousin still utilizes the same tailor. Pity. In my absence, I thought he might have acquired a modicum of grace." He lifted his arm. "Shall we see what he has to say?"

They casually circled the room until they stood near Cecil behind a large Chinese urn on a tripod of bronze legs that afforded them some privacy. Becca asked, "What shall we do?"

Adam studied his cousin, who craned his neck to see over the dancing couples, a difficult task since Cecil stood no taller than Becca. "I wish to garner his attention. Laugh loudly as though I said something witty."

Becca's laughter was rich and melodious, and it shot a ripple of awareness down Adam's spine. She sounded like a sea siren, the sort that lured men into dangerous waters, then left them distracted and powerless. She looked the part as well. The bodice of her dress accentuated the fullness of her breasts, the creamy expanse of flesh rising with each breath she took. Her hair, which shone like spun gold in the candlelight, was piled on top of her head in a simple knot with a few wispy curls at her nape and forehead. A single strand of pearls enhanced the delicate lines of her neck. And her lips parted charmingly.

Lips he had begun to covet and consider his.

Adam forced his thoughts from the topic as he saw his plan had worked. He stepped to the side of the urn, content to wait and watch as Cecil quickly closed the gap between them.

"Lady Rebecca, a delight. Are your parents here?"

"Unfortunately, Father is battling a nasty cold."

"I won't be put off, you know. It is high time Kerrick Castle be released to my care. If your father forces me to wait much longer, I'm prepared to take my case to the House of Lords."

Smiling innocently, she said, "Surely that is not my father's intent. Aren't you the least bit saddened by the news of your cousin's death?"

"Not particularly."

"But Adam was your family."

"He was a chaperone worse than any nursemaid, and a tiresome banker who chose to dole out my pitiful allowance only with a number of lectures on my sins. He cared more for England than his relatives." Shrugging, Cecil added, "Besides, they say he abandoned his command and turned traitor."

"Adam was brave and honorable and dependable. He would never have done those things!"

Gone was any pretense of cordiality. Sneering, Cecil snapped, "Ah, yes. Adam Hawksmore, Earl of Kerrick, a living saint. I see you still harbor tender feelings for him. A shame he died before he could reap the benefits."

Angry color raced up Becca's neck to her cheeks. Her hands fisted at her side. If Adam didn't do something, he knew she was likely to knock Cecil on his shimmering gold arse, herself. He briefly considered letting her.

"You're insufferable. You should be whipped just for thinking he was guilty."

"My dear Rebecca," the man said. "It's a moot point. He is dead. Your father saved us the humiliation of a trial and a hanging. I shall have to remember to thank him."

She really was going to slap the smirk off the fool's face. Deciding it was time to intervene, Adam stepped forward and patted Becca's hand. Tsking several times, he faced his cousin. "That was poorly done, sir. You've upset the young lady. I think she's trying to decide how to separate you from this earthly world."

"Who are you?" Cecil asked, surprised.

Becca answered between gritted teeth, "Allow me to introduce Francis Cobbald, a friend of mine. He was with us when Adam returned to Kerrick Castle."

Cecil gave him a passing glance, but obviously decided Adam was nothing more than a minor nuisance; he proceeded as his usual obnoxious self. "It is of no consequence. All I want now is my inheritance."

"Nasty business, it was," Adam said, wrinkling his nose. "So much blood. A shot right through the chest." He clapped his hands together twice. "But enough. This is not an appropriate discussion for such refined company. I must rescue this young damsel before she crumples at my feet. She's positively blotchy. Perhaps fresh air or food will help. Yes. A bit of squab to restore her vigor."

Cecil nodded in dismissal. "Only make sure my message is relayed to Lord Wyncomb," he said, then moved away.

Adam watched his cousin slither into the crowd without so much as a good night. The man was an

ill-mannered leech, blinded by greed and not to be
trusted. Pity. Adam had no choice now but to make
his cousin disappear before he could make any claim
to the House of Lords. More interest in the Kerrick
situation was the last thing Adam could tolerate.

Guilt reared up inside him. Perhaps Adam should
have sold his commission and remained in England
to help and guide his cousin, should have been more
generous with the boy's allowance. Now it was too
late; Cecil's hatred burned too deep.

"How can you just stand there?" Becca asked.

Sighing, Adam watched her pace back and forth.
A nearby couple with little else to do was beginning
to notice. He draped her hand over his arm and casually turned toward the French doors leading to the
terrace. "Would you have me go and shoot him down
in front of two hundred witnesses? Tomorrow will
be soon enough to deal with my cousin. Would you
like to be the one to tie him up?"

"This is not funny."

"No. It is not. Try being in my shoes. 'Tis rather
unsettling to know that a member of your family,
someone you provided for, even if only financially,
detests you. I never realized he hated me so."

She hesitated. "Oh, Adam. I am sorry. It's not your
fault. The man is an ass."

"Becca Marche, watch your language," he hissed,
smiling at a passing gentleman whose expression
was one of shock.

She glanced from side to side. "It is the truth. And
you sound like my mother."

"You sound like your father."

Ignoring him, she asked, "Tomorrow, you say?"

"Indeed. The only question is what time of day
should we expect Cecil?" He whirled about and

marched in the direction from which they had just come.

"What is the matter with you?" she asked as she hurried to catch up.

"Lady Winshim is fast on our heels with her daughters. If we hurry, we might escape with our sanity intact."

Chapter Thirteen

Adam heard Becca giggle as he led her through several small groups of chattering females, behind a seated row of scowling matrons, around the orchestra, up the stairs, down the hallway and into the dining room. Only then did he stop, pausing to peer around the corner behind them. *Success.* The rabid mother hen and her chicks were nowhere to be seen. He decided that since they were already near the buffet, they might as well eat.

He'd just finished heaping his plate with an array of delicacies, and Becca's too, when a fair young man barely old enough to sport a beard approached.

His hair was of the palest yellow, near white in fact, and his skin was the color of paste, without a hint of red in his cheeks. He wore neatly tailored beige trousers, waistcoat and cravat. Although he had a sensible face that held a politely contained ex-

Thrill to the most sensual, adventure-filled Historical Romances on the market today...

FROM 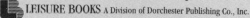 LEISURE BOOKS

As a home subscriber to the Leisure Historical Romance Book Club, you'll enjoy the best in today's BRAND-NEW Historical Romance fiction. For over twenty-five years, Leisure Books has brought you the award-winning, high-quality authors you know and love to read. Each Leisure Historical Romance will sweep you away to a world of high adventure...and intimate romance. Discover for yourself all the passion and excitement millions of readers thrill to each and every month.

SAVE AT LEAST $5.00 EACH TIME YOU BUY!

Each month, the Leisure Historical Romance Book Club brings you four brand-new titles from Leisure Books, America's foremost publisher of Historical Romances. EACH PACKAGE WILL SAVE YOU AT LEAST $5.00 FROM THE BOOKSTORE PRICE! And you'll never miss a new title with our convenient home delivery service.

Here's how we do it. Each package will carry a 10-DAY EXAMINATION privilege. At the end of that time, if you decide to keep your books, simply pay the low invoice price of $16.96 ($17.75 US in Canada), no shipping or handling charges added*. HOME DELIVERY IS ALWAYS FREE*. With today's top Historical Romance novels selling for $5.99 and higher, our price SAVES YOU AT LEAST $5.00 with each shipment.

AND YOUR FIRST FOUR-BOOK SHIPMENT IS TOTALLY FREE!*

IT'S A BARGAIN YOU CAN'T BEAT! A Super $21.96 Value!

LEISURE BOOKS A Division of Dorchester Publishing Co., Inc.

GET YOUR 4 FREE* BOOKS NOW—
A $21.96 VALUE!

Mail the Free* Book
Certificate
Today!

4 FREE* BOOKS 🌸 A $21.96 VALUE

Free * *Books Certificate*

YES! I want to subscribe to the Leisure Historical Romance Book Club. Please send me my 4 FREE* BOOKS. Then each month I'll receive the four newest Leisure Historical Romance selections to Preview for 10 days. If I decide to keep them, I will pay the Special Member's Only discounted price of just $4.24 each, a total of $16.96 ($17.75 US in Canada). This is a SAVINGS OF AT LEAST $5.00 off the bookstore price. There are no shipping, handling, or other charges*. There is no minimum number of books I must buy and I may cancel the program at any time. In any case, the 4 FREE* BOOKS are mine to keep—A BIG $21.96 Value!

*In Canada, add $5.00 shipping and handling per order for first shipment. For all subsequent shipments to Canada, the cost of membership is $17.75 US, which includes $7.75 shipping and handling per month.[All payments must be made in US dollars]

Name _____

Address _____

City _____

State _____ *Country* _____ *Zip* _____

Telephone _____

Signature _____

If under 18, Parent or Guardian must sign. Terms, prices and conditions subject to change. Subscription subject to acceptance. Leisure Books reserves the right to reject any order or cancel any subscription.

(Tear Here and Mail Your FREE* Book Card Today!)

Get Four Books Totally
F R E E* —
A $21.96 Value!

(Tear Here and Mail Your FREE* Book Card Today!)

PLEASE RUSH
MY FOUR FREE*
BOOKS TO ME
RIGHT AWAY!

Leisure Historical Romance Book Club
P.O. Box 6613
Edison, NJ 08818-6613

AFFIX
STAMP
HERE

pression, the lad's movements burst with excitement.

"Rebecca, my beautiful flower petal. I have found you."

Adam arched a brow. The familiarity of the man's greeting triggered a none-too-pleasant thought. Was this . . . ?

Becca managed a choked greeting. "Barnard! What are you doing here?"

"I planned to wait another week, but, without my rosebud to freshen my day, I languished at home. I thought to surprise you, yet I arrived to discover rather distressing news. Is it true?"

She neatly avoided the question. "How did you find me?"

"Kismet, my tender leaf. I accompanied my third cousin, Lydia, who shares the same modiste as the niece of Lady Grayson. It seems I arrived here none too soon. There is such talk. Lydia's friends suggested that you were sponsoring another poet, some Francis Cobbald fellow. I quickly reassured them the notion was pure whimsy. You would never do such a thing without consulting me first."

Dabbing a stray crumb from her mouth with her napkin, Becca cleared her throat. "As a matter of fact—"

"Francis Cobbald at your service," Adam interrupted, bowing.

After assessing him most thoroughly, Barnard squared his bony shoulders and formally introduced himself. "I have never heard of you," he added.

"I was thinking the same thing about you." The arrogant young pup positively bristled. Nonchalantly, Adam tossed a raspberry into his mouth.

"Lady Becca neglected to mention your name to me. You say you're good friends?"

When Becca sent him a nasty glare, her warning none too subtle, Adam shrugged. This was the most fun he'd had all evening.

"Becca? He calls you Becca?" Obviously smitten and surprisingly possessive, Barnard's eyes widened in shock. "What is the meaning of this?"

"A simple misunderstanding, nothing more."

"Is he"—Barnard cocked his head in Adam's direction—"or is he not, a poet?"

"Yes. Sort of."

"Are you or are you not his patron?"

"More or less."

"You engage in riddles, my precious. Which is it? More or less? Poet or not?"

Surely, Adam thought, Becca felt no real attachment for this fellow preening before him. Grand passion, hah! Higher plane. Rubbish. Adam would wager a month's earning that Barnard Leighton was barely out of the schoolroom. The boy was incapable of knowing his own thoughts, let alone how to make Becca happy.

"Truth to be told," Adam said with a smile, "I'm merely dabbling with verse and rhyme at the moment. Lady Becca generously offered to introduce me to Polite Society. Of course, her aunt, a woman of the first consequence, has extended her support as well. I am forever grateful and in their debt."

"Haven't you somewhere to go?" Becca asked Adam peevishly.

"Have I offended someone? A thousand apologies." He waved his napkin in the air. "I will consume this delectable feast, a silent woolly lamb in a room full of wolves. Pay no attention to me."

Adam was as much a lamb as Barnard was a wolf, Becca thought. She fought an urge to dump her food on Adam's arrogant head. The man was purposely baiting Barnard, behaving like a snob. Granted, Barnard wasn't behaving much differently. *Men.* She had a feeling both were fulfilling some male ritual of sorts, one she didn't understand.

With his thumbs hooked beneath the lapels of his jacket, Barnard regarded Becca expectantly. Adam munched on a stalk of celery, watching Barnard. Becca stared at both men. Suddenly overcome by the bizarre nature of her predicament, she giggled. "The tale is really quite amusing," she said. Neither man laughed nor even smiled.

Becca had thought to tell the entire story, at least the parts she could reveal, but decided the abridged version might be better. "Mr. Cobbald was attacked by thieves near Kerrick Castle. One thing led to another, and here we are. Imagine, all of us in London together."

"Modesty becomes you, sweet Becca," Adam cooed. "Without your tender care, who knows what would have become of me."

Fuming, Becca no longer tried to conceal her irritation. Adam was purposely baiting her!

He made an odd squeaking noise, then pressed his fingers over his mouth. "Dear me, I forgot. I promised to be silent." Becca was not amused.

"This is alarming in the extreme," Barnard said to her. "I thought we had an understanding. I thought we meant something to each other. Was I wrong? Have I hoped falsely?"

Sadly, seeing Barnard again had made Becca's decision so very simple. While he was sweet and caring, gentle and kind, she felt nothing for him. Damn

Adam for awakening her passions, those feelings she knew she'd never feel for Barnard. Adam fixed his gaze on her, obviously as curious to hear her answer as Barnard was. But she'd give him no satisfaction of knowing what he'd done. "You and I are the best of friends; you know that."

Barnard clasped his hand in hers. "We've been more than friends, my precious."

Adam cleared his throat.

"I believe my aunt is looking for you, Mr. Cobbald," Becca said. Adam didn't budge. Instead, he tossed a raspberry into his mouth, his fathomless blue gaze fixed upon her. Closing her eyes, she willed herself to calm down, all the while praying for a miracle. When she opened her eyes, the solution was barreling down the hall in their direction.

"Mr. Cobbald, you scamp," came Lady Winshim's shrill voice. "You've been the very devil to find. Now that I have, you shan't escape me." The matron propelled her daughters before her and practically thrust them in Adam's face.

Becca watched Adam's lips draw into a tight smile. His eyes, filled with promise, lit on her for one moment before he said, "Lady Winshim. How lovely to see you again."

Becca felt a moment's pity but wasn't about to lose the opportunity to talk with Barnard alone. "Excuse us, Mr. Cobbald, it appears you are needed here. I shall discuss the other matter with you later. Shall we, Mr. Leighton?"

Laughter tumbled through the air as the partygoers consumed more wine. Mothers, matrons and dowagers seated in gilded chairs surrounding the dance floor kept their daughters at the forefront of the crowd, staging and primping, their silent bartering ever present in the scene. Adam needed a quiet place to hide. And he wanted Becca.

He wanted to strangle her for abandoning him. It had taken nearly an hour, four glasses of punch, two waltzes and a promise to call in two days before he escaped the clutches of Lady Winshim and her brood.

Circling the ballroom, Adam's mouth fell open when he finally found her. The blasted chit was shamelessly flirting with Benjamin Seavers! This was not part of the plan. He'd left her alone for only a short time and already she'd pounced on trouble like a six-week-old spaniel. Adam fought the impulse to stomp to her side and stake his claim; such forthrightness would surely draw unwanted attention.

But evasive behavior was often misconstrued as nervousness, and that, too, prompted speculation. There would be safety in being aggressive, he knew. His opponent would never expect direct confrontation. And yet, he couldn't risk Becca. Adam had to proceed very carefully.

He draped the handle of his cane over his sleeve, gathered two glasses of champagne from a passing servant and sashayed in Becca's direction like her personal errand boy. Borrowing a white rose from a floral arrangement the size of a small table, he forced his speech an octave higher and warbled over her shoulder, "A rose for a rose?" Damn, if he wasn't beginning to sound like a blasted cuckoo bird. He grinned like a lovesick fool and extended a drink toward her. "And here I thought I had misplaced you, Lady Rebecca."

Her spine went rigid before she relaxed and accepted his offering. Good; she knew enough to be self-conscious of her interference.

Accepting the flower, she widened her smile. "Not at all, Mr. Cobbald. May I introduce Lord Seavers?"

Meeting Seavers's direct gaze with one of his own, Adam asked, "Have we met before?"

The nobleman cocked his lips to one side, thankfully more amused than anything else. "Highly unlikely."

"Hmmmm." Adam pursed his lips together and tapped his finger on his chin. "Perhaps last year at the . . ."

"I was in France."

"A soldier?" Adam bristled. "I admire your tenacity for bloodshed and heroism, but in all honesty I cannot applaud your efforts. I fear our opinions would likely differ greatly. I prefer to leave our neighbors to their own devices." Adam remembered something the poet Shelley had said. "Why must there be war in the first place, but to provide men with opportunity to garner pretty gold medals?" He gave Seavers a treacly smile. "Perhaps we met in the fall at the—"

Though Seavers returned Adam's smile, a dangerous glint lit his eyes. "Impossible. I remained in France until recently. And you are correct. Our opinions *do* differ."

"I see I've upset you. A thousand pardons." Adam turned to Becca, remembering Barnard's ridiculous endearments. "My sweet petunia, you promised me a dance. Shall we?"

Becca bid Seavers good night, along with an open invitation for him to call on her. To Adam's horror, the man had the audacity to accept. Adam thought he'd choke her right there on the spot. He did not want Becca anywhere near this man.

His irritation had nothing to do with the fact that Seavers was an eligible bachelor, and a handsome one at that, known for his charm with the ladies. He was a possible spy! A reprimand lay on the tip of Adam's tongue as he led Becca to the center of the ballroom floor. He swung her into his arms, opened his mouth and—

"You may thank me now," Becca said.

"*Thank* you?"

"Yes. You now know when Seavers returned from France. Had you not interrupted, I would have discovered what he has been doing over there for all this time. Don't you find it coincidental that he returned shortly after you escaped?"

"I do not remember us discussing approaching Seavers."

"You talked with Cecil," she pointed out.

"I have not seem my cousin for three years. The odds were in my favor that he'd not recognize me. He is also an idiot."

"Don't be a spoilsport. I was standing there minding my own business when Seavers happened by. I grasped the opportunity. And before you say another word that is liable to force me to do something we'll both regret, was the information helpful or not?"

Adam refused to answer. Becca needed no further encouragement as a spy, accomplice or whatever it was she imagined her role in this was. He snapped his lips together and slipped into a silent graceful glide with the music. His body began to relax, aware of the fact that he held a beautiful woman in his arms. When he glanced at Becca, he discovered a

167

whimsical, almost dreamlike expression on her face. "What are you smiling about?"

"I've never waltzed before."

"In that case, I shall endeavor to make the experience memorable. Though it has been a long time, I imagine it's like shooting a pistol. Once you learn, you never really forget."

"Can we, for at least a few moments, forget about guns and knives and traitors and spies?" Becca felt the muscles in Adam's shoulder bunch and ripple. He pulled her tighter in his arms, waltzing as he did everything else, with skillfulness and grace. The gentle pressure of his hand on her lower back burned through the silk of her dress. They turned and swirled, their gentle movements a heady combination with the wild thoughts in her head. She itched to thread her fingers though the ebony mane curling slightly behind Adam's ears. Beneath the candlelight, dark flecks in his otherwise sea blue eyes sparkled. His neatly trimmed beard beckoned her fingers to test its course texture.

She closed her eyes. The rhythm of the music, Adam's breathing, his familiar spiced scent, all flowed over her like a fine mist, sweet and intoxicating. She felt as though she floated in the air, safe within his arms, knowing he'd not let her stumble. In the deep recesses of her mind, although aware of what she did, she ignored reason and pressed herself even closer, mesmerized by the heat of his body. From behind half-opened eyelids, she found Adam's gaze burning into hers. She stumbled. "I'm sorry," she mumbled into his shirtfront.

"Don't be," he whispered.

His voice was husky, and it held a promise Becca had not fully understood until he'd kissed her a few weeks earlier. She found herself thinking of the candy forbidden her two weeks before Christmas, forbidden and therefore all the more enticing.

All at once, Becca realized the music had ended, and they hovered near the entrance to the French doors. More than anything, she wanted Adam to whisk her away beneath the stars and press his lips to hers. Her silly edict on not kissing seemed years ago, bloody ridiculous when her body thrummed with anticipation as it did now.

He extended his arm. "Shall we?"

Incapable of speech, Becca placed her hand on his and followed him through the doors into the brisk evening air. Her heart pounded and her pulse quickened. He led them to the far end of the balcony, farther into the darkness, where their bodies easily blended with the shadows.

Adam stood very close. She could feel the texture of his jacket against her hand, his breath upon her ear. She tipped her head upward. Her eyes drifted shut.

"Wait here," he whispered against her ear.

She kept her eyes closed. The pulse in her brain hammered, matching the pounding in her chest. It took several seconds for her befuddled mind to realize that something was wrong. Her eyes popped open and she scanned the balcony. Adam was nowhere to be found. Heat flooded her cheeks. Oh, Lord, she'd thrown herself at the man and he'd fled like a March hare.

"One dance and I offer myself like a sacrificial virgin," she muttered to the starlight sky. "I don't even *like* the man," she complained. Mortified, embarrassed beyond belief, Becca stared out into the darkness. There, in the shadows, skirting the balcony steps toward the garden, was a very familiar body. Anger overwhelmed the feeling of abject foolishness. For all she cared, the fool man could traipse into the night and—

What if he found trouble—or, more likely, trouble found him? She would never have the opportunity to tell him what she thought of his rude behavior. She braced on the edge of the marble wall for one minute, then paced for another two. When he failed to return, she made sure that she was alone, lifted the hem of her skirt and scampered down the stairs in the same direction Adam had gone.

Wandering aimlessly between the topiary animals, she passed a fountain with Cupid spouting water from his bow and arrow, a bed of roses that smelled like heaven and a lovely gazebo. Each step took her farther into the darkness, farther away from safety. That one thought had her stop to consider whether to proceed or return to the ball.

On her left, behind a tall hedgerow, she heard muted voices, one distinctly male. She crept forward, thinking to find Adam.

A hand clamped over her mouth suddenly and unexpectedly.

"Say one word and I'll wring your neck." Before Becca could interrupt the very conversation he'd been trying to overhear, Adam dragged her behind a matched pair of ivy lions.

He shook his head, marveling at his body's reaction to touching her and the lack of discipline that indicated—a rare and unexpected occurrence for him. Becca had felt so damn pliant and subtle in his arms as they waltzed. Her breasts had risen and fallen with each expansive sigh. The gold flecks shimmering in her eyes had warmed with passion.

She fit in his arms perfectly. Damn, he could nearly forget his disguise and his reason for being at the ball in the first place. He'd almost missed Jeremy Oswin sneak onto the terrace.

This woman had no common sense. She was a plague, a direct assault on a man's need for order and authority. Unfortunately, now was not the time to offer the lecture formulating in his mind. But later, oh yes indeed, she'd hear his opinion of her lack of obedience. Once they'd made it safely back home.

Now he had two problems: try to discover Oswin's purpose, and try to keep Becca safe. Actually, he had three problems. If they were caught alone together, there would be hell to pay.

Becca fought his hold, wriggling her backside in a manner that was most distracting. He bent so close to her ear, he swore he could taste the lilacs on her skin. "Be still."

She froze. Slowly he removed his hand and spun her about. Fire blazed in her eyes. She had the audacity to be angry when she was the one who refused to stay put?

Ready to tell her just that, he heard nearby whispered tones. He signaled her to be quiet, and for once, thankfully, she seemed to grasp the seriousness of the situation. If he were wrong, if Oswin had slipped into the garden for a simple assignation, Adam and Becca could move back to the house with no one the wiser.

A dog barked in the nearby alley. The wings of a bird, disturbed by some other creature of the night, flapped overhead. An occasional burst of merriment from the party drifted outdoors, reminding Adam to be careful. He crept forward.

Bending slightly, he found a spot with blessedly

fewer leaves. One man stood opposite Adam. Unfortunately, his back was turned. However, with the smattering of several garden torches, Adam saw Oswin perfectly. The man had his arms crossed over his chest and looked none too happy. Bits and pieces of conversation drifted through the hedge.

"What do you mean he disappeared? Do you realize the consequences if he is not found?" Oswin drew his hand through his hair. "Dammit! What else can possibly go wrong?"

The other man, small and wiry, dressed like a common thief, was not one of Lord and Lady Grayson's guests. He mumbled something about a woman from Paris.

"We must find her," Oswin whispered. "Otherwise all will be ruined."

The smaller man nodded, and spoke more softly. Adam caught the word "why," or was it "spy?" Bloody hell, he wished he could hear—

"We'll meet tomorrow. You know where." Oswin handed the man a scrap of paper. "See what you find here. Be careful, for goodness sake. We can't afford to be caught. Not yet."

The stranger headed toward the back wall of the gardens. Prepared to follow, Adam remembered Becca's presence and muttered several searing curses under his breath. He whirled back to see Oswin roll his shoulders and casually light a cigar, then stroll back to the house.

Nothing unseemly about a gentleman taking a walk in the gardens, was there? Adam thought ironically. The man was confident, certainly. And too much confidence led to mistakes. That one thought eased a portion of Adam's frustration.

He slid back to Becca, grabbed her hand and silently inched his way in the other direction. They would take a more circuitous route to the house.

A twig snapped beneath Becca's feet. The brittle crackling echoed through the garden like the crash of a felled tree. Adam froze, listening. The rustling of leaves and the pounding of feet sent Adam into a sprint, dragging Becca behind him. The last thing they needed was to be caught. The social repercussions would be tremendous, but more importantly, Adam did not want to raise Oswin's suspicions.

Seeking the deepest shadows, they dashed around the hedges, past a fountain carved to look like chariots and three white horses and farther into the darkness. Adam could hear the following footsteps gaining. Becca's heavy breathing rasped in his ear. She'd never make it with her fancy gown and shoes. He spied the outline of the stable, hoped that was the first place Oswin would search.

Adam veered in that direction, flung the door open, then ran back toward a nearby elm. He whipped Becca around so that her back pressed against the rough bark of the tree. His body covered hers in an attempt to conceal any and all of the glittering fabric of her dress. Watching the path leading to the barn, he saw a shape race forward. It was Oswin. The shiny barrel of a pistol glinted in the moonlight.

Neither moved, nor spoke. Time seemed suspended. At last, Oswin exited the barn, surveyed his surroundings once more, then stomped back to the house.

"Is he gone?" Becca asked, sensing that the immediate danger had passed.

"I believe so."

She felt as if her heart might tear right through

her chest. Adam remained still, his body pressed intimately against her chest, the bark of the tree rough on her back. Mercy, her feet were spread apart and she practically straddled his thigh. All the wicked, horribly wanton sensations she'd felt while dancing with Adam settled uncomfortably and inexplicably between her legs.

As she raised her head to speak, her breath lodged solidly in her throat. Fire flared in Adam's eyes. To her horror, her nipples tightened in response.

Her gaze strayed longingly to his mouth. She swallowed convulsively, like a kitten eager for a taste of the cook's cream. Whimpering his name, she melted into his arms. *I've lost my wits*, was her last thought as his lips descended to hers.

His kiss was everything she remembered and more. Perhaps because there was no gentle sparring this time, simply raw need. She answered with equal ardor, her hands clamped behind Adam's head as if she feared he might disappear.

She worried needlessly.

His breath scalded the tender skin of her throat as he traced a gentle path from her chin to the curve of the breasts brimming over her bodice. She nearly expired when his tongue circled her nipple through the fabric of her dress, laving the tiny bud with the most excruciating tenderness. She arched her body to greet his caress with a whimper.

The sound cut through the haze of Adam's need. Still aching, he pulled back. Becca nuzzled closer, and Adam suddenly knew that she was possessed by passion, that she would deny him nothing. That single thought spurred him to resist the sweet bounty of her body.

Sweet mercy, Edward had entrusted his daughter

into Adam's care and Adam had near lost control like a green lad. He should have been lecturing her on her foolhardiness rather than plying her with kisses. Nothing he did could take back his actions . . . but truth be told, he wasn't sure he wanted to.

He lifted his head to see her eyes pool with questions. He gently cupped her chin and pressed one last tender kiss to her lips. "We had best go. Unfortunately, your dress is beyond repair. You can wait in the carriage while I find Lady Thacker and your cape. We can talk once we're home."

...

Chapter Fourteen

"Good night, dear lady," Adam enthused as Jeanette ascended the stairs to the upper level of Wyncomb House. When Becca followed, he slid directly into her path. "You, I wish to have a word with."

That was certainly no surprise, she thought. Adam had found Jeanette, offered the lame excuse that Becca had tumbled down the stairs, then brooded the entire ride home, nodding occasionally as Jeanette chattered ceaselessly about his successful debut. Becca had hoped to escape this inquisition tonight, had prayed her parents would still be awake. She needed time to think. But Adam obviously had other ideas.

She wouldn't behave like a frightened goose. Wandering into the library, Becca did not bother to close the door, knowing Adam would. She perched on a blue satin chair set apart from the others and fixed a rebellious glare on the cobalt sky and billowing clouds painted on the ceiling. Thinking the defensive was a good place to put Adam, she asked, "Are you going to explain your behavior?"

Astonished, he froze beside the Raphaelesque motif of three nymphs decorating the wall beside the door. "You dare to ask *me* for an explanation? If you were a soldier in my company you would be receiving severe disciplinary action. First, you nearly attack my cousin Cecil. Then you abandon me to that Winshim woman. That alone is unforgivable. But then you approached and flirted shamelessly with Benjamin Seavers. Worse still, you followed me into the garden, alone, in the middle of the night without a care. We were almost caught by Oswin!"

"But we weren't."

"That does not mitigate your actions. What do you think would have happened had we been seen alone together in the garden?"

"There might be a bit of gossip."

He stomped to her side. "Your reputation would be in tatters, any and all future marriage proposals an impossible dream. Not to mention the damage to your parents' good name. Heavens, your father would have no choice but to see you immediately wed."

"He would never force me."

Leaning over her shoulder, a resolute expression set on his face, Adam snapped, "Dearest Becca, he would not have to. I'd see to the task myself. I would never stand by and allow their names, or yours for that matter, to be dragged through the rumor mill. Surely you know your actions reflect upon them?"

She hated the fact that he spoke the truth, that society would condemn her as well as her parents because of an endless list of petty rules created by ignorant socialites. "Why can't I be judged for *me?*"

"That is not the way of things. You know that. I can't believe you would purposely hurt your mother and father."

"Of course not."

"Then why would you risk all these things?"

She couldn't believe he was really so cork-brained. Then again, he'd tried his best not to rely on anyone in his entire life. As far as she was concerned, it was high time he grew used to the idea that friends helped one another. She stood and thumped him in the chest with her finger. "I thought you might be in danger, you bird-wit."

"There is no need for name calling," he groused, dragging his hand over his face. She was so damn sincere. With the uncertainty of the next few weeks looming before him, he had to make her understand. She had to obey his orders; otherwise he would never be able to keep her safe. That was, above all else, his most pressing concern.

"Thank you for your worry. I, better than anyone, know what is at stake. It is my duty to clear my family name and, trust me, I have no desire to play the martyr. I want to save my name, my life and all that those things entail. But I have managed to survive so far with a minimum risk to those who need not be involved. Until my name is cleared, other dangerous situations will likely arise. You cannot gad about simply because you want—or feel the need—to help. You *cannot* follow me."

"What if you die?"

"I would rather die than have any injury to you on my hands. Your parents would never forgive me. By thunder, I would never forgive myself."

178

"I'm not defenseless. You, yourself, taught me how to shoot a pistol. I've practiced ever since and often carry the weapon in my purse."

"Men are supposed to protect women."

"Men, men, men," she snarled in frustration. "A woman can do anything a man can, if she so desires. I am sick to death of hearing what men can do and women cannot."

"Because men know what is best for women."

"That is the same as saying I am not capable of thinking for myself."

"After tonight, I'd say your actions validate that point pretty damn well."

"You arrogant boor!"

They stood nose to nose, each trying to stare the other down. "Promise you will not follow me again," Adam demanded.

"No."

He stared incredulously at her. No one refused his orders. *Except Becca.* He studied the firm set of her mouth, the resolute gleam in her eyes. She wasn't about to heed his warning. The frustration of the last few weeks near bested his patience. The residual adrenaline from the chase and raw, unfulfilled desire fired his blood. By the stars, she would agree. He stepped closer. She retreated behind the chair. He quickly circled behind and, with his arms braced on either side, effectively trapped her with her back to the desk.

"Listen well. There are innumerable dangers that threaten a young lady foolish enough to traipse about unprotected. Shall I show you the main reason not to follow me again, the most dangerous reason of all, something you should already realize after our adventure in the garden?"

All he needed was one kiss to prove her danger. One taste to satisfy a fire unlike any he'd known before. Her eyes darkened as she realized what he meant to do, and damn if she didn't meet him halfway. Their mouths met, and he opened his over hers. He intended to stop, truly, just as soon as she'd learned her lesson.

Then she timidly touched her tongue to his.

His good intentions vanished like a breath of fresh air on a battlefield.

Thrusting his hands into her hair, he plundered her mouth. He nibbled, then stroked; teased, then tormented, all while his hands caressed the creamy flesh of her shoulders and neck. Angling his head, he plunged his tongue into the moist heat of her mouth, again and again, swallowing her passionate whimpers, wishing he could make love to her. He'd meant to teach her a lesson. Instead he found himself the student, bound to her by the innocence of her kisses, the ardor of her response.

Adam pulled away. "Tell me to stop, Becca," he gasped.

Stop? she thought wildly. When liquid fire pulsed through her veins? When every inch of her skin craved his touch? "Not yet," she whispered, her voice distant in her ears.

With a growl, Adam clasped her about the waist, set her on the desk and boldly stepped between her legs. He pressed close, and Becca could feel a hard ridge rest intimately against her body. His gaze locked with hers, silently challenging her to stop him. Not a chance, she thought. This was far to wonderful.

She felt him edge the dress from her shoulders, one finger slowly dipping below the bodice, tormenting her, until finally the silk slipped free to pool at her waist. He lowered his head, his mouth tracing a path of fire from her neck, over her collarbone, to the hollow between her breasts. Finally, his tongue circled a distended nipple, the heat of his mouth sweet torture.

She tried to wriggle closer. He raised his head and kissed her with a wild hunger, his hands massaging and caressing her breasts. Air swept across her feet as he slid up her gown, exposing her ankles, calves and thighs.

Mesmerized, she watched his hand slide across the bare flesh above her rose-colored garters. She throbbed in her very core. Self-conscious, she tried to press her legs together, but his body prohibited the action. Then, again, he kissed her.

Lost once more in a sea of longing, Becca realized where she wanted his hands to touch her. She wasn't completely ignorant of the way of things, but this stirring deep within, this knowledge of what she wanted, was totally unexpected. And Adam seemed to know, too. His hand slid up to cup between her thighs, and she shifted restlessly, seeking something that lay just beyond her reach. Wanting. Needing.

Thankfully, Adam understood. He plied her body with tender probing strokes. His mouth and tongue began a magical rhythm that his clever fingers matched. Becca's heart raced. Her breath hitched. At last, every inch of her body tensed as she pitched into wave after wave of sensation that was unlike anything she'd ever imagined.

A breathy shudder eased from her chest as her pulse slowed. She felt as if she floated on the very clouds painted on the ceiling above. Adam tenderly held her. The room came into focus: the wall clock ticking away the minutes, the paintings of ships on the high seas, the cool night air. He clasped her to him, stroking her back until her breathing calmed. When she dared peek, she saw his jaw was clenched. Moisture dotted his brow. As if he felt her eyes upon him, he opened his own. Raw passion burned in their depths.

Becca swallowed convulsively.

Turning to put her clothing to rights, he asked, "Now do you understand the danger? I cannot deny the fact I want you. If pressed to the limit again, I'm not sure I could stop myself. And if that happened, you and I would marry. Doubt it not."

His touch had been shattering, a life-changing experience Becca was sure. Never again would she be able to sit at this desk without remembering the way Adam's tongue had laved her flesh, the eager way her body responded to his touch. There was no recrimination in his voice. In fact, it sounded as if he blamed himself completely. Suddenly, she felt angry. Why the devil had he had to ruin this moment with a bloody lecture, a reminder of their irreconcilable differences?

She slid off the desk, her skirts fluttering to the floor. "Why would I marry you?" she hissed. "If and when I do marry, it will be to someone I love. You are not a very loveable man. Right now, I don't even like you."

Her arrow struck home, but it brought with it a reprisal. "You liked me just fine a few moments ago when my mouth was on your breasts and my fingers touched the very essence of you."

Heat flooded her cheeks. A twinge of shame wrestled with her newly founded beliefs regarding men and women. She would not give in to it. "Fine. For the second time, you proved that I am weak when it comes to your touch, your kiss. But that only proves me right. A woman can feel the same passions as a man, experience the same lust, possess the same needs. Why can't she do so without the benefit of the marriage bed?"

Striding to the crystal decanter on the table, Adam poured himself a brandy. "You don't know what you're saying."

"If you tell me that one more time," she snarled, "I swear I will not be responsible for my actions. In my naivete, I never fully understood what poets meant by grand passion, or the bond lovers share. Now, thanks to you, I have a far greater understanding.

"However, wanting someone with an animal's appetite and loving them are as different as sea and land. Passion is the most fleeting of emotions. True friendship and compatibility come with the acceptance of intellect. A kiss does not a marriage make. Nor should it. You have not managed to change my belief of that. Good night."

Thank heavens he didn't try to stop her. She managed to hold back her tears until the stairway, then she let them fall, utterly weary and thoroughly disheartened. Until Adam returned, she had been so certain of what she wanted in life. Now confusion seemed a constant companion. Her body still thrilled from Adam's kisses, still throbbed with some unknown ache. And it was his fault. Damn Adam Hawksmore all the way to his honorable big toe for making her feel such things.

A glass shattered against the library wall. Good. She wasn't alone in her frustration.

* * *

His foil dancing through the air, Adam advanced across the Wedgwood Room toward Edward. From the corner of his eye, he studied his cousin. He had known Cecil would come today, and the timing of his visit was perfect. With his face concealed behind a wire mask, Adam could observe the fool without difficulty.

Dressed in a ridiculously tailored suit of black and red, his lips thinned to a straight line, Cecil drummed his fingers together as he pondered Edward's most recent revelation. "Shame on you, Edward. You never told me that Adam made changes to his will. That was very naughty." He flicked a scrap of lint from his trousers as he roosted on the tapestry chair like a vain barnyard cock. "What do I care if Adam left a spot of change here or there for a loyal servant as long as the amount is of no great consequence? My cousin had more than enough money to spare. He simply refused to share it with me. I am in line to inherit everything else. You cannot alter that fact."

A laugh came from Edward's mask.

"My request amuses you?" Cecil snapped.

"No, my boy," Edward answered. He lunged around a grained beechwood screen, barely avoiding Adam's thrust at his chest. "*You* amuse me."

Adam darted to the right of a gilded pedestal displaying a fancy enameled vase. Cecil glanced in his direction. The action wasn't lost on Edward.

"As I explained when you arrived, there's no need to worry about Mr. Cobbald. Feel free to speak your mind. He won't reveal any of your nasty secrets."

Cecil puffed his chest with indignance. "I want my cousin's will read immediately."

"Are you asking or telling? You know how contrary I can be."

Slapping his hand on the arm of the chair, Cecil blurted, "I need that money. There is no reason for delay."

Edward tsked several times, the clicking matching the rhythm of the rapid parry of swords as the men danced lightly on their feet back and forth across the room. "Having a bit of financial trouble again? You should really quit gambling. Desperation is most unbecoming; makes men consider all manner of things. How desperate are you, Cecil?"

"What are you talking about?"

"The need for money or power often provokes men to blackmail, cheating, stealing and lying. Even murder."

"Are you suggesting I performed some crime? Now it is you who amuses me." Chortling, Cecil said, " 'Twas not I who murdered my cousin."

Turning, Edward made a movement as if he might knock Cecil to the floor. Adam redirected his friend's attention by executing a forward thrust, then darting around a large potted palm. "If I may speak?" he asked rather nasally. "Mankind, on the whole, is weak in nature. Weak, weak, weak. Its very history is rife with familial conspiracies. Murder is no stranger to even men of good breeding."

Cecil frowned. "True. However, in this case I've killed no one. I admit I considered it on several occasions when my cousin was being his typical autocratic self, and I once imagined him trampled beneath his horse. But murder? Me? No. I fear I haven't the stomach for violence."

"One does not always have to do the task oneself," Edward prompted.

"No, that's true. I actually hoped Kerrick would die on some mission in Spain or France." Cecil paused. "I should be furious that you are suggesting that I would stoop to such a level, Edward, but I forgive you. After all, you accomplished the task for me." Cecil crossed one leg over the other and laughed. "Have I thanked you?"

Adam had heard enough. His cousin was a pitiful specimen of mankind, guilty of nothing more than cowardice, stupidity, bad taste and gluttony. Just the same, he needed to be dealt with. Judging from the grip Edward used on his sword, he, too, was eager to offer a proper lesson. Making the final decision regarding his cousin's future, he whirled. He sliced his sword through the air, stopping a half-inch from Cecil's suddenly quivering chin.

"Let *me* be the one to thank Edward," Adam said. With that, he tossed his mask to a nearby chair.

The color drained from Cecil's face. His cocky grin vanished, replaced by shock. He opened his mouth to speak, but no words escaped.

"Surprised to see me, cousin?" Adam pressed the tip of his sword into Cecil's flesh. "Sorry to disappoint you. I'm quite alive."

"But Edward said . . . the authorities . . . I don't understand."

"I'm sure you don't." Adam directed the deadly point of his sword to the floor. "Edward, pour my dear cousin a brandy. He looks faint."

Having removed his mask as well, Edward beamed. He fetched the drink and thrust the glass into Cecil's hand. "Now, Cecil, you pompous jackass, this is amusing."

With trembling hands, Cecil downed the contents

in one gulp. He immediately slipped into a fit of coughing. "You tricked me. Why?"

Adam saw many things in Cecil's eyes. Hate, anger, confusion. The smell of desperation oozed from the poor bastard like the stink of a skunk. "You see, cousin, someone decided to eliminate me from this earth. That makes me very angry. Since you were in line to inherit my worldly possessions, and considering your greed and incompetence with money, I considered you a possible candidate."

Cecil's gaze darted to Adam's sword. "You think . . . surely you can't mean that I . . ."

Fear overwhelmed the man, and suddenly Cecil was back to stammering like a dimwit. Adam scratched his beard thoughtfully. "If you are asking if I believe you capable of murder, the answer is no. Not any longer. You yourself admitted you haven't the guts for it."

Cecil flushed bright red.

"Do not be insulted, cousin. I merely state the obvious. You should be pleased. Otherwise, I'd skewer you like the animal you are."

Cecil squirmed in his seat. "Why am I here, then?"

Adam crossed to the window and stared outside. "I needed to make sure you weren't involved in any of this. Now that I know for certain, I have a problem. Given your need for money, if you remain in London, you might decide to turn me in."

"Never."

"You forget, cousin, I heard every malicious word you spoke last night and today."

"Fine. I wish you had died. I would have been the earl. People would have respected me."

"Fool," Adam snapped. He lay his weapon on the windowsill and moved back toward his cousin. "The title doesn't make the man. You'd still have been the same whining excuse for a noble, unfit to bear the honor of the Kerrick title." Adam sighed and glanced to Edward.

"Indeed." Edward nodded, still grinning with such delight that Adam wondered the extent of his cousin's machinations in the past year. "The sooner we deal with him the better."

Like a cornered squirrel, Cecil swung his head back and forth between the two men. "What are you going to do to me?"

"You are going to take a trip," Edward said cheerfully.

"You can't just kidnap me. I have rights, you know."

Adam squeezed Cecil's shoulder. "If you remain here, you would be tempted to waggle those lips of yours to anyone who might listen. Then, Edward or myself would have to kill you. A few months at sea and you can return to England hale and hearty."

"The sea? I hate the sea. I become deathly ill at sea," Cecil whined. His petulance was growing as he grasped his true circumstances.

Adam leaned within an inch of his cousin's ashen face. "Listen well. Two of Edward's men will escort you to the *Wild Orchid*. They have orders to ensure your safe arrival at the ship. Do not test their patience. They have fewer morals than I do. One false move and you will be sorry. The opportunity for a pleasant trip is yours. The captain is a good man, but I recommend you do not tax him with your sniveling."

Edward waited at the door, flanked by two burly seamen with arms the size of table legs. Cecil slunk to the door, his insolence completely gone, but when he turned back, hate shone clearly in his eyes. "I will never forgive you for this."

"No doubt, but I happen to know I'm doing you a favor. It is my understanding that you owe money to some rather nasty men. The plantation on St. Kitts will be at your disposal, under the supervision of my very loyal, very competent solicitor, of course. I have ordered him to begin to pay your debts. You may like the Caribbean and decide to stay. Look at this as a second chance."

As Cecil was escorted out, sadness overwhelmed Adam. Suddenly weary, he dropped into the seat his cousin had vacated. "You'd think I had just sentenced him to death."

"It had to be done," Edward said.

"Why do I feel like such a bastard?"

"Because you are an honorable man. Decisions do not come easily to those in positions of authority. But such responsibility is incomprehensible for individuals like Cecil. It is always far easier to blame someone else than yourself. What now?"

Adam sighed. "With my cousin out of the way, I can concentrate on Jeremy Oswin and Benjamin Seavers. They are the keys to this mess. I am sure of it."

"What about Becca?" Edward asked.

Adam considered. "Are you asking me my intentions?"

"Damn right I am. I trust you implicitly, but I also know my daughter. She's beautiful, headstrong, passionate and curious, a dangerous combination for a young woman—especially when thrown together with a man like you. And don't think I don't know about that little incident before you left. The girl fancied herself in love with you then. I doubt that has changed."

"I wager she'd disagree on that point."

"Becca doesn't know her own mind these days. All that rubbish about women's rights. I should never have taught her to read."

"She would be a challenge for any man. She's willful, stubborn and disobedient."

"I am well aware of my daughter's character. Do you intend to marry the girl or not?"

"I have no future to offer her," Adam began. When Edward snorted, he added, "I'm bloody serious. No matter how noble everyone thinks I am, I will not allow myself to hang. If faced with no other choice, I will start a new life elsewhere. Alone. I refuse to drag Becca along as the wife of a fugitive."

"We'll straighten this mess out soon enough. In fact, I intend to call on that pompous little arse Lord Archibald today. We know Seavers talked with the war department. I want to find out exactly what information he gave them."

"There are two rational explanations for his testimony. Either he is the Leopard and he wanted to frame someone else, or he simply misinterpreted my presence at the Red Goose Inn. I don't know what you'll learn by questioning Archibald."

"We'll see, won't we?" Edward asked. He crossed his arms over his chest. "Now, answer my question. If this were settled, would you intend to marry Rebecca?"

Adam thought about the night before, pressing Becca against the desk . . . the sleepless tossing and turning later, alone in his bed. Of all things, he had actually considered the possibility of marrying her. Cursing, he faulted Mac for planting the notion in his head in the first place. Then he blamed Becca and her damnable impetuous behavior. He'd never met a woman who could obliterate his calm and reason like she did. Yet it was his own fault, his own lack of discipline that was responsible. In this one thing, he could not overcome.

"I must be insane," he finally admitted. "My life would be a constant sparring match, but yes, the thought has crossed my mind. If—and I say if—we clear my name, I would marry Becca. The trouble would be convincing her of the idea."

Edward slapped Adam on the back. "Nonsense. She needs to be wooed. You are a master tactician who thrives on challenge. The way I see it, this is the ultimate war."

Chapter Fifteen

"Only one outshines the moon. Our gracious hostess"—Adam paused for dramatic affect—"Lady Witherspoon."

"My turn now, Mr. Cobbald. Please. You promised."

Adam nodded to the young lady flapping her arms as she sat on the stone bench beside him. "Indeed, I did. Let me think."

He studied the chit and the other three relentless matrons who surrounded him, each awaiting the opportunity for a snippet of verse dedicated to what he now referred to as their beauteous attributes. Thank the stars these women were easily pleased, finding delight in words he considered utter rubbish.

From his spot on the balcony, Adam searched the small garden below for Becca. She wandered the row of caged animals in the company of none other than

Jeremy Oswin. He had to have been out of his mind to agree to her idea, but desperation had settled the matter. That and Edward's endorsement.

Four days of parties and teas had provided no new developments. If Becca could glean any bit of information while conversing with Oswin, so be it. She would interfere with or without his approval anyway. But she might place herself in danger at any moment, and Adam planned to keep her within his sight—a difficult task since he could only see her with the eye not covered by a patch.

"I am particularly fond of my eyes, sir." Leaning forward, displaying a fair amount of bosom in the process—likely her motive in the first place—the debutante batted her lashes several times.

Bloody hell. What had happened to sensible young girls? Quelling a less than flattering remark, he said, "Magnificent. Your blue eyes it shall be." He stood, one thumb looped beneath his lapel. "A lagoon of endless depths, where secrets lurk and glide." He glanced down to the caged animals, the center of Lady Witherspoon's circus-theme party. Neither Becca nor Oswin were anywhere in sight. "Like the night sky, they sparkle, a challenge for men to deny." Scanning the expansive lawn, he saw several small groups circling about a juggler and a clown, but no Becca. "Damn and blast."

A female gasp dragged him from his reconnaissance.

"Not you, my dear lady," he ameliorated. "What can I say? A mental lapse, a burst of frustration as I struggled to quantify perfection. Certainly you understand. Now, where were we? Ah, yes, your eyes."

He scanned the terrace stairs. Empty. The balcony? Though dozens of people milled about, Oswin and Becca were conspicuously missing. There was no hope for it. "A thousand pardons, ladies, but I suddenly remembered an appointment."

A hand caught his coat. "Mr. Cobbald, do finish my poem, I implore you. I shall perish if you abandon me."

"Good grief," he spat, not in the least bit penitent. "Fine. Blue eyes are yours—Not brown, not green but blue. And now your silly poem is through. Good night." He left the circle of matrons with their mouths gaping like a heavenly choir in a verse of hallelujahs.

Perhaps Becca had decided to return to her father. He veered toward the ballroom when he glimpsed a scrap of pink linen disappearing between several cages full of dogs. He bounded down the stairs, two at a time. By the time he caught up, he was furious. "What the devil are you doing? Where is Oswin? Did he hurt you?"

"Do be quiet. We must leave immediately." She turned back in the direction she'd been going.

"We are going nowhere until you explain what you are about."

"For your information, the man with a face like a bulldog from Lady Grayson's garden is leaving by way of the alley. I believe Oswin intends to meet him somewhere. But if you would rather debate whether or not to pursue the fellow, then what do I care? 'Tis not my neck in the noose."

"The man from Lady Grayson's garden? Pray tell, how did you unearth that information?"

"A servant delivered a note to Lord Oswin, at which time he rudely abandoned me with some flimsy excuse about his mother. When he turned toward the garden rather than the front door, I knew he was up to some mischief. Naturally, I investigated."

"Naturally." They would discuss that later. "What did you discover?"

"You understand I feared being noticed, so it was rather difficult to hear exactly what they said, but Oswin mentioned a meeting in fifteen minutes and off he went, back toward the house. I can only assume they intend to rendezvous somewhere. Of course, I intended to come to you directly, but then I thought I should determine in which direction the man went. If we leave immediately, we might just catch him." She whirled toward the back gate. "What are you waiting for?"

Adam was asking himself the same question. If he hoped to catch the man, time was of the essence. He hesitated because of Becca. If they gave chase, he would place her in the midst of danger. Granted she would be with him, under his protection . . . and this *was* one of the first tangible leads he'd had. If need be, if he felt their lives were truly in peril, he could always retreat.

"You will do exactly as I say. If you so much as bat your eyelashes without my consent, no matter how strong my need to clear my name, I will dump you on your doorstep and try to find Oswin on my own."

"For all your chattering, the dog-faced man could be halfway to Dover by now."

Growling under his breath, he grabbed her hand and raced along the hedge. The gate leading to the alley was slightly ajar. Adam glanced toward Park Lane in time to see a man, slight in stature, turn the corner. It might be either the chap they sought or a footpad, hoping to strip a lord or lady of their coin.

"Was that him?" Adam asked, wondering if he

could still deposit Becca with her father.

"How should I know? I saw nothing except the back of your shoulders."

They crept along the ivy-covered wall, concealed in the shadows created by an umbrella of vines, leaves and limbs. Laughter from the party floated on the evening air, replaced by the rumbling sound of carriages as they neared the main thoroughfare. At the end of the alley, Adam glanced in both directions. A block down the street, a short, thin man dressed in dark, serviceable clothing climbed into a coach.

"There he is!" Becca cried excitedly, but just as Adam thought he might dump her in her father's lap after all, she quickly added, "At least I think it was. He seems to be the same height, but I won't really know for sure until I see his face more clearly."

Wondering if she'd realized his plan, Adam murmured, "No doubt."

Without another word, he hailed a passing hackney and practically tossed Becca inside as he issued orders to the driver. Slamming the door behind him, he took the seat opposite her and removed a lethal-looking knife hidden in the lining of his knee boots.

"Surely you don't expect to use that, do you?" Becca asked.

"Considering the fact that we do not know exactly where we're going or who we shall encounter, I'd rather not helplessly stumble into trouble." He closed the curtains, enclosing them in darkness once again. From time to time, he peered outside, but otherwise remained silent.

"Do you know where we are going?" Becca asked.

"East."

As the conveyance rumbled through the city for another quarter hour, the noise on the streets filled the quiet confines of the carriage. Since Adam was being annoyingly close-mouthed, Becca decided he was likely irritated that he had brought her. Pity. She'd had absolutely no intention of staying behind.

After counting to one hundred, she itemized fourteen reasons why Adam's behavior was insufferable, deciding she would ignore him as well. Unfortunately, she'd never quite mastered the art of patience. "Even young debutantes carry a better conversation than you, which is not a compliment. What is the matter? I would think the prospect of finding a clue would be thrilling."

Leaning imperiously against the side of the carriage, his face shadowed, he asked, "Do you remember our conversation about placing yourself in danger?"

"Indeed I do. You told me I was not to follow you in times of danger. I didn't. I followed the dog-faced man."

"You understood what I meant. You purposely twisted my instructions to suit your fancy."

"Yes, I did."

An unpleasant rumbling sound came from his mouth before he slipped into silence once again. After several deep breaths, he said, "Other than your conversation with Barnard Leighton tonight, you spent most of your time with Lord Oswin. Much of it alone. What did he have to say?"

"This and that." When Adam growled a second time she added, "Truth be told, I talked more than he did. He finally began to respond when he received the note. Surely if we hadn't been interrupted, I'd have learned more. He did say the oddest thing, though. When I asked him if he spent much time in the social world, he said this season was different from most and that he was searching for something he had lost. Does that mean anything?"

"No. What else did the two of you discuss?"

"Very little. However, he plans to attend Lady Featherstone's costume ball on Thursday. He promised me a waltz. I shall interrogate him then."

Though Adam's manner appeared calm, almost bored, the air between he and Becca crackled with tension. His satin trousers slid against the leather seats as he uncrossed his legs and leaned forward. "You *will not* interrogate him, nor will you flirt or dance with him. I've changed my mind. You can forget about Seavers as well."

"Just like that?"

"Just like that," he repeated matter-of-factly.

Typical, she sneered. Like the bloody King of England, Adam offered no explanation for his decision. He simply expected her to obey. And just last night, he had called her unreasonable. Would the man never learn that she despised blind dictates as much as she despised society's rules? When would he see that a polite request ensured so much greater success?

An absurd notion popped into her mind, which she dismissed as pure female whimsy. The idea returned in greater clarity. A prudent young lady would ignore such foolishness, but Becca admitted she had never cared much for caution, especially when she wanted a direct answer. Squeezing her hands in her lap, she blurted, "I think you are jealous."

Adam gurgled like a small brook before he managed to speak. "That is by far the most ridiculous bundle of flummery I have ever heard. You've taken to those idle-headed musings you read and write about in your poems. Jealous? Poppycock."

"The concept is not so preposterous. Why else would you be so contrary about my visiting with Oswin and Seavers in public? I think you are afraid to admit that you don't like to see me with other men."

"More likely, this is a stretch of your wild imagination that ignores the obvious fact that I choose to keep you out of danger. Though your behavior often drives me crazy, do not confuse my attraction for you with your lack of judgment."

She had actually warmed to the idea that Adam might be jealous. Now she wished she'd kept her mouth shut. Dripping with sarcasm, she said, "I'm so glad I brought it up."

"I should think so. The day that I am jealous of a few men—most of whom are indolent, high-stepping dandies who waste their lives on the sentimental whims of ladies of the Ton—is the day I resign my commission or cock up my toes. To be jealous, I would have to doubt my ability to win you. If I remember correctly, it was *my* arms that held you the other night in the library, *my* lips on your flesh, *my* caresses that brought you pleasure."

Fire flared in Becca's belly. Wicked images, real and imagined, had haunted her the last few days and nights, causing all manner of unladylike cravings. And damn Adam for knowing he had such an effect on her. "A brief and momentary lapse on my part," she said coolly. "I doubt it shall happen again. But no matter the excuse for your change of heart, since you still think to order me about, you're in for a rude awakening."

He leaned his face within inches of hers. A wicked gleam shone in his eyes. "I think I could convince you otherwise. With little effort."

Even though Adam spoke the truth, she couldn't

allow him to have the last word. Surely a clever retort lay on the tip of her tongue, but the sweet warmth of his breath against her cheeks muddled her thoughts. Thank heavens the carriage lurched to a stop.

The trap door slid open and the weasel-like face of the coachman, complete with beady eyes, peered through the small opening. He beamed a toothless smile at Becca, then spoke to Adam. "The hack ahead stopped, guv. I pulled around the corner, figuring ya didn't want to be seen."

Adam lifted the curtain. "Exactly where are we?"

"Near Hound's Ditch and Ratcliff Highway. The Tower's not far. Neither are the docks. The gent stopped near a warehouse ahead."

When Adam stepped from the carriage, Becca climbed down as well. "Back in that carriage this instant," he insisted.

"Before you go creeping into the night, I thought you might like to know whether we followed the right man or not. You also need someone to watch your back."

Adam sighed. "And if I refuse to take you with me, you'll likely disobey my order and follow anyway."

"That is a distinct possibility." She smiled innocently at the driver, then leaned toward Adam to whisper, "I have no intention of staying here alone with that man. I'd rather take my chances with you." She clutched her purse to her chest. "Besides, I have a gun."

Adam's mouth formed a nasty snarl, and his eyes narrowed with anger. He dropped his head to his chest. She supposed she should have kept that bit of information a secret. When he looked up, he extended his hand. "Give it to me."

She thought about arguing. The firm set of his jaw suggested she shouldn't. Grumbling the entire time, she pulled the small hand pistol, no more than four inches in length, from her purse and placed it in his hand. As he stuck the weapon in the waistband of his trousers, he closed the carriage door and tossed a gold coin to its driver. "We'll be back. There are three more where that came from if I find you waiting when we return. Toss me your cover."

The hack driver reluctantly parted with the old blanket draped over his knees. Adam wrapped the scrap of wool around Becca like a cape. "Your dress shines like a rose-colored beacon. This will help a bit."

Hand in hand, they inched their way to the end of the alley. Malevolence seemed to breed in this part of town. Wind laced with moisture from the Thames gusted, sending particles of grime into the air. Ghostly fingers of fog blanketed the dirt track, curling around Becca's ankles. Across the street, raucous laughter breached the silence as a sailor stumbled from a tavern and veered east toward the docks. Lanterns nailed to wooden posts cast small pockets of light, but, past them, uninviting darkness prevailed. As if in eerie warning, a woman wailed a prayer from some unseen shelter where a baby cried. Becca shivered as she whispered her own silent plea.

They slid into the shadows as another carriage passed. Luck was on their side tonight, for from the corner, they watched Oswin abandon his coach and slip between the two buildings.

When they reached the narrow space between the two warehouses, Adam tried the first door. It was securely locked. The second opened without a noise, the pungent aroma of coffee and spice spilling out into the alley. Inside, hulking crates lined every wall and corner of the cavernous wooden building. Smaller casks and boxes of merchandise were stacked six feet high in the center.

Becca had her own opinion on how they should proceed, but Adam neglected to consult her. He simply wended his way toward a dim light shining near the back of the building. Becca had no choice but to follow; her hand was locked in his. They reached a set of stone steps that led down. The muffled voices of two men rose from somewhere below, Oswin, she assumed, and Dogface.

"If something goes wrong," Adam whispered, "do exactly as I say. No matter what."

"Wait." Blast his soul, the man had grabbed a candle and flint from a nearby shelf and was moving before she had time to speak. She bolstered her nerve and tiptoed silently behind him until they reached the bottom of the stairs. A heavy wooden door was ajar.

Wasting no time, Adam peeked around the corner, then pulled Becca through the doorway. They were surrounded by six-foot-high shelves lined with bottles of champagne and wine. The brick floor and walls allowed only cold, damp air into the room.

Becca and Adam crept along the wall, until they stood behind a shelf with their quarry on the other side. Adam pressed his back into a corner and pulled Becca against him.

Dogface and Oswin were replacing the lid on a big wooden crate, talking in hushed voices. Once finished, they lifted the box and moved it farther into the shadows.

Oswin wiped his hands and brow with a handkerchief. "I had best return to the party before anyone notices I'm gone. I want a solid alibi for tonight."

"What do you want me to do?" Dogface asked.

"Make sure everything is out of sight and locked up. Then we wait a few days to see what develops."

Oswin departed, while Dogface placed smaller boxes on the larger crate, then covered the entire cluster with a tarp. He came and went twice before finally extinguishing the lamp. The ominous click of a lock signaled his final departure.

Still Adam stood immobile, his arms wrapped about Becca, the hardened muscles of his chest and thighs pressed intimately against her backside. When she thought her arm would surely cramp, Adam unwound his body from hers. "Stay here."

He didn't need to ask twice. Save wiggling her arm about, she wasn't moving. She had no desire to stumble about in the dark. And here she had thought the business of intrigue would be exciting. On the contrary, she was frightened all the way to the shiny silver buckles of her slippers. Even her breathing sounded horrifyingly loud.

The soft pad of Adam's footsteps sounded across the room, followed by a rattling noise. Just when she was beginning to worry, she heard him curse most profoundly. A light flared as Adam struck a match, then lit his candle, which provided enough light to better study their surroundings.

Grim was the one word that came to her mind.

This dingy, dank cellar was long and narrow, with endless racks of wine and not a window in sight. Adam's expression was grimmer yet. He scanned the tiny storeroom one more time, then said, "It would appear that we are trapped."

"What?" Becca's voice sounded a bit hysterical

even to her own ears as she ran to rattle the door several times.

"I assure you the bolt is quite secure. And I don't think I can break it down."

She kicked the door for good measure, then clumped over to Adam's side. "I had no desire to creep down here in the first place. If you had asked my opinion, we would be safely upstairs."

"Little did I expect to be locked down here."

"Humph. I'll have you know I'm not enjoying myself in the least. What do you propose to do?"

Adam groaned. She made it sound as if their circumstance was entirely his fault. Hell, she'd practically begged him to allow her to come. "Unless you know a secret way out of here, we have no choice but to wait for someone to open the door—which will likely be in the morning. If it makes you feel any better, I'm not particularly thrilled with our circumstance either."

Eyeing her surroundings another time, Becca shuddered. "Mother and Father will be frantic with worry."

"I imagine so."

He didn't bother to mention that her reputation would be ruined, or that he found their situation as alarming as she did. Becca stood, tousled and flushed, worrying her lower lip in a manner that made Adam think the most undisciplined thoughts. The two of them were completely alone for the entire night. And her father considered them as good as married. Such realizations were hell for a man who'd pondered little else but bedding a woman for the last few days.

Distraction, Adam decided, was necessary. He crossed to Oswin's stash, whatever it was, removed the tarp, the smaller boxes and finally the lid off the large hidden crate.

"What are you doing?" Becca asked.

Trying to forget about your lips, their taste, the satin texture. He cleared his throat. "Since we're here, I might as well take a closer look at the items that interested our friend."

Lifting a velvet-covered bundle from the box, he leaned the package against the crate, knelt down and removed the cloth. Becca leaned over his shoulder, her sweet scent teasing his nostrils and adding to his torment. His body began to throb.

"Dear heavens, Adam. I believe that painting is by Rubens, the Flemish painter."

Adam lifted four more bundles from the box. Once all their coverings were removed, he crouched on his heels and stared at the collection of masterpieces.

"I do not understand this at all," Becca said as she knelt beside a Raphael, her derriere enticingly pointed into the air as she studied the signature. "Where did they come from?"

Adam focused on a painted horse's right hock. "In all likelihood, from France. Napoleon was notorious for confiscating paintings and sculptures from other countries during his conquests."

"However could someone steal these from him?"

"Near the end of the war, Paris was in turmoil. Anything was possible for a clever enough person with the right connections. I'd wager that the owner of these is the man I seek, the Leopard."

"But why go to all that trouble to smuggle them out, then hide them here?" She shrugged in confusion, her makeshift cape slipping from her shoulders and revealing a creamy expanse of flesh.

He realized he was staring at a small mole on the

left side of her neck and shook his head. "To buy or sell, who knows which? Did Oswin smuggle them from France or is he the buyer? Do they belong to Dogface? If so, why are they here? I'd like those questions answered myself. Since they are not yet hanging on someone's wall, my guess is they are recently arrived, or the owner intends to sell them to the highest bidder."

Becca moved to wander the confines of the storeroom, gathering discarded tarps and muslin sacking and arranged them in the driest corner; then she sat, her knees tucked beneath her. A few curls had loosened from her ribbons and nestled against her breasts. He wanted to free the remainder of her curls and rummage his fingers through the silky cascade. Hell, he wanted her naked, beneath him and afire with passion.

In order to keep his hands and mind otherwise occupied, he meticulously covered each painting again, and carefully replaced them in their original order, taking far more time than was required. When he had completed that task, he stood in the middle of what he now considered his own private torture chamber.

Yawning, Becca shifted to the side, her head cradled in her elbow. The bodice of her dress dipped lower. "If we're here for the night, you had best make yourself comfortable. There is room for both of us."

Comfortable, indeed. He was near bursting from his trousers and she invited him to sit with her on a makeshift bed when he wanted to offer his body as both blanket and pillow? He reminded himself that he wasn't a green lad, lacking self-control. On the other hand, Becca tended to have adverse effects on his discipline. The little innocent seemed oblivious to her appeal or the existing danger of it. He thought he would be best off sleeping on the damn stairs.

Grabbing the candle, he stomped two strides forward until he towered above her. "Don't you see the problem here? Depending on the actions your mother and father take, the entire town might learn of this disappearance. There will be talk."

"I wondered when you would broach that subject. The fact that a man can indulge in any vice whatsoever without any consequence while a woman makes one tiny mistake to wind up at the altar is bloody unfair! I've told you before. I won't be forced into marriage. *If* I marry, it will be because I share mutual respect and love with a man who allows me the freedom to educate my character and my mind. Rather than be some man's puppet, I would rather spend my life alone, content with my writing."

Alone? Never. Not in my lifetime. "You would never be content without passion," he found himself saying.

"Perhaps." She tightened the woolen blanket about her body. "Do stop glowering and sit down. Truth be told, I could use your heat. It is downright freezing."

"If I take that place beside you, we won't sleep. Do you understand what I'm saying?"

She blinked several times before her eyes flickered with a captivating mix of a woman's understanding and wide-eyed insecurity. Her breasts rose and fell as she gathered several breaths, then nodded.

He fought to find a final argument not to bed her. *In the name of honor.* That was the first absurd thought that leapt into his mind. He nearly laughed. It was one of those rare moments that he actually envied the sluggard's life, a dull, complacent existence that believed in little but one's own pleasure. He was so damn tired of behaving honorably.

She could become pregnant.

But picturing Becca, her belly swollen with his child, his heir feasting at her breast, did nothing to dissuade him from bedding her. If anything, a wave of pure masculine pride surged through him. So much for that argument.

We aren't legally married, not even betrothed. Becca had even claimed she might remain a spinster. Yet, in Adam's mind, he believed she wanted—and even belonged to—him. No other man would ever touch her.

The possibility that he might not regain his title, that he would desert his past, Becca included, posed the most compelling argument. He watched as she wet her lips, then tentatively smiled, a mute siren's call laced with innocence that wove an invisible web of attraction he was powerless to escape.

Right or wrong, Adam suddenly knew they would make love. He placed the candle beside her on the lowest shelf. "Be sure, Becca. After tonight, the game changes."

Becca's heart jolted beneath Adam's unwavering stare. His smoldering gaze ignited a tiny spark in her belly. Her fingertips tingled with the thought of touching him, of him touching her. She had never expected to feel the things she did, these wild, wanton emotions, especially for the man who had rebuffed her so many years ago. But he drove her to distraction. They had nothing in common. Their life together would be a daily battle.

The thought of making peace suddenly sent hot shivers tumbling down her spine.

In all likelihood, Adam already had his wedding

vows written, and Becca wasn't ready to march to the altar just yet. That was a problem she would deal with tomorrow. Right now, this moment, she only knew she wanted his lips on hers, his hands caressing her body as he had before. She was truly wanton, filled with desire and passion.

Though her mind was set, she couldn't quite bring herself to say anything more, or meet his gaze. She slowly rose to her knees and pulled several pins from her hair.

"Let me," Adam murmured huskily.

She dared not speak for fear her voice would fail her. After all, she was supposed to be a liberated woman. She nodded.

In no apparent hurry, Adam knelt beside her. One by one, he removed the silver pins from her hair. He began to whisper wicked suggestions: promises of all the ways he meant to pleasure her. Some she understood, others were uncharted territory. She liked his suggestions. His fingers sifted through her hair until the curls drifted past her shoulders and down her back. Her breath hitched, and he had yet to really touch her! She recognized the dull throbbing between her legs for what it was, knowing that Adam would ease the ache.

"Are you afraid?" he asked.

Surely he didn't expect an answer. Her mouth was as dry as summer straw. She was afraid he'd find her lacking in some way, horrified she'd disappoint him and terrified he might change his mind. She knew he was waiting for her to answer. Now was not the time for cowardice. She met his unwavering gaze with a shy, welcoming smile. That was all the invitation he needed.

In a slow, deliberate motion he melded his lips to

hers in a gentle exploration. He feathered his tongue over her lips until she opened to him. Even then he teased her with quick flicks of his tongue—shallow thrusts, delicate laps that left her wanting. He laced his hands in hers and caressed her with his lips until she thought she would perish if he didn't kiss her fully. She writhed against him, and only then did he lock her hands behind her back and boldly thrust his tongue deep into her mouth.

Gone were the damp walls of the cellar, their grim surroundings. Becca felt only heat, like a burst of sunlight warming an autumn day.

Trailing one finger slowly up her arm, over her shoulder and down to the valley between her breasts, Adam teased her. Up her arm and down again. Each time his finger dipped lower beneath her bodice, edging the garment off her shoulders and down her arms until the fabric clung to her swollen nipples. Surely the flames that enveloped her skin were capable of incinerating every tree in the king's forest. One final swish of his hand and her dress pooled at her waist.

"You are beautiful," Adam rasped. Gloriously naked from waist to neck, Becca possessed breasts that begged for a man's touch—but only his. Her pale ivory skin tantalized him. Her eyes were luminous, misty with passion, her breath quick and her lips slightly parted, moist and ripe from his kisses. He wanted to bury himself to the hilt in her, and yet also desired to dawdle over every luscious inch of her flesh at the same time. Most importantly, though he knew little about virgins, he desperately desired to give her pleasure.

With the backside of his hand, he brushed his fingers across her nipple, first one, then the other, until she moaned in ecstasy. Arching her back, she pressed herself up to him.

He traced the curve of her brow, the silky skin of her cheek, the rim of her ear, the delicate crook of her neck. Greedily, he suckled like a babe. He was filled with pride, knowing he was the first man to ever love this beautiful woman like this.

"May *I* touch *you?*" she asked, her voice resonating with passion.

"By all means."

With shy, tentative movements, she freed one button, then another, until his shirt hung open, exposing the muscles of his chest. He guided her hand down to the bold outline of his erect flesh. Commanding his frantic body to be patient, he allowed her to trace the size and shape of him, her caresses tender, hesitant and curious at first, growing bolder with each stroke. She was a virgin goddess, testing her newly discovered power. His control was slipping away.

He felt himself jolt as Becca's hand came to rest on the waistband of his trousers. He clamped his hand over hers. "Not yet, darling, or we'll be finished before we've truly begun. Patience will benefit us both."

His hands trailed down her abdomen, over her hips, dragging her dress and shift lower. He wanted her completely bare. Achieving his goal, he felt his breath lodge like a brick in his throat. She was more beautiful than he'd ever imagined.

Here she was, offering herself to him with such trust that he felt humbled. By the stars, he would make this first time for her a memory to treasure. Lowering her to their makeshift bed, he began a sensual caress that began with her feet and slid up every inch of her skin. Each trail of his fingers skirted where he knew she ached most, and each time, she seemed to part her legs in silent invitation. At last, he slid his hand to the juncture of her thighs, testing her body's readiness. She shuddered beneath his touch. "Are you cold?" he asked.

"Surely you jest," Becca said with a throaty laugh. Moisture beaded Adam's brow, his chest. Tension lined his eyes. His mouth drew into a tight line. He was being so incredibly tender, calling on every ounce of self-control at his own expense, and she recognized that. A delicate thread of magic wound about her heart, overpowering judgment and reason. There would be no regrets; this was *right*.

His lips traveled down her neck, and she tipped her head to the side. His tongue drifted down to the valley between her breasts, and she groaned. Still he teased her, building her desire. His fingertips, like fluttering butterfly wings, brushed her nipples, circled her navel, skirted the apex of her thighs only to repeat the torture. The torment was too great to bear, too divine to refuse.

Somewhere in the midst of his lovemaking, he had managed to shed his clothes. Through half-lowered eyes, she stared at his swollen manhood, trying not to lose her courage.

My goodness, she thought. That was what she had caressed? He gave her plenty of time to ponder the differences in their anatomy. With a wry smile, he extended his hand. The final choice was hers. She opened her arms and her heart to him.

His hands gripped her hips and pulled her flush with his body. She could feel his hot male flesh pressed against her abdomen, reveled in the fact that she could arouse such a reaction. She wrapped her hands about his neck and held on through the storm of sensation as his fingers caressed her own wet heat. She knew his body promised her satisfaction. She had thought she'd experienced all there was to know in the library the other night, but that encounter was a mere shadow compared to this. Just when she thought her heart would sprout wings and burst from her chest, Adam eased into her, joining his body with hers. Currents of pleasure electrified her naked flesh.

Liquid fire poured through Becca's veins as he began to move—ever so slowly, as if he feared the moment might be suddenly lost. She climbed an imaginary hurdle, the destination unclear, but certain the reward would be well worth the effort.

All at once, she peaked and cried out, and his lips took hers in a near-savage kiss. Then and only then did he unleash the power of the beast trapped within. Levering himself up on his knees, he buried himself completely within her, thrusting until he had finally purged the devil spurring him to completion.

Spent, neither moved, as if they feared the harsh reality of separation. Becca's racing heart calmed in increments. As she trembled, Adam lifted himself on his elbows and pressed his lips to hers. There was both possession and shared intimacy in his kiss. As he slid to the side, he covered them both with the blanket and stroked his hand up and down her arm. Becca immediately found herself guessing his thoughts. The last thing she wanted was a lecture, yet his continued silence worried her.

"I stand corrected, my lord. I cannot imagine a woman who would refuse herself the pleasure and satisfaction of lying with a man to live the life of a spinster."

Adam looked, if possible, more pensive. She lifted a finger to his lips. "What is done is done. Do not ruin the memory with worries or lectures. Not tonight. Please."

When he nodded, she reached for her shift. His hand stayed her action. "I promise to keep you warm through the night."

Chapter Sixteen

Becca climbed from the carriage behind Adam. All she wanted was a bath and a few hours alone to untangle the web of emotions choking her heart. She doubted she'd get either. Even if by some chance her parents were asleep, Adam, her newest self-proclaimed keeper, would never let her sneak upstairs to her bedroom, not with the unresolved issue of marriage lingering over their heads.

Throughout the night, she had lain in Adam's arms as they shared kisses and easy conversation like careless young lovers. The unyielding soldier's veneer had vanished, revealing the side of Adam she had always known existed.

When she woke, the predictable, systematic tyrant had returned with a vengeance. Already dressed, he had ordered her to do the same, wrapped the blanket around her head, then hidden her behind the wooden shelf closest to the stairs. There had been no tender good-morning or even a how-are-you. She had been prepared to offer her opinion when she'd heard footsteps in the warehouse above. Then she had willingly hid, peeking out between the bottles of wine.

Armed with her pistol in one hand, a bottle of wine in the other, Adam had waited beside her as the lock clicked. The door creaked as it opened. A bearded man, carrying a wooden box on his shoulder, rounded the corner at the bottom of the stairs. He managed three steps before Adam smashed the bottle on his head. The worker crumpled to the floor. Adam managed to grab the box before it crashed as well, then clasped Becca's hand in his, and together they'd made a mad dash for the exit.

Miracle of miracles, their carriage was parked in exactly the same place. The coachman had apparently stayed for the other three coins, either that or the return of his horse blanket. Once settled on the hack's leather seats, Adam had made his proclamation. He was honor-bound to do the right thing.

Becca watched the muscles of his legs and buttocks as he now climbed the steps to her home. She had an entirely new appreciation for his body. The memory of him naked created a pulsing knot at her very center. She admonished such foolishness as both reckless and nothing but trouble. Unfortunately, her body seemed drawn to that particular kind of trouble. For the love of Shakespeare, she would simply have to try harder to ignore such impulses. At least enough to allow her space to figure out exactly what it was she wanted.

One thing was certain. She refused to marry simply because some proud, domineering man was telling her it was the right and honorable thing to do. Arriving home at seven in the morning, she hoped she still would have some say in the matter.

Without the slightest hesitation, Adam shoved the front door open and waited for Becca to cross the threshold. She took two steps into the foyer and froze. Seated on the bottom of the winding staircase, a pistol in his lap, was her father. Jasper was sprawled across his feet.

The dog raised his head and sniffed the air. Since Becca obviously presented no threat, he resumed his nap. Her father, on the other hand, bounded to his feet. "It's about damn time. Where the hell have you been?"

Splendid. Given her father's bellow, the Prince Regent along with every nosy matron within a mile radius likely knew she'd just arrived home.

Her mother rushed from the salon, her eyes strained with worry. She enveloped Becca in a fierce hug, then laid a gentle palm against her cheek. "We were terribly worried."

Becca's maid, Molly, and another servant trotted down the stairs, while three others scurried from the kitchen. No doubt they were as curious as they were concerned. There was finally enough excitement to merit Jasper's attention; the dog sat on his haunches and howled.

Becca thought she just might do the same.

Though she teetered on the verge of tears, she pasted an overly bright smile on her face. "As you can see, Mr. Cobbald and I are perfectly fine." Everyone in the room exchanged worried glances. Even the blasted dog looked skeptical. Changing her tactic, she said, "Molly, I desperately need a bath and could use a bite to eat." She inched toward the stairs, closer to escape, and yawned. "And I'm exhausted. So, if you don't mind, I'd like to talk later."

Adam, back in his role as Francis Cobbald for the benefit of the servants, turned to the downstairs maid. "I, too, am hungry, and I imagine we all could use some refreshment. I suggest we move to the salon."

Arching one bushy brow, Edward cast a knowing glance to his wife, then withdrew to the parlor. Miriam obviously detected her daughter's hesitation and clasped Becca's hand. Becca had no choice but to follow. Besides, she knew Adam would never allow her to retreat. He was eager to confess his sins.

Coffee and cocoa were immediately served, along with fresh buttered biscuits and marmalade. The remaining food was placed on the oval table in the middle of the seating area. Except for the ticking of the winged lantern clock on the mantel, the clinking of silver and china was the only other sound.

Over the rim of her cup, Becca watched her father. Quietly sitting in his favorite armchair, complete with carved lion heads for hand grips, his arms crossed over his chest, his expression grim, he presented an imposing figure. She decided she preferred his thunder to his silent brooding.

Adam moved to the fireplace, where he could remain standing while Becca chose to sit on the blue damask settee, close to her mother, who had the greatest chance of persuading her father to listen calmly.

Once the servants cleared from the room and the door was closed, Edward said, "I'll not waste time asking questions. Simply start at the beginning. And you had best have a damn good reason for keeping my daughter out all night."

Before Adam had a chance to breathe, let alone speak, Becca blurted out her version of events, purposely eliminating the most incriminating scraps of information, hoping that Adam might change his mind and keep his mouth shut. *And ships will sail across the skies,* she thought miserably. When she finished, everyone stared at her expectantly.

After two sips of cocoa, three nibbles on her scone, and the clearing of her throat, silence still reigned. "*What?*" she finally snapped.

"Is there anything you wish to add?" Adam prompted.

"No. I am quite satisfied with my telling of our adventure." She yawned. "Now, shall I go have my bath?"

As imperturbable and unyielding as ever, Adam calmly stood beside the mantel with his feet braced apart and his arms laced behind his back. She recognized the expression on his face and knew he'd not changed his mind.

"Edward, it is my duty to inform you that Becca and I were placed in a terribly compromising position last night."

"I see," murmured Edward, comprehension in his gray eyes.

"That is absolute nonsense," Becca objected.

Staring straight ahead, Adam continued as if she hadn't spoken. "My behavior is reprehensible, I know. I accept full responsibility. My only excuse is a lack of discipline. The damage to her reputation will be irreparable, but given your permission I shall find a way to rectify the situation."

Becca leapt from her seat. "This is absurd. I do not consider myself ruined or damaged in any way. And don't you dare allude that I was some naive church-mouse unaware of my choices. I knew exactly what I was doing. I wanted you to make love to me and as I told you earlier, I have no intention of marrying you! No one else besides us knows what happened, and I certainly have no desire to scream our behavior to the world."

Her mother clasped Becca's hand and drew her back to the settee. "There is one problem," Miriam said in her tolerant but no-nonsense manner. "Lady Witherspoon and two other matrons saw you venture into the gardens with Adam—Francis. When neither of you returned, the tongues wagged faster than the time Lydia Littlemore was discovered backstage with that actor fellow. I hate to say it, darling, but in the eyes of society, your reputation *is* ruined."

Becca forced herself to breathe. "I refuse to equate myself with damaged goods."

"Of course not," Miriam added gently. *"Ruined* is a harsh word. But we must be prepared for the worst. Society has been gracious and up until now has excused your impetuosity to your father's eccentricity." When Becca started to argue, her mother held her hand in the air. "Not that you care, I know. But surely even you realize the consequences of last night."

Though she saw no accusation in her mother's eyes, Becca felt her world begin to tumble. She looked to her father, who wore a similar expression as his wife's. As Becca began to fear the worst, several tears fell unchecked down her cheeks. "Mother, please don't force me to marry."

"One lone woman could possibly be ignored, but not an entire ballroom of scandal-seekers." Miriam fingered the gold locket dangling about her neck as if that loving gift from Edward might provide an alternative solution. After all, Becca's situation was not so different than her own had been. She shook her head. "The task is near insurmountable. I have already received four visitation cards for today. No doubt people wish to discover the true circumstance."

Becca could no longer sit still. Neither would she cry. Swiping at her tears, she skulked about the room, stopping before a side table where three miniatures of her father's ships were set. He had been a common dock worker. Now he spoke in Parliament when he felt so inclined. He had defied society, thrown their rules and strictures back in their pompous faces. But he was also a man.

"Tell everyone I was kidnapped by Corsican raiders or knocked unconscious by a thief. Say I fell from a tree and knocked myself senseless. I prefer insanity over a marriage of convenience."

A choking sound came from Adam's mouth. She was a little surprised to see he looked hurt. "Pardon me, but I feel like a lame horse at Tattersall's auction, one no one wishes to buy. Granted, I am not prone to spontaneous poetic exclamations, but neither am I a bumbling oaf. I will provide and care for you. Your vehemence to my proposal completely baffles me."

Again, like this morning, declarations of love were conspicuously missing from his words. Doing her best to stay calm, Becca fisted her hands in her dress and pivoted to face him. "That is precisely the problem. I will not marry a dunderheaded fool who does not understand his feelings. Or mine, for that matter."

"Fine," Adam snarled. "If you're lucky, I shall be killed or unable to clear my name—then I will leave

221

England and live my life as a fugitive, therefore alone. You would be free to spend your life as a spinster, hiding from society in the country."

She trembled at the thought. Her hand clenched the black queen on her father's chess set. "You would ruin me, then abandon me?"

"Of course that is what I mean. Though I don't understand how I can bloody abandon you when you refuse to marry me in the first place." He dragged his hands through his hair. "Thunderall, Becca, I do not understand what you want."

Your undying devotion, she practically shouted. *Your love.* Her knees nearly buckled. Mercy, she really did need time alone to sort through this mess. "Exactly the reason we should not marry."

Edward raised his hand in the air. "Be quiet. Both of you. We have not yet even considered the greatest obstacle. The Earl of Kerrick is dead. Adam, even if you want to marry Becca, you can't. At least not yet."

Her father's commanding tone alerted Becca that she had won a brief respite, but there was no doubt in the man's mind that she and Adam would marry.

"So where does that leave us?" Miriam asked, massaging her forehead.

"With an engagement," Lady Thacker chimed from the doorway.

Edward slapped his hands down on the armrests and stood. His lips thinned to a tight line. "How long have you been eavesdropping like a common thief?"

Jeanette stepped into the room and closed the door again. She wore a violet wrapper covered with peacocks. A white lace cap covered her red curls. "You forget, brother, I *was* a common thief. If you hadn't shouted like a ruddy costermonger hawking his wares, I might have slept through all the excitement.

Actually, I think your howling mongrel woke me. As I was saying, we will announce Becca's betrothal to Francis Cobbald at Lord and Lady Featherstone's masquerade."

"Impossible. There is more to this page than you can read," Edward said gruffly.

Jeanette's robe billowed as she crossed the room to the tea service and toast, using an excess of blackberry jam. In no apparent hurry, she poured herself a cup of cocoa, then sat beside Miriam. Jeanette sipped her drink, then pursed her lips. "I imagine you are referring to that little lie about Francis Cobbald not being Adam Hawksmore." She winked at Adam, then giggled gleefully as every person in the room gasped.

Adam eyed her curiously. "How long have you known?"

"Four days after Mr. Cobbald arrived at Kerrick Castle, I noted a striking resemblance between him and the portrait of that handsome devil Lord Hawksmore. Maybe it took me a day after that to piece the puzzle together."

"Why didn't you say anything?" Becca asked, as shocked by the revelation as everyone else in the room.

"I didn't want to spoil everyone's fun. My feelings were horribly bruised when I first discovered the truth, but then I rather enjoyed watching the maneuvering to keep Adam's identity a secret. I thought I played my role at his funeral magnificently."

Massaging the back of his neck, Adam crossed to the window and stared at the street below. Edward huffed as he plopped back into his chair.

"Edward, you of all people should have known I am not easily deceived. I was the best glimmering mort on the London docks, conning more men than I can count out of their purses before you sent me off to that fancy private school."

Waving her napkin in the air, Jeanette added, "Of course, there will be talk. But if handled properly, every debutante will wish she were Becca, and every mother envious of her newfound love."

"Aunt Jeanette," Becca said, "what are you talking about?"

"Love," Jeanette cried dramatically. "True romantic love. The profound adoration every woman dreams about all her life: the melding of two hearts, two souls." She was all business now. "For all appearances, Edward will reluctantly agree to the engagement and a fall wedding. The dust will settle while Adam clears his name. Once he does, he will resurrect himself from the dead. Mr. Cobbald, brokenhearted and distraught, shall flee. I envision Francis so inconsolable the poor man will likely move to the Colonies, never to be seen again. Does anyone have any questions?"

No one spoke for the longest time; then Miriam said, "You just might be right about this. Not two years past, Lady Milton successfully saved her daughter's reputation after that mangled elopement with much the same tactic."

"Exactly. Several matrons, Lady Grayson included, are enamored with Mr. Cobbald. We shall exploit every romantic notion they possess. The story will be something like Francis aspiring to sweep Becca off her feet, but, in his excitement, pushing her into the fountain. Mortified, they fled through the back and so on and so forth."

"No one with an ounce of intelligence will believe that fustian," Edward said.

"Of course they won't believe the story. They'll think the young couple made wild, passionate love in the gardens. They'll be green with envy because women dream of love matches and they happen so infrequently. Because Adam and Becca will portray the most enamored of young couples, society will accept the excuse we offer."

"You truly expect society to roll over on this?" Adam asked, his skepticism clear.

"Trust me. In two weeks' time, with a wedding looming in Becca's future, some other chit will earn the unpleasant honor of being the target of the Ton's gossipmongers. In the meantime, we shall prepare for a wedding." She stomped to Adam's side and shook her finger in his face. "And you, young man, will sort this matter out immediately."

Adam nodded briskly. "And if I am unsuccessful?"

Without hesitation, Jeanette said, "You had best not let that happen."

Like the woven flowers in the rug, Becca stood rooted to the floor. This was her future they were discussing. *Her life.* Not once had anyone asked her opinion. She wasn't even sure they wanted to hear what she had to say. "Since it seems everyone in this room has my immediate future and life planned for me without a care as to what I want or think, I am going to take a bath, then a nap."

Jeanette shook her head. "A bath is in order, but there will be no nap. We shall spend the day spreading your tale of love in the more powerful drawing rooms of London. Tonight we can celebrate with an intimate family affair. You can sleep then. Come along, Miriam. We must decide who shall have the honor of our company today."

Adam followed Becca to the door. "You may think

this a high-handed tactic, but I did not plan any of this," he said softly. Wishing he could kiss the forlorn expression from her face, he offered a warm smile. "Enjoy your bath. We can talk more this evening."

When the door closed, Adam ambled back to the window to peer down through the sheer curtains at the streets below, just coming to life. "I truly intended to keep my hands off her," he said to her father.

"You are not the first man to tumble a maid before marriage, and you certainly won't be the last. At least you agreed to make things right. Granted, I wish you'd managed to hold the honeymoon after the nuptials—and I just might knock a tooth loose on principle—but what's done is done. In the end, all this may have been for the best. My daughter needs a husband, someone to take her in hand. In my mind, there is no better man for the task than you."

"Most men have claim to their lives. I may not. I told you before. I won't swing from the gallows. Nor will I spend my days as Francis Cobbald. Aside from the glaring fact that I don't even like the man, Cobbald possesses none of the requirements essential to care for a family: no money, no property. Then there is the problem of Cecil. He won't remain silent indefinitely. There would always be the risk that someone might discover the truth. That leaves only one choice. Though life would be difficult, they say there are opportunities in the Americas. I will not drag Becca with me."

"And if she chose to follow?"

Adam's laugh was devoid of humor. "She'd more likely celebrate my departure."

"I'm not so certain of that. Right now my daughter's pride is standing in the way of her clear thinking. It's this free-woman nonsense, and Lord knows what else. Her irritation sometimes stems from something as simple as the sky is blue when she expected it to rain."

"Edward, if you are trying to advise me, then speak plain English."

"Woman are complicated creatures laden with depths and layers a mere man can never comprehend. You best not even try. Miriam and I married twenty years ago, and I have yet to understand all her moods. Nevertheless, I thank God every day for the opportunity to try. Do you love Becca?"

"Love her?" Adam practically choked on the words. Her welfare mattered to him. And he obviously desired her. She would be a good mother, run his household efficiently and provide intelligent conversation. But *love* her? He crossed the floor in four long strides and dropped to the settee, his chin cradled in his hands. "What a question, Edward. Do you love Miriam?"

A glimmer of something Adam didn't quite comprehend shone in Edward's eyes. "I'm absolutely beef-headed for the woman. Have been since the first time I saw her, standing on the docks, trussed up all prim and proper like a Puritan. Something about those deep brown eyes of hers tugged at me. Good thing she knew what was what, because it took me a while to sort through my feelings. I imagine you'll see reason soon enough."

"I have heard countless confessions of young sergeants who missed their lady friends or wives, but they always excused such ramblings to loneliness. I've seen lords pledge love to their wives, but most spend more time with their mistresses. Mother and Father seemed to care for one another . . . but *love?*

That is strange, uncharted territory for me. I will give the matter more thought, but first I must concentrate on clearing my name."

"Ah. I think I see the problem. A word of advice. Don't go telling Becca you are giving the matter *consideration*. She'll likely hang you herself."

"You suggest I lie to her about my feelings?"

Edward chuckled. "You? Lie? Impossible. I suggest you avoid the topic altogether. You'd be wise to remember one thing. Love does not follow a timetable. Now, I heard Becca mention stolen paintings. I want you to tell me what you're thinking."

"Oswin is up to something, but do the paintings have anything to do with me? I wish I knew." Adam shrugged his shoulders. "If Oswin is the Leopard, I need proof."

"What of Seavers?"

"He resigned his commission and seems content. Besides our being friends at one time, his service record is rife with citations and his reputation is impeccable. Nor have I been able to dig up any signs of mischief."

"Unless you consider the murder of his French mistress less than respectable?"

At the sound of the familiar voice, Adam whirled. Insolently lounging in the doorway was Macdonald Archer. The man offered his typical cocksure smile, obviously pleased with himself.

"I didn't expect you this soon," Adam said. He crossed to his friend and extended his hand in greeting. "Now what's this about Seavers?"

Chapter Seventeen

With her eyes closed, Becca soaked in the rose-scented bathwater, her muscles absorbing the heat. Before, when she was disturbed or upset, the pastoral scene painted on her walls in soft pastels had always provided solace and a sense of freedom. Today her bedroom felt like a prison. No matter how hard she tried, she couldn't relax. The last twenty-four hours played through her mind over and over, bombarding her with explicit images best forgotten.

Aunt Jeanette sat at Becca's writing table, furiously scribbling notes and lists while muttering about this dowager or that matron. Her mother offered an occasional suggestion to Jeanette as she washed Becca's hair with gentle, soothing strokes, the epitome of patience.

"Go ahead and ask your questions, Mother. I know you're dying to interrogate me."

"You must be feeling particularly contrary to snipe at me. Wait until you have a daughter of your own. Then you will understand a mother's plight." Miriam rinsed the soap from Becca's hair, then offered her daughter a towel. "Do you love Adam?"

Becca's hand froze in midair. "Couldn't you have started with a simple question?"

"Considering you spent the night in his arms and gave him your virginity, I would think the question easily answered. Unless he forced you?"

"Of course not."

"In that case, I assume you harbor feelings for the man. Even given your recent fascination with women's rights, you are not prone to gooseheaded decisions."

Becca dried herself, noting the tenderness between her legs, a blatant reminder of her loss of innocence. Skulking to her canopied bed, she slipped into her robe, then plopped down with her legs crossed beneath her. She stared at the vase of fresh white roses on her dresser. They immediately reminded her of Adam and their first waltz. She couldn't seem to escape the man. He had overrun her life with the same thoroughness an army of ants pervaded a picnic. And she had let him. "I thought I considered all the possibilities."

Shaking her head, her mother stood and began to comb the tangles from Becca's hair. "Do you remember the first Christmas Adam spent with us?"

Becca nodded, pondering the meaning of her mother's question. "His parents died the previous year. Father became his guardian."

"He gave you your first dollhouse. You positively glowed. Later that night, after endless hours of placing furniture in it with Adam, you retired. Do you remember what you said to him?"

Becca remembered the moment all too well. It was one of those memories that never faded, but grew more powerful as time passed, more poignant with maturity and understanding. Adam had stood before her, dressed in black evening clothes, thanked her for a wonderful Christmas day and kissed her hand. She'd thought him the most eloquent of men. It had taken her mother three days and the threat of no horseback riding to persuade Becca to wash her hand. "I was a child."

"I don't believe I've heard this story," Jeannette said, her writing suddenly forgotten. "What happened?"

"Adam was fourteen," Miriam explained. "Not only did he blame himself for his parents' death, he was forced to handle an earl's responsibilities at such an early age. Duty, honor, right and wrong, they were already his daily tenets. Becca was five. Yet even then, she spoke her mind when she wanted something." Her mother gazed into a shaft of light beaming through the window and seemed to drift far away, a gentle smile tugging at her lips. "Becca practically floated up the stairs. When she reached the landing, she turned about and curtsied. She stated, most authoritatively; "Adam Hawksmore. *After* we marry, you will build me a house just like the one you gave me today."

Feeling unsettled by a memory she had always treasured, Becca wanted nothing more than to change the topic. "Must we reminisce on a child's silliness? I thought we were discussing my fall from innocence."

Her mother ignored Becca's protest. "You have

adored Adam since the first day you met him. When he spent time with us, I could barely drag you from his side. You even proposed to him. Granted, Mary Wollstonecraft may have a valid point or two about a woman's education and her intellect, but surely you do not prefer a life without children of your own, a life as a spinster, shunned by society? Why are you so set against this marriage? What are you afraid of?"

Jeanette watched from the corner of her eye as she added another name to her growing list of matrons to woo. Becca's mother, content to wait, leaned against the bedpost. Faced with the direct question, one she knew she had to confront sooner or later, Becca stood and paced the cozy confines of her bedroom and shuddered. She lingered before the damask drapes and toyed with a tassel tieback. "He writes his daily activities on paper, for goodness sakes. He expects everyone to behave exactly as he says. He wants a lady who will sit quietly by his side like a hound. I would make a horrible pet."

"He's a man," Jeanette said. "They're born with those expectations."

"What if a man expected you to change and you couldn't? What if he was disappointed because you acted differently than the way he expected? What if he stopped loving you because you couldn't make him happy?"

Studying Becca in the way only a mother could, Miriam said, "I think you had better explain precisely what troubles you."

"Take Millicent. She was my very best friend. We shared everything. Now I cannot see her because her husband thinks I'm an inappropriate companion. Millicent actually obeys!" Seeking two silver combs,

Becca searched her dresser, then continued to pace back and forth between her desk and the door. "All my friends have married, changed into ladies I no longer recognize. It's as if we never shared our dreams with one another. I would never abandon my friends because my husband demanded it."

"They hurt you terribly, I know." Her mother patted the spot on the bed. "Wearing the carpet thin won't help. Come here."

When Becca reluctantly sat beside her mother, Miriam clasped her daughter's hands. "Believe it or not, for a variety of reasons, some women prefer acquiescence and conformity. They see it as security, often believe it to be love. You are not one of them. You are a shining star, pulsing with energy and brilliance. You possess your father's spirit, his pride and loyalty, even some of his arrogance. You will never be content with mere existence. And I do not believe Adam would be content with such a docile creature either."

"But what of love? I'm not sure Adam is capable of such. He said so himself."

"I thought the same thing of your father."

"My Raymond was an even bigger idiot," Jeanette chimed in as she penned and sanded her final note. "Men are such hardheaded beasts. They rarely understand their emotions, and speaking of them is near impossible. You might as well wait for a goat to talk. It is a woman's responsibility to guide men, to teach them how to express themselves. There are some men who never quite learn the knack of it. Adam loves you. He simply hasn't recognized his feelings for what they are."

"You see, darling," Miriam added. "Men confuse love with many things. Lust, obedience, responsibility, duty, the list is endless. The truth is, a woman recognizes those traits for what they are. A man may excuse the notion of love as frivolous. Flowery words are nice to hear, but most men are incapable of speaking them. It doesn't mean his heart is not full. And even if Adam admits he cannot love—which I highly doubt is true—he has at least admitted to being human. You see, a person cannot begin to change unless he recognizes the problem in the first place."

"How can Adam truly love me when he said himself that he would leave me? You heard him downstairs."

"Adam is a decent, honorable man. Nothing will ever change that . . . and don't make the mistake of trying to change him. His pride is wrapped around his ability to take care of you."

"Doesn't he see that it would hurt more if I gave him my heart and then he left me?"

Miriam clasped her daughter's chin. "I'm not so sure your heart isn't already given."

Tears filled Becca's eyes as she finally admitted the truth to herself. She did love him. All the way down to his methodical big toe. Her heart would break if Adam left her again. "What am I going to do?"

Molly rapped on the door, then entered. "Pardon me, madam, but your husband requested I fetch you downstairs."

Miriam winked at Becca. "I best not keep him waiting." She kissed Becca on the forehead. "Only you can determine what you are willing to risk. Life offers no guarantees. Neither does love. But I believe, if you take the chance with Adam, the rewards will be far greater than you ever imagined." She kissed Becca on the forehead. "I will return shortly."

Jeanette drummed her fingers on the desk as the door shut. She pursed her lips together, then studied the emerald wedding ring on her finger. "You know, if I was worried about the man I loved leaving me behind, I'd find a way to make sure he took me with him."

"I don't understand," Becca said, a bit wary of the twinkle in her aunt's eyes.

"If your mother and father truly believed you would be miserable, they would never force you to marry. Right now, they are acting in your best interest because they've watched you and Adam together. Before I offer my suggestion, think on this. Do you want Adam as your husband? Do you love him enough to fight for him and perhaps lose everything that is familiar to you? Your family, your home, England?"

Tugging a loose string on the blanket, Becca said, "Like blackberries. I savor them, yet they give me the hives."

Practically hopping from the stool, Jeanette clapped her hands together. "I take that to be a yes. Adam made the mistake of making love to you once. Chances are he has vowed since to maintain his distance. You, on the other hand, must provoke the man without mercy. You must seduce him."

Becca's pulse raced and her skin flushed. Her body obviously liked the suggestion. "Why? What if he refuses me?"

"As pitiful as it seems, as strong and disciplined as men appear, there is one trait consistent to the poor beasts. They think with their cocks."

"*Aunt Jeanette*," Becca gasped.

"This is not the time for priggish sensibilities. We are at war. Once a man has tasted the fruit, 'tis difficult to refuse another taste. If we must bind Adam to you until he realizes he loves you, then we shall use every wicked trick."

"But what do I do?"

"Considering the way I've seen Adam stare at you, I doubt you have to do much at all. But, just in case, I shall tell you all you need to know."

Becca stood in the hallway, her ear pressed to Adam's bedroom door, listening for the slightest sound or movement. Once she crossed the threshold, there was no turning back.

True to her word, today Jeanette had led Becca and her mother in a veritable siege on three of the most powerful matrons in Polite Society. When Becca first entered Lady Featherstone's salon, she'd noted the rigid set of the matron's mouth and feared the worst. Then Jeanette, bless her conniving, manipulative heart, had spilled the most outrageous tale, mixed with half-truths and pure romantic prattle. She had thrown in a goodly dose of flattery. Somehow, against all odds, by the end of the afternoon, after a somewhat scathing lecture on common sense, Becca had been rewarded with the matron's congratulations and support.

She was also now exhausted.

It was partly due to the lack of sleep the night before, but also because of the battle she waged with her heart, her fears and her beliefs. In the end, her heart had won, which meant she planned to take her aunt's advice.

She had confined herself to her bedroom until the entire household retired, then waited another hour for good measure. Standing at Adam's door, listening one last time for any disturbance, she nibbled her lower lip and made up her mind. If seducing Adam forced him to take her with him should he leave England, so be it.

Cautiously, without the slightest noise, she opened the door. The dim circle of light from her candle pooled on the floor around her as she silently tiptoed toward the bed where Adam lay asleep. The covers lay low on his chest and high on his legs, exposing glistening bits of skin and muscle that she had once kissed and caressed. All the unimaginable suggestions Jeanette had made sent a rush of excitement down Becca's spine. Her body thrilled with anticipation. She set the brass candlestick on the table and gently tapped his shoulder.

Adam reared from the mattress, grabbed Becca by the waist and tossed her onto the bed. Suddenly she lay flat on her back, staring at the cream-colored canopy, Adam's hand wrapped around her throat. His face hovered above hers, his breath coming in ragged spurts, his eyes narrowed dangerously, almost wild. Sweet mercy, he looked like a feral dog wakened from its nap. She couldn't seem to move, let alone think about seducing the man. When she tried to speak, no sound escaped.

Blinking rapidly, Adam appeared to shift from some dark, faraway place and into the present. He jerked his hand away, glaring at her with a mixture of anger and disbelief, then he rolled onto his back to stare overhead. A guttural sound, part grunt, part groan, slid from his lips. "Are you mad? What the devil are you doing here?"

She lay perfectly still for the longest time, her heart pounding like a kettle drum, finally exhaling the breath of air she hadn't realized she'd been holding. "I hadn't seen you all day. I wanted to talk with you."

"In the middle of the night? I might have killed you."

"Never."

Shaking his head, he said, "You have no idea what I'm capable of."

He sounded so detached, so matter of fact, she wasn't quite sure how to respond. She nearly blurted out that she loved him. Jeanette's stern warning froze the words on her tongue. Many men, it seemed, even those inclined to act nobly, often fled for another continent when a woman mentioned love. Her aunt suggested Becca save that proclamation for another time. Tonight was about seduction.

Leaning on her elbow, allowing the thin strap of her nightrail to slip from her shoulder, she all but purred, "I know you would never harm anyone you cared about. I wanted to talk."

"Dear Lord, save me," he muttered. Turning his face toward hers, Adam spared her a passing glance before he swung his gaze to the canopy once again. Rebecca was near naked. What was she thinking, traipsing into his room wearing little more than a scrap of gossamer? The dusty outline of her nipples, already swollen, beckoned his lips. The curls between her legs tempted him to touch them. With one swift movement, he could drag her across his body, ply his mouth to her breasts, and teach her to make his dreams a reality. His eyes nearly crossed with the image.

By the stars, he'd vowed to leave her be until he'd proven his innocence. He was a cad, the worst kind of libertine. He'd lost hold of his senses last night, had known where his caresses would lead. And he hadn't cared. Her innocent admission that she wanted him as well, though likely offered without true understanding of what it meant, had not stopped him. He *would not* lose control again.

Especially since he'd decided not to force the marriage, that she deserved someone better than him, someone who could give her all the love and devotion she deserved. She deserved a man who would not break her heart.

She had cried—not those tears of women who used them as a tool of manipulation, but tears born from honest-to-goodness sadness. That fact had brought him no end of discomfort, for he was not equipped to deal with a woman's tender feelings.

Adam had given the matter a great deal of thought. If he disappeared, so would Francis Cobbald. Edward would have no trouble maligning the poet as a scoundrel, a debaucher of innocents and perhaps even a thief. Granted, there would be talk, but given time and Jeanette's tenacity, Adam felt Becca would find happiness.

As long as he didn't touch her again.

There was already the chance she might be pregnant. Testing the Fates a second time was far too risky. Indeed, he and Becca did need to talk. When fully dressed, in full sunlight, with one or two dozen people in the room. Maybe then he'd manage to keep his hands to himself. He rubbed his hands across his face one last time, sat up, wrapped the covers about his waist and swung his legs over the side of the bed. "I think we had better continue this discussion in the morning."

She trailed a fingernail across his neck, down his arm and across his back, where the blanket covered his buttocks. "If forced to wait, I doubt I will sleep at all."

Her voice was low and seductive. He felt her breath against his shoulder. Hare 'n hounds, she had actually touched her tongue to his ear. He dared not look.

His body ignored his brain.

Peering over his shoulder, he found Becca perched on her knees, directly behind him, every delectable inch of her flesh exposed through her sheer gown. If he moved a single inch, her breasts would press into his back. If he tipped his head lightly to the right, he could meld his lips to hers. "Becca, are you trying to seduce me?"

"Is such a thing possible?"

"I think you know the answer to that, but I have to wonder why . . . especially when earlier today you were ready to banish me to hell and back."

"I was angry. You know I despise orders, and I'm not yet convinced that I wish to give any man control of my life. I'm thinking Percy Shelley and Mary Godwin have the right of it. Nevertheless, I lay in bed tonight, unable to sleep, and I wondered if you suffered from the same malady. I *want* you."

She had managed to drag his discipline to the edge of the bottomless precipice of longing. Any normal man would toss her on her back, bury himself in her and damn the consequences. Unfortunately, he wasn't any man—regardless of the arousal that threatened to send him to his knees.

Clutching his blanket around him like a shield, he escaped to the foot of the bed and pointed to the door. "Rebecca Marche, remove yourself from this room immediately."

The blasted chit ignored him. She fell to her hands

240

and knees, arching her back like a feline in heat. Her gown gaped, exposing the creamy flesh of her breasts, belly and below. Where the devil had she learned to do that? He didn't have time to discern the answer. In horror, he watched her creep over the mattress toward him, inching closer and closer. She suggestively dragged her body upwards against the carved mahogany bedpost, pointed to the bulge his sheet failed to conceal and purred, "I would much rather take care of that."

His swollen shaft twitched, liking her suggestion just fine. Adam swallowed convulsively and pulled the sheet tighter against his body. "You could become pregnant."

"Hmmm," she purred as she ran her tongue over and around her finger. "My aunt said there were ways for men and women to pleasure one another without the danger of conception."

Now he knew how Becca had gained her newly acquired skills in seduction. First thing tomorrow morning he would throttle Lady Thacker, maybe even tonight. If he lived that long. True, he could make love to her with his mouth, let her pleasure him in the same manner, but he knew he'd never be content without complete possession of her body.

Becca's cheeks were flushed with excitement, and he could smell the sweet scent of her desire. She wasn't leaving, which meant he needed an entirely different approach. By all that was holy, he was going to have to touch her after all. He prayed for strength.

Strutting forward, he pulled her torso flush with his and lifted her from the bed. "Wrap your legs about me." She eagerly complied, and he felt her heat pressed against his erection. All he needed to do was drop the sheet and press into her, then both would know ecstasy.

You have no future.

"Kiss me," he said. Their lips met with a bold thrusting of tongues. Slowly, he inched toward the door. He ravished her mouth, drowning her in sensation, hopefully fogging her mind. He recited all the reasons not to take her. With one hand, he clasped the doorknob and cracked open the door. His hand inched toward her breast, teasing the hardened peak of her breast. He kicked the door fully open with his heel and prayed that no one lingered in the hall. This would be more than difficult to explain. He cupped her buttocks, kissed her one last time, then leaned against the wall and let her feet slip to the floor.

"Adam," she murmured. A question hovered in the way she said his name, but thankfully her mind was still befuddled enough for him to escape.

He pressed a gentle kiss to her lips. "Checkmate." He slid inside his bedroom, closed the door and turned the lock. "Good night, Becca. We shall talk in the morning."

He waited for her reaction, the kicking of the door or a curse or two. Several moments ticked by. Maybe she had gone to bed. Then he heard the telltale sign of movement and a whisper. "You may have won the battle tonight, but I intend to win the war. Sleep well, Adam Hawksmore."

Damn. He needed to resolve this mess, and soon. He needed a new plan.

Chapter Eighteen

"And you didn't bed her?" Mac asked incredulously.

"Not so loud. Do you want every gossip in London to hear?" Adam leaned against the trunk of a large elm tree and peered beyond Mac's gaping mouth at their surroundings. Luckily, no one lingered in the immediate vicinity.

Lords and ladies paraded about, flaunting their charms, enjoying the vast array of entertainment, all in the name of charity. Lady Ashby had opened the back gates of her stately home to Green Park, transforming a section of the grounds into a country fair to raise money for her latest altruistic endeavor, an orphanage near St. Giles.

Flanked by her family, Becca and Adam were making their debut as the newest love match of the Season. Becca, Miriam, Edward and Jeanette were now strolling around the vendors as if a breath of scandal had never been whispered. That left Mac and Adam to their own devices, which suited Adam just fine. He wasn't in the mood for idle conversation.

"Explain this to me," Mac said as he leaned against the other side of the tree. "You already made love to Becca. Edward gave you his blessing, the two of you you are engaged and you obviously want the girl." He shrugged one shoulder. "Sorry, but I'm confused as to why you didn't take her."

"I have decided not to force this marriage," Adam whispered as two giggling young ladies passed by.

"May I ask why?"

"I have my reasons."

"That I'm sure of." Mac squinted against the sunlight. "You don't look pleased. Were it me threatened with marriage, no matter the lady's charms, I'd dash for the nearest ship and sail to a deserted isle in the Indies. But you, my friend, are meant for wedlock, constancy and serene evenings before a fire with slippers on your feet and a hound at your heels. Your decision baffles me. But I can tell by the set of your jaw, you don't intend to tell me why."

Overhead, several rooks cawed noisily as they passed in and out of the trees. The clear blue sky was a sharp contrast to the morning that had begun with shades of gray and dense fog. Sunlight drifted through the canopy of trees, warming the air with a fresh earthy fragrance. The gloom had better suited Adam's mood.

Especially since he had slept little last night after depositing Becca in the hallway; he'd gone to bed aroused and awakened even more so. And this very morning over breakfast, she'd had the audacity to act as though nothing had happened. As if she hadn't slithered across his bed with her derriere perched in the air like that of a trained courtesan. That alone was enough to irritate a man.

Now Mac had placed another unbidden image in Adam's head, one just as disconcerting as a naked Becca, writhing in pleasure, begging for his touch. He could easily picture himself sitting in his study at Kerrick Castle beside a fire complete with dog, book and slippers. And seated beside him was Becca. They would share a brandy and intimate conversation before he stripped her of her clothes and made love to her, bathed in firelight on that soft Persian rug he favored so much.

Adam commanded his mind to clear. He needed no distractions today. From the corner of his eye he spotted Lady Grayson, sporting a bright yellow parasol and matching hat, provocatively swaying those hips of hers in a manner meant to entice. She stopped before Adam and wound one of her auburn curls about her finger. "My dear Mr. Cobbald. I hear congratulations are in order, though I admit I experienced keen disappointment when I received the news. Yet Lady Wyncomb was most persuasive in her argument that I offer my support."

"You are a diamond of the first water among a heap of common stones."

Her lips formed a sensual pout. "One must be careful these days where they lend support. I considered asking you for a private meeting to ensure your sincerity toward the girl."

Flat on her back and with very little conversation, he imagined. He scrunched his nose like a rabbit and laughed to himself. "Your wisdom and generosity extricated me in my hour of need. What can I say? Cupid pierced my heart. Becca is my soul, my sun, my moon and stars."

"Pity," Lady Grayson said, suddenly eyeing Mac. Obviously liking what she saw, she thrust her bosom out a good two inches farther in silent invitation. "Should your circumstance change, you know where I can be found."

After the woman had moved onto her next prospect. Mac touched his forehead in a mock salute. "What a performance, Mr. Cobbald. A vast improvement since last I saw you." He nodded toward Lady Grayson's retreating back. "You've an interesting friend, there."

"You'd do well to stay away from her. I have a feeling she'd not be content with one quick tumble. She's more like a shark with breasts. She won't be happy until she's completely devoured a man."

Grinning, Mac added, "A shark with lovely plump breasts, if I say so myself. But never fear. I learned my lesson and rarely make the same mistake twice."

That was of no surprise to Adam; he'd heard the story. Long ago, as a dangerous, titillating diversion, Mac had played bedroom games with many of the bored wives of Polite Society. Until his heart became involved and he nearly lost everything that mattered, including his life.

"Good. Come along. We have business to attend." Mac pushed away from the tree. "Where are we going?"

"I have decided to lure the wolf from his lair. What do you suppose will happen if Cobbald catches Oswin's or Seavers's attention, perhaps makes them curious about his past?"

Mac's brows furrowed. "If they make the connection between Cobbald and Hawksmore, they just might shoot you. Or possibly go directly to the authorities. Either way, it's a dangerous game. Are you sure the time is right?"

Adam waved his handkerchief at some matron whose name escaped him. He distinctly remembered her request for a poem about her dead finch, Romeo, and purposely lengthened his stride. When Mac glanced over, Adam said, "Do not so much as hesitate. No matter what."

When they reached a roped area where pony rides were offered, a pence apiece, he stopped and feigned interest in the children's antics. "I'm tired of waiting. I have been in London for too long and all I have to show for it is more questions. I was positive Oswin was guilty. After your news about Seavers, I can't be sure of anything. Becca's little visit last night has prompted me to change my tactics. I'm not sure how long I can keep my hands off her, and if there is the remote possibility that I must leave, I dare not touch her again."

"The ship is ready to sail if and when it's needed."

"Sail?" a voice asked. "Are you leaving us, Mac?"

Becca. How did she always manage to be within earshot of the things that she wasn't supposed to hear? Thunder and turf. She was worse than a gossipmonger on race day. Shaking his head, Adam swung about. "Mac was born ready to sail."

"Lucky you." She gave her parasol a jaunty twirl, doing her best to hide her distress. *Infernal man.* Adam had tossed her from his room as if she were a sack of grain, as though she hadn't offered herself to him like a common tart. This morning, she'd dressed with the utmost care, selecting a lovely poppy-colored dress with a flattering neckline, and he'd practically ignored her.

And still he talked of leaving. *Stubborn fool.* If he

thought he could march back into her life, make her fall in love with him, then simply sail away, he had another think coming. "I envy your freedom, Mac. Mercy, I envy the freedom that all men have and take for granted, the fact they can virtually come and go as they please."

"Now, now, *my fuzzy peach.*" With his hand under her chin, Adam gave Becca a devoted look meant for the eager eyes watching them. "This is not the time or place for such a discussion."

"Pardon me, *my turtle dove,*" she whispered with a smile of adoration. "But I disagree. Do you wish to know what I really think you and Mac were discussing?" She raised her brow, challenging Adam to dismiss her question. "How quickly you could leave the country should your plans go awry. Perhaps I shall stowaway. I haven't sailed in years."

Mac chuckled.

Adam growled, "We can discuss this alter. Right now, I wish to court my *lady love.*"

Instantly suspicious, Becca strode between Adam and Mac along the promenade. They passed a fortune teller and a dancing dog. Adam bought her a raspberry tart and a pair of lovely white lace gloves. They paused to watch a fencing exhibition, then moved toward a group of bystanders in which, every now and then, someone gasped or giggled. The trio inched their way to the front of the crowd, where a bench was positioned to keep everyone back. Beyond, a large board covered with black fabric was balanced against a tree trunk. Attached to the fabric were miniature drawings of Napoleon. Nine months after the fact, it seemed society still delighted in the enemy's downfall. When a man dressed in tight-fitting black pants and a flowing white shirt hurled a wicked-looking dagger at one of the pictures, Becca knew Adam's purpose. She glared at him. "You wouldn't dare," she whispered. "Not with everyone here. What if Oswin or Seavers see you?"

"There is that possibility," he admitted from the side of his mouth, grinning all the while.

The devilish idiot. What did he possibly hope to gain? Studying Adam, she thought for a moment. "You hope Seavers or Oswin *do* notice, don't you?"

"Smile, darling. People are watching." He waved the tall chap with the knives in his direction, paid several coins and stepped over the bench and into the ringed area.

She might have had a chance, or so she had hoped in some deluded recess of her mind, until Barnard found her.

He clasped her elbow and blurted, "Lady Rebecca. I must talk with you. It is most urgent."

With a silver dagger in one hand, Adam placed his other hand on his hip and struck a pose equal to any strutting barnyard rooster. He even crowed like a damn bird. "Why Mr. Leighton, we meet again. Do you wish to offer your congratulations?"

"I wish to talk with Lady Rebecca. The matter is most urgent."

"Sorry. My fiancée is preoccupied. And if you wish to keep your hand," Adam added, "I suggest you remove it from her arm."

Barnard eyed his dagger, then gasped and turned to Becca. "Are you going to allow him to talk to me in such an awful manner?"

To Becca's mortification, Barnard's voice carried and was garnering the unwanted attention of people standing close by. Adam was probably thrilled. "He's teasing. He means nothing. Now, what were you ask-ing?"

"Tell me that someone is spreading heinous tales, malicious lies that wound me to the depths of my soul. Are you *engaged* to this person?"

Sensing he meant to stay until she answered, no matter what, Becca offered a serene smile, one meant to calm and placate him. She thought she'd explained to him that she was not interested in his suit. "Yes, the rumor is true. Considering what grand friends you and I were, I was hoping you would share my happiness."

Barnard tugged on his crisp white cuffs, then blinked several times. The muscles around his mouth quivered. *Please don't let him weep*, was all Becca could think. *Not in front of these people.* Added speculation was the last thing she needed.

Barnard nervously glanced toward Adam, then back to Becca, his eyes pleading. "You do not un-derstand the ramifications. I have information."

Becca had never seen Barnard so demonstrative in all her life. And he was positively splotchy from ex-citement. The crowd had grown quiet, eager to hear every sordid detail, she was sure. Massaging her forehead, she softened her voice to a whisper. "Come by the house in a day or two. We can talk then."

"Do come by and visit," Adam added enthusiasti-cally, eager to wrest away control of the conversa-tion. "We can share a poem or two."

"I have no desire to share poetry with you, Mr. Cobbald. I wish to speak with Lady Rebecca. Alone."

"I see," Adam murmured as he searched the faces of the curious onlookers. God bless Polite Society. They could smell gossip or scandal from across the Thames. The whispers had begun when Barnard made his sudden appearance. Adam was more than willing to use him as a pawn if it meant drawing Oswin and Seavers into the game.

Adam's irritation had nothing to do with his powerful urge to punch Leighton in the face, or the fact that Becca always seemed to fawn all over the fellow. Nor did it bother him that she had never admitted she didn't love Leighton, or that she'd cried when she'd been ordered to marry Adam.

A ghastly prospect struck Adam like a stray rock to his head. He was jealous.

"Adam?" Becca asked.

"What?" he snapped before he remembered the prying eyes of their audience.

"Are you all right? You look . . . odd."

He felt odd. He'd never experienced these childish inclinations before he met Becca. But they would pass. He'd make damn sure of that. An irrational impulse such as jealousy was for lovesick, addlebrained pups. He was neither.

Exhaling a deep breath, he pulled his handkerchief from his pocket and dabbed his brow. He began to twirl the knife he held between his fingers with increasing speed. One moment he faced the crowd, in the next he spun on his heel and hurled the knife into the center of Napoleon's face. To his delight, the crowd gasped. He nonchalantly turned and bowed.

Several ladies in the audience giggled. Adam saw money being exchanged, bets no doubt, though of what exactly Adam had no idea. He also noted that Jeremy Oswin stood near the perimeter of the crowd. "Mr. Leighton," Adam asked. "Are you refusing my generosity?"

Sniffing as though insulted, Leighton said, "You shan't threaten me."

"Threaten?" Adam asked. "Dear me, I hope not. I abhor violence, but admit I have a penchant for knives. I simply hoped to impress my fiancée before you interrupted us."

Becca twittered between clenched teeth. "In that case, my dear, consider me duly impressed. May we go now?"

"Wait," Leighton cried, almost hysterically. "I had hoped we might speak about this in private. . . ."

Adam thought the lad might collapse with the vapors. Selecting another two knives, he said, "Good grief, sir. You have managed to garner the attention of everyone here. If you have something to say, please do so."

Leighton tipped his chin in the air, rolled his shoulders, then blurted. "This man is a fraud, an imposter. There is no poet named Francis Cobbald from Lincolnshire."

Tare'n hounds! Adam had considered several reasons for Leighton's odd behavior. This announcement had not been one of them. Stalling for time, deciding how best to proceed, he strutted in a small circle.

Edward, a concerned expression on his face, appeared from the shade of a nearby elm with Jeanette and Miriam. Becca worried her lower lip but thankfully kept silent. Mac looked as though he just might send the lad straight to hell and back. And strolling together down the path was Lady Grayson and Lord Benjamin Seavers. Adam had certainly achieved his goal. Retreat at this point was unthinkable.

Simultaneously, he launched two knives. They both landed with a resounding thud in the center of Napoleon's chest. Adam whirled about, pointed his toe like a dandified jackanape, set one hand on his hip, dangled the other in the air and bowed to wild applause. "It seems I have been found out."

More curious than ever, the crowd quieted as Adam stepped to Becca's side and clasped her hand. "Dare we tell them the truth, my sweet?"

Becca merely nodded.

"My good people, I fear Mr. Leighton is correct."

Whispers swept through the crowd. Leighton, the interfering buffoon, puffed up like a Christmas goose, one Adam would have just as soon stuffed at the moment.

Staring directly at Seavers, Adam continued. "I admit I am not what I seem. My life has been a masquerade of sorts." When Becca dug her fingernails into his hand, Adam gazed into her eyes. She wasn't the least bit happy with his plan. "I am not from Lincolnshire but possess humbler beginnings. I am the son of a tavern maid, abandoned and scorned by a titled father who refused to acknowledge me."

Adam heard a muttered "Poor dear" and a "Bloody shame," even a "Not the first time." He reminded himself to thank Mac for inspiration. "Alas, you see before you a self-made man who believes in universal kindness and the limitless gift of forgiveness by humanity. Lady Rebecca, as well as her parents, were aware of my heritage and still accepted my suit."

Thoroughly pleased with himself and his performance, Adam kissed Becca's hand. "All in the name of love."

Several women sighed. The older lords eyed one another as if Adam's father had always been within their tight circle of friends. By the stars, one woman actually dabbed tears from her cheeks. Jeremy Oswin was nowhere to be seen, but Benjamin Seavers stood as still as a stick, his eyes narrowed and focused directly on Adam.

That was that, Adam thought. The punch was in the pudding now. All he could do was wait.

Eager to prolong the discussion, Barnard sputtered several times. Thankfully, Edward handled the situation most eloquently. He stepped to the front of the circle and snapped, "Shut up, Barnard. I, for one, would like my future son-in-law to toss another knife or two. I bet he can throw three knives at once and hit three separate drawings of Ol' Nappie. What do you say? Do I have any takers?"

Nothing could possibly have turned the tide faster than a wager. For the moment, Barnard was forgotten. Later, behind closed doors, in their salons or bedrooms, with nothing else to do, people would talk, but Adam was accustomed to that. One thing was certain, Lady Featherstone's masquerade party tonight would certainly be interesting.

Chapter Nineteen

Adam passed through the great west doors of Westminster Abbey, following the footsteps of every monarch crowned since William the Conqueror. A feeling of solemnity engulfed him the moment he stepped into the sacred building. A perfect place, he mused, for a mysterious meeting, and one that could very well be his last.

As his eyes adjusted to the dim interior, he fingered the paper in his pocket. A messenger had delivered the note shortly after Adam had returned from Green Park. The instructions were very specific. Meet in the Poet's Corner of the Abbey at four.

Edward and Mac had argued against the stupidity of going alone until Adam had finally relented. He'd allowed Mac to leave early and hide himself somewhere near the proposed meeting place. Adam wasn't the least bit worried. Wary, yes. But he was more excited that he might finally have answers to his questions. Or so he hoped.

He could also end up dead.

He sauntered beneath the vaulted ceiling that made one think of heaven's gate. The clicking of his boot heels on the stone floor marked his progress past monuments to deceased kings and queens, beneath the exquisite stained-glass windows, until at last he reached the south transept, home to the greatest poets of England's past. Their words had granted them immortality.

The scent of candle wax permeated the smaller chamber, and cool draft of air fell across Adam's shoulders. He tugged the collar of his greatcoat higher on his neck, then fingered the knife in the pocket. Glancing from side to side, he waited beside the tombs of Chaucer and Spenser, each fellow poet paying homage to his esteemed predecessors. He briefly wondered where Mac hid himself.

"I see you received my invitation."

A rush of adrenaline exploded in Adam's veins, clearing his mind and sharpening his wits. He knew the feeling well and welcomed it. Slowly, he turned toward the left, where Lord Benjamin Seavers lounged against a marble bust. His face was hidden by shadow, but the pistol neatly tucked into the waistband of his trousers was easy to spot. Unable to discern Seavers's mood, Adam simply cocked his head to the side. "Interesting place for a meeting, sir."

"I thought it appropriate since I intended to meet both a dead man and a poet, Mr. Cobbald. Or should I say, Adam Hawksmore, Earl of Kerrick?"

The air stilled, as if the tomb's occupants held their breath in anticipation of Adam's answer. "An interesting theory, Lord Seavers. The earl *is* dead."

Seavers stepped closer, his footsteps on the stone floor reverberating off the walls. "Exactly. Pity, though. Dedicated soldiers are hard to find these days."

The choice was his; Adam knew that. Seavers was allowing him to speak his mind or walk away. Adam decided he had nothing to lose, and much to gain if Seavers agreed to help prove Oswin's guilt. Adam slid toward the monument to Shakespeare. When Seavers followed, Adam quietly asked, "What did you hope to gain by this meeting, Lord Seavers?"

"I would ask you the same thing. I assumed your display this afternoon, reminiscent of our days together at Oxford, was directed toward me. Was I wrong?"

Adam chuckled. "No. I need your help."

"Considering the War Department has declared you a traitor, that is a gross understatement." Seavers's voice was as cool as the marble slab upon which his hand rested, devoid of any indication that he and Adam had once traveled in the same social circle. "Though I found the information hard to believe, when I first heard the news, I was furious. The Leopard caused England innumerable problems and lives. I wanted to find you myself and put a bullet in your head. But I've had time to cool down, to think. Since you're in London, I can only assume you have something to prove. My hope is that it is your innocence. Since we were friends, I decided to give you the benefit of the doubt before I contacted the authorities. You have five minutes. Shall we walk?"

They ventured toward the stairs that led to Henry VII's chapel. Just beyond the bronze gates, the banners of the Order of Bath lined the walls like two rows of brightly colored soldiers. They framed the graceful curve of the vaulted stone ceiling, its delicate fanlike design a work of art in itself. Adam stopped at the entrance to the chamber. "I was framed."

"An interesting proposition. By whom? Why?"

"Those are the very questions I have asked myself for the last few months. I believe I am close to the answers. The problem is, I have no proof. My performance today was designed to lure the real spy into the open."

Seavers's spine went rigid. His eyes narrowed dangerously as his hand slid to the handle of his gun. "Surely you don't think I—"

"Actually, yes. I considered the possibility."

"I should shoot you for that alone."

A soldier through and through, Seavers wore his pride like a well-tailored uniform, his temper like a shield. Adam casually crossed to the elaborate tomb of Henry and his wife, Elizabeth. "I had my reasons. Do you remember that night at the Red Goose Inn?" When Seavers nodded, Adam added, "Lord Jeremy Oswin was there."

Seavers stood silent for a moment, rubbing his chin. "Yes. He, too, met a woman. I didn't speak with him, though. I remember thinking that it was odd that he was there and not at the Duchess of Richmond's ball."

A hooded priest shuffled into the chamber and proceeded to replace candles. He slowly worked his way toward the late king's tombs.

"Precisely." Adam whispered, moving to the opposite corner of the chapel and wondering whether Mac had suddenly found religion. The possibility made Adam smile.

"You think Oswin is the Leopard?"

"The idea occurred to me. He was there that night with a dark-haired woman. The Leopard supposedly had a dark-haired female accomplice. Oswin was privy to the details of the English military and could go virtually anywhere he wanted. He could easily have planted the evidence in my belongings at camp. I briefly spoke with him that night, and even then I thought he was acting oddly. I didn't put two and two together until I returned home and discovered I had been framed."

Circling an elaborate iron stand of candles, Seavers said, "If what you say is true, I have done you a great disservice. I informed the War Department that you and I met at the inn and a woman accompanied you. I intimated that she could have easily been the Leopard's accomplice."

"May I ask why?"

Seavers ran his hand through his hair in apparent frustration. "Like everyone else, I wanted that bastard caught. I'm sorry. I acted out of turn."

"If it makes you feel any better, I already knew about your testimony."

"Why didn't you say something?"

Adam waved his hand in dismissal. "I'm not very trusting these days. I wanted to see if you would mention the incident. I am to the point of desperation. I have allowed myself only a few more days to clear my name. If I cannot prove my innocence, I will leave England."

"That's rather drastic."

"The longer I delay, the less likely it is that the truth will ever come to light. Which brings us to the real reason for my performance today. Oswin saw me as well. Let's see if he takes the bait. Since you

259

stepped forward, are you willing to offer your assistance?"

Seavers squeezed Adam's shoulder. "Of course. Though I'll do you little good if Oswin shoots you in the back."

"The fact that you believe me is enough for now. As for Oswin, I shall be doubly careful. If something happens to me, then you will know for certain that Oswin is the traitor. You can go directly to the War Department." He paused. "I have one last question. There are rumors that you murdered a woman in the village of Cherbourg, possibly your own mistress."

Seavers made on odd sucking noise with his teeth. "You of all people should understand the danger of such tales. Though I don't believe I owe you any explanation, I will tell you all the same. The woman was a common whore who thought to rob me of my purse and attack me. She was unsuccessful."

The story would be difficult to prove on short order. Adam nodded. "Will you be at Featherstone's masquerade?"

"I have a previous engagement." Seavers pulled a watch from his coat pocket. "In fact, I must leave immediately. But come by my house tomorrow at five. We can talk more then."

Watching Seavers's retreating back, Adam leaned against a stone support. After a moment or two, wearing a priest's robe, Mac crawled from behind Henry VII's tomb.

"Nothing like hovering near a dead king to make one question his mortality. I recognized Seavers. Is he friend or foe?"

Pausing to consider the brief encounter, Adam wished he felt more confident with the outcome. Seavers had said all the right things, reacted exactly as expected. He appeared wholly supportive of Adam's plight. Nevertheless, a small visceral reaction made him uneasy. "I think he'd be a hell of a gambler. Come along. I'll explain."

Candlelight glittered off silk and satin in a palette of colors a painter would envy. The lords and ladies of London had outdone themselves tonight. They wore costumes that ranged from the mundane to the outrageous, the wicked to the sublime. Since there were far more people present than the ball and supper rooms could accommodate, Lady Featherstone's masquerade would undoubtedly be heralded as a rousing success. And it seemed that each and every person there was fascinated with Becca's sudden betrothal. Thank goodness her shepherdess costume kept some of the curiosity-seekers at bay.

Everyone except Barnard.

"My dearest periwinkle, I cannot believe that you have forgotten the truly remarkable union of our senses." Barnard paused momentarily. "Surely *he* won't make you happy?"

"Time will tell," Becca muttered, barely aware of Barnard's ramblings. In rapt fascination, she watched Lord Oswin. The man was dressed as Faust's Mephistopheles. She'd happened on his identity quite by accident when they nearly collided with one another in the foyer. As he apologized, he hadn't bothered to conceal his identity. Since then, she'd done her best to keep track of the man.

"As eternal spiritual beings, we walk this earth in mere physical form to share our love with others. Can you honestly tell me this Cobbald fellow loves you in *all* ways?"

"Francis is unique."

She watched Oswin as he sneaked a glance from side to side and set his glass of champagne on a passing servant's empty tray. Like a red serpent, he slithered around the marble pillar at the top of the stairs and disappeared from sight. He was definitely up to some sort of mischief.

In search of reinforcements, Becca quickly ran her eyes around the crowded oval ballroom. She easily spotted Adam. Dressed as a dashing Spanish pirate, he wore his eye patch, black satin pants, a red linen shirt with flowing sleeves, and a brightly embroidered vest and black boots that fitted snugly well above his knees. A saber and a knife added the final touches to his costume. He looked dangerous and remarkably handsome. And he was dancing with Lady Grayson, of all people. He certainly wouldn't be of any help.

Her father was trapped in a conversation with Lord Ashby. Mac, dressed as a Viking warrior down to the fur leggings and horned headdress, was flirting with a Grecian princess in a corner near the terrace. Becca's mother and aunt, wearing identical blue dominoes, were available . . . but what could they possibly do?

That left Becca with one choice.

"Come along, Barnard."

"Where?"

"I understand Lord Featherstone recently acquired a grand statue of Mercury. I wish to take a peek."

At the top of the stairs, the entrance hall split in three directions. One arched doorway led to the dining area, for those who wished to eat. In the opposite direction was the library, where people played cards. Becca spotted Oswin just as he rounded the corner of the third passage, which wound beneath the grand curving staircase and led to who knew where.

"Are you sure about this?" Barnard asked. "Do you know where the statue is? This is highly irregular. Perhaps we should we find your mother first. Or my cousin."

"We'll only be a moment. Where is your sense of adventure?" Becca shot a wistful glance toward Adam one last time. Unfortunately, he was too busy laughing at something witty that Lady Grayson had said.

From beneath the staircase, Becca peeked around the corner. Oswin was nowhere to be seen. She scurried past two marble benches, a large wooden chest and a row of gilded mirrors. Barnard followed along, mumbling as he came. The hallway ended and split in opposite directions, the left definitely darker and less inviting than the right. If she were searching for a place to hold a secret discussion, wouldn't dark be good?

Suddenly, Barnard pushed her against the wall, raining sloppy kisses on her face and neck. "What a fool I was. I thought you were angry. You clever, clever girl. You do love me, my golden iris!"

"Barnard. I *do not* love you."

"Be still, my heart. My love enflames my soul."

Becca shoved her hands against his shoulders. "Good grief. Stop this nonsense immediately, Barnard, or I shall be forced to hurt you."

"Hurt me? Never, my heart mate, my essence of life, my sweet water lily. We shall elope for Gretna Green tonight."

"I don't think so," thundered the voice of an avenging angel. Angrily, Adam lifted Barnard away from Becca and hurled him across the hall. The young man bounced off the wall into Adam's fist, then collapsed into a pool of black and white satin.

"Rebecca Marche, I ought to take you home and lock you in your room until every hair falls from your head. Maybe then you will remember what I have told you about sneaking out alone."

Relief cleared her wits. Oxygen filled her lungs. Her heart crawled back into her chest. "I will have *no* hair if you continue to scare me to death."

"Then do as I say. This is the last time you wander off by yourself. Do you hear me?"

She hurried to Barnard's side and patted his cheek. "I wasn't by myself."

"Now there's a persuasive argument, considering I found that coxcomb wrapped about you like a bloodsucking vine."

"Be quiet. I think you killed him."

"Good. You should know better than to sneak away with a man."

"For your information, this is all your fault. I was doing you a favor so that maybe, just maybe, you won't scurry away like a whipped dog with its tail between its legs with the likes of Macdonald Archer. Besides, until tonight Barnard has always behaved as a gentleman. I don't know what came over him."

Adam offered no rebuttal to her accusation about his leaving London. As for Leighton, he easily understood the man's motivations. Adam, himself, had thought about putting his hands on her all night. Ever since she'd stepped into the foyer wearing that forest green creation that laced at her waist and emphasized her breasts. Delightful breasts, firm and ripe. Yes, indeed, he remembered them all too well. "I guess Barnard lost sight of his communion with that *higher plane* of his. Which way did Oswin go?"

"Don't you dare throw Barnard back in my face. Anyway, you were absorbed in conversation with Lady Grayson."

"Amazing as it seems, I can converse and observe at the same time. You wasted little time in following Oswin." He raised a dark eyebrow high on his forehead, as if he dared her to argue. "Where did he go?"

"I'm not sure. He's obviously hidden away in a room somewhere. What about Barnard? We can't very well leave him in the hall. We should at least make him comfortable."

Adam's expression became a stony mask. Grabbing Barnard by the heels, he dragged the limp body to the chest, lifted the lid and tossed the lad inside like yesterday's linen.

"That was not what I had in mind," Becca grumbled, torn between guilt and annoyance. Adam merely shrugged and veered toward the brighter corridor at a clipped pace. "Shouldn't we go in the other direction?" she asked.

He looked at her curiously. "Why?"

"Because if I were trying to hide somewhere for a private conversation, that is where I would go."

"That is exactly the reason why you should listen to me. Oswin knows better than that. He's likely in a chamber in which his presence could easily be explained."

"Shouldn't we be a bit more discreet?"

"We look like two lovers seeking a place for privacy. Better that than sneaking around having someone think we're after Lady Feathertone's diamonds."

He draped her arm over his and slowly walked down the corridor, past three small alcoves with floor-to-ceiling windows edged with wine-colored brocade curtains. Five mahogany doors lined the other wall. Adam stopped in front of the first door and adjusted the sash of his costume. When he heard nothing, he moved onto the next room. Beneath his cool facade the fury he'd felt when he saw Barnard plastered to Becca like a wet blanket still simmered. "Do most engaged women traipse off alone with other men?"

"Only when their fiancés leave them unattended for long periods of time. What did Lady Grayson have to say?"

"The usual." Adam had simply been curious about Seavers's and her relationship. Unfortunately, he'd been too busy defending himself from her advances to find out anything.

Then he'd seen Becca leave with Leighton. "You have no reason to be jealous, you know," he said.

"Just as you have no reason to be jealous of Barnard."

Before she could say anything more, Adam turned the knob and peered inside a second room, which was empty. Farther down the hallway, from the direction they'd just come, he heard the light sound of footfalls. He grabbed Becca, dragged her into the farthest corner of the alcove—as far behind the open drape as possible—and waited for the person to pass. In the name of caution, he wrapped his arms about Becca, pulling her flush with his body. She raised her head. Her lips parted as she prepared to speak so to ensure her silence, he caught her words with his lips. To erase any memory of Barnard, he devoured her mouth.

She returned his kiss with even greater ardor, drawing him into a vortex of need. Every time he touched her, held her, kissed her, greed reared its ignoble head. One kiss was never enough. Dragging his lips from hers, he tucked her head into the curve of his shoulder. The fact that it might not be so easy to leave Becca behind burned foremost in his mind. With that thought, he watched a familiar shadow sneak past. Pulling back the drape, he cleared his throat.

Edward froze, hunched his shoulders and swayed from side to side. Swiveling about, he grinned like a bloody bosky well into his cups. One look at Adam, and Edward's lips thinned. "Are you trying to give an old man a seizure?"

Becca peered from behind Adam's shoulder. "Father? What are you doing?"

"I might ask you the same question."

"We were following Lord Oswin," Adam hissed, trying his best not to lecture the grown man who should have known better than to traipse off into possible danger alone.

As Lord Wyncomb rubbed his hands together in delight, his eyes filled with mischief. "I knew you were up to something. Where is he?"

"He's probably long gone and settled in a game of poker by now. Nevertheless, stay here and be quiet. Both of you." Shaking his head in frustration, partly due to Edward's interruption and to his unabated desire for Becca, Adam continued down the hallway to the third door. Warm breath and the scent of lilacs tickled his neck and ear. One quick glance over his shoulder told him what he already knew. Becca and Edward were right on his heels. It was a wonder the woman ever listened to him at all. She'd learned disobedience from her own blasted father.

Muted voices drifted down the corridor. "Sweet Hebrides," Adam muttered. "Who could be coming now?" He shoved Becca toward her father, then studied the seascape painting on the wall. His companions in crime quickly aped his action.

"I'm telling you, they sneaked off like common thieves."

Damn if Adam didn't recognize that voice. That fact barely registered in his mind when, strolling around the corner, arm in arm, as if they hadn't a care in the world, came Lady Thacker and Miriam. Becca's mother wore an expression that was part curiosity, part disbelief. Jeanette positively glowed with anticipation.

Throwing his arms up in surrender, Adam scowled at each and every person before he stomped back to the previous room. He shoved the door open and waited for everyone to file inside.

Becca quietly slid behind the door and waited. Her mother, not knowing what she'd interrupted, seemed to know enough to keep silent. Her father was suddenly fascinated by the assorted wooden boxes on a table at the far side of the parlor. Jeanette, completely nonplussed by Adam's ire, sailed into the room, humming.

Adam shut the door. "Sit down."

Edward perched his large frame on the spindly-legged stool beside the pianoforte. Miriam sat on a small settee with Jeanette beside her. Becca chose the padded bench closest to the door.

Obviously deciding where to begin his lecture, Adam circled the room. He halted before an ornate chimney face with a rather sad-looking lion and looked at everyone like a general inspecting his troops. "This is the final straw. I have had it. Tonight is the last silliness I will tolerate. Never in all my days have I witnessed such gross insubordination. What were all of you thinking?"

All four people began to speak at once.

He held his hand in the air. "Do not say a word."

"But you just—" Becca began, but Adam's mouth locked in a scowl of the like she had never seen. And his eyes . . . well, if it were physically possible, Becca thought he just might scorch each and every one of her family into cinders. She decided her question could wait.

He paced another three times, circling the rosewood pianoforte twice before finally settling back at the fireplace. "I shall make this very clear. None of you are to follow me again. Nor Lord Oswin, or Lord Seavers. This is *my affair*, and I will not have your lives endangered. That is an order."

Edward stood, bristling with indignation. "The day I hide from trouble is the day my body goes into the cold earth. I've faced worse ruffians on a Sunday in the park. You are my future son-in-law. If you think I will stand by like a dandified lapdog, you are sorely mistaken."

Adam stacked his hands on his hips. "If I am not cleared, you will be accused as my accomplice. All of you. And have you forgotten that we are dealing with a possible murderer? You will not put yourself in jeopardy again."

"And if we wish to help you?" Miriam asked.

"*Unwish* it."

Jeanette chuckled. Actually chuckled. Once Adam recovered from his astonishment, his final thread of patience unraveled. Sweet mercy, he thought, he just might bellow like Edward.

"My dear boy," Jeanette continued, ignoring the obvious clenching of his jaw, "it is not as simple as that. You would never let anything happen to us. We know that. And even if you failed in some way, we would still care for you. But that just makes it all the more imperative that we see after you."

The brass knob on the mahogany door turned. Everyone in the room fell silent.

Chapter Twenty

With a bottle of brandy in one hand and an empty glass in the other, Mac swaggered into the room as if he owned the house. "Thought I heard Edward. That bellow of his is rather distinctive."

"I do not bellow," Edward proclaimed, loud enough to warrant a warning scowl from his wife.

Adam pressed his fingers to the bridge of his nose. "Thunder and turf, Mac. Not you, too."

"Did I miss something?" his friend asked, setting his bottle on the marble side table near Becca.

"Only a comedy of errors that Shakespeare would envy. Oswin left the ballroom. Becca decided to follow him—just as a precaution, mind you. With Barnard, no less. I followed her—a good thing, since Barnard decided to plead his case for true love. Lord Wyncombe thought he might miss the excitement, so he followed me. Then, just in case we needed help, along came Lady Wyncombe and Lady Thacker. So here we are, my merry band of lunatics, waiting to be caught and sent to Bedlam. I was trying to explain the benefit of prudence, but no one agrees with me. They seem to believe I am capable of moving mountains if need be to clear my name. This discussion is more tedious than trying to talk to a herd of mules. Perhaps you can explain the wisdom of minding their own damn business."

Mac shrugged as he sprawled in a cushioned chair, parking his feet on its small footstool and placing his hands behind his head. His lips curled insolently as he winked at the grinning Jeanette, who sat across from him. "Why would I do that?"

Sputtering, Adam stared at his best friend, the one person he believed he could always rely on for reasonable thinking. "What the hell is that supposed to mean?"

"Give over, Adam. In all the years I've known you, you never allowed anyone an ounce of responsibility. You're not alone here, like Moses in the desert. You have friends who believe in you. Friends who are willing to help you. You've always been so hell-bent on taking care of others that you've forgotten how to let anyone take care of you."

"I am the Kerrick heir. It is my job to be in charge. I refused to be a burden when I was a lad, and I'm certainly not going to start now."

"Yet you willingly allow everyone else to be a burden to you."

As if Mac's declaration cleared the pathway to truth and wisdom, Edward crossed his arms. "Damn right. Every man reaches a point where he realizes he can't do it all himself."

Miriam's face was soft and motherly. "We face our

problems together and expect nothing in return."

"Like it or not, you are part of our family now," Jeanette cheerfully added. "It is our duty to protect you."

"I don't recall any wedding ceremony," Adam snapped.

Becca had the gleam in her eye that always meant trouble. Sucking in a deep, fortifying breath, she stood and waltzed the length of the room with slow, deliberate steps. She stopped directly in front of Adam. "But I'm sure you remember the honeymoon."

"I can quickly unremember it."

"Personally, I am sick and tired of hearing you rant and rave about *our* interference in *your* personal matters. You cannot open and close a door and allow people into your life only when you deem it possible. Life is messy. You may not want to hear this but, when a person loves someone, they will do anything they can to help that other person."

Miriam glanced over her shoulder toward Edward. "I told you she loved him."

"I knew it all along," Jeanette said as she dabbed at a tear.

With his back to Becca, Adam braced his hands against the cold marble of the fireplace. Struck with the disturbing realization that everyone was frightfully serious, a sense of inadequacy washed over him. What if he failed their expectations? Dear Lord, he'd spent his entire life trying to honor his father's dying words: "Make me proud." And what had Adam done? Blackened the Kerrick name, failed his troops, turned his cousin against him.

Even more disturbing was Becca's *declaration.* He certainly wasn't going to discuss *that* in front of everyone. This called for retreat and lengthy meditation. "I fear we have strayed from the matter at hand and should save this discussion for another time. Oswin is undoubtedly gone by now, so I suggest we return to the ball."

"Just like that?" Edward snapped.

"Just like that," Adam returned, leaving no room for negotiation.

Mac set his feet on the floor. "Before we join the festivities, you might like to know what I discovered while all of you were busy solving Adam's familial needs. Oswin met a fellow. Would you like to know whom?"

"Would you like to simply tell us?" Adam prompted, without bothering to hide his irritation.

"No need to cob on, my friend, just because you're having trouble adjusting to the way of things. Anyway, Oswin met the same man whom I saw asking questions about Adam Hawksmore in Portsmouth. Now, what do you think of that?"

"Are you certain?" Edward asked.

"I'd recognize that face anywhere. Little fellow reminds one of a rottweiler."

"Dogface," Becca gasped. She turned to see Adam's reaction.

"So it seems," he said, his fingers steepled beneath his chin. What little evidence Adam possessed all implicated Oswin. The meeting at the Red Goose Inn, Dogface, the secret meetings, the paintings in the warehouse. If only Adam could find tangible proof of the man's guilt.

It was time to mobilize the troops.

"All of you wish to be involved. Call me a fool, but here is your chance. Edward, you must find out if anyone else talked with the War Department. Find

Lord Archibald and pry the information from his teeth if you have to. See what he knows about Oswin.

"Jeanette, Miriam and Becca, you will keep Lord Oswin occupied for the rest of the night. Dance with him, play cards, whatever. Given my experience with you three, I trust you ladies will think of something, but keep him here."

"What are you and Mac going to do?" Becca asked.

"A bit of burglary. It is high time I see what Oswin's hiding. Every man keeps personal records. If we're lucky, we'll find the proof I need."

A hush fell over the salon before everyone voiced a new wave of objections. Adam simply answered, "As you all so eloquently put it earlier, you can choose to help me or not, but I have made up my mind. Now, if you please, I wish to speak with Becca. Mac, I'll find you shortly."

Everyone retreated from the room, no one particularly happy with the sudden turn of events. Adam crossed behind them, bolted the door and remained there. Becca stood beside a marble bust of Lord Featherstone, her hair glimmering from the light of a nearby lamp and her hands worrying the ties of her green shepherdess dress. Heaven help him, but she was beautiful, and he wanted her. Talking about this was likely a foolish thing to do, but he couldn't simply ignore her earlier announcement.

With her declaration came a sense of longing, a particle of hope that wedged itself into his heart along with a lingering fear that he would hurt her. "About what you said . . ."

She swung around to face him. "I love you. There. I said it. I feel the way I do and I am tired of pretending otherwise."

"Be reasonable. I'm not a loveable man. You've said so yourself."

"Usually because you've made me angry. You are not at all what I envisioned as a husband, but unfortunately my heart refuses to listen to logic."

"You called me a boor. Said I lacked spontaneity. I make lists and adhere to them."

"I don't."

"Order and discipline are essential to the running of a household. I can't change who or what I am."

"Neither can I."

"You're not in love with me. You're confusing Adam Hawksmore with Francis Cobbald."

Becca grimaced. The poor man seemed determined to find an excuse to change her mind. He didn't realize it was too late. Shaking her head, she stepped forward. He retreated. "For an intelligent man, you are an idiot. And to say I don't know the difference between Cobbald and Hawksmore makes me sound an even bigger idiot. Try as you might, you can no more control the way I feel about you than my father can control the tides. I *love* you. Every irascible part of you."

"I'm not sure I want your love, that I'm capable of love, or even if I know what love is."

"I believe in love with all my heart. I believe in you." She placed the palm of her hand on his cheek. "Let me help you learn."

"That would be a mistake. I can't be anything but what I am."

"You're right. But true love doesn't dictate who or what someone should be to their partner. I was afraid to let myself love you for fear I couldn't be the woman you wanted. Please don't make the same mistake. Don't shut me out."

"Becca, I know battle strategies and war plans, a dozen ways to kill a man. I know nothing of love."

"The fact that you are worried proves you care, at least a little. I think falling in love is like learning to walk. Everyone stumbles and falls from time to time. Mother said the first step is recognizing a problem exists. Next you must want to believe." She held a finger to his lips. "You can accept my feelings or ignore them, but you can't change them. Take what I offer, nothing more, nothing less, and let's see where we go from there."

She pressed her lips to his. With a groan, he dragged her against him, almost roughly, and returned the kiss in almost wild desperation. He had never needed someone in his entire life, had survived because he refused to allow anyone too close. Becca was the brave and courageous one. He was the coward, afraid to let himself hope that she could truly love him. He'd been taught to believe in honor, responsibility and duty. Those fundamental beliefs had ruled his family, his childhood, his life.

He had the feeling she was offering the missing piece to a puzzle, a contentment and happiness he'd never really known, a cure for the lonely ache he felt so often, even when surrounded by a company of men or a room filled with people.

He lowered himself to his knees, inched the hem of her dress higher and slid the palms of his hands up over her bare legs. Callused soldier's hands against tender feminine flesh. He kissed the spot behind her knee, the flesh above her garter. He plied her body with kisses, his mouth seeking that for which his body hungered.

Becca ceased to breathe. Cool air brushed her skin. But Adam's hands, his lips, sliding sensuously up her legs, left fire in their wake. When the heat of his mouth nuzzled the tender flesh between her legs, it was all she could do to remain standing. She hadn't quite believed her aunt's story of men and women making love in this manner. Evidently Jeanette had spoken the truth. Adam's probing tongue was all the proof she needed.

She leaned her head against the wall and stared into the mirror on the opposite wall. Wicked as it was, she couldn't remove her gaze from the image of Adam, his head tucked between her thighs. Feeling what he did to her beneath the yards of fabric bunched at her waist almost drove her wild.

He eased one of her legs over his shoulder, and her body went rigid with the increased intimacy. Maidenly restraint urged her to stop such madness. Womanly passions demanded she stay as she was. Becca bucked against his mouth as his tongue teased her with gentle strokes. He was returning her declaration of love with physical pleasure. Adam had to love her. For no man could be so gentle, so blissfully deliberate with his touch unless he knew love—even if he knew not how to say it.

A tingling pulse vibrated through her, down her legs. Her skin prickled with the coming of ecstasy—wave after relentless wave of it. Still, Adam demanded more from her. One hand massaged her buttocks. The other hand, with its clever fingers, masterfully tantalized her swollen flesh. Her body, which she thought had experienced the ultimate in pleasure, apparently had further to go. All at once her body shook harder than ever, a blinding explosion of joy. She cried, then, wholly sated, her muscles relaxed. Her wild convulsions and her breathing steadied.

Ever so slowly, Adam edged the fabric of her dress to the floor and levered himself to stand before her. He kissed her mouth, the very essence of her fresh on his lips. Her hand crept to his trousers and stroked him through the fabric. He strained into her hands, molded her fingers around him.

She wanted more. The strain on his face showed he needed more. Before he could stop her, she had opened his trousers and freed him. The velvet length of his shaft leaped to life with her tender care. His breathing rasped against her ears until he jerked free.

"No, Becca. I can't stand it—"

She clasped his face between her hands. "Look at me. In the end, if you must leave, there will be no regrets. I am giving myself freely. I *love* you."

With a groan he pressed her to the wall, lifting her, guiding her, until she clamped her legs about his waist. She felt him probing the entrance to her womb and rejoiced in the sensation, knowing they would join as one.

He slowly, torturously, eased into her. There was no tightness like the first time, only a gentle pressure coupled with the sense of rightness. Her hands clasped about his shoulders, she felt the brocade wall against her back, the hardness of his chest against her breasts, and she wished they were naked. Their image in the mirror was shocking. Thrilling. Stirring.

"I dreamed of us. Like this." He withdrew his sex from her. Slowly. Drawing out the pleasure to a level of near-pain. She bit his shoulder and cried out. His breathing rasped in her ears. "Just like this. Buried deep inside you." He pulled out again. "I can't be gentle, Becca."

His eyes burned like the banked embers of a fire, ready at any moment to burst into flame. With understanding and acceptance and a passion as hot as his, she said, "There's no need to be."

Then and only then did he plunge home, thrusting again and again, taking her roughly against the wall. She met his every movement, gripping his hips with her feet, kissing his lips with her tongue and teeth. It was madness. But both were trapped within the same cage until the insanity was purged from their bodies. And then, gloriously, it was.

Spent, Adam stood holding Becca, his breath mingling with hers. What could he say when he was unsure of what he was feeling himself? He eased her legs to the floor and righted their clothes, stepping back to stare into her amber eyes filled with compassion and love. He couldn't deny her love. But for now, he had to ignore it.

"Mac is likely wondering what happened to me," he said gruffly.

"Adam—"

"Shhh. There are a great many things to resolve. I promise we will talk when all this is over. Come on."

He cracked the door open. The hallway was vacant, and darker than he remembered. When they moved down the hallway, a breeze from the nearby window brushed his shoulder.

As he turned, a knife sailed through the air. His reflexes took over. He tackled Becca and crashed with her to the floor. The weapon lodged in the wall where they had been standing a moment before. Standing, he rushed to the window. Whoever it was had gone.

He turned back to Becca. If he'd delayed one second longer, made the smallest error in judgment, she would have been killed. The image of her lying on the floor, bleeding to death from an attack meant for him, was too much. The blood in his veins froze. Someone was going to pay.

Chapter Twenty-one

The lane was cloaked in darkness; there was no moonlight, no visible stars, only small auras of light from the windows of the houses lining the street. Fog swirled and eddied around the bushes in the garden below. A low blanket of clouds overhead poured forth a steady drizzle. All in all, it was a good night for a thief.

And Adam needed to steal back his life. He had to have proof and information. In order to find both, he was prepared to take drastic measures. Why else would he be creeping along this ridiculously narrow brick ledge twenty feet above the ground like a stray cat?

Mac, two feet in front of him, easily managed the crawl the same way he'd managed climbing the bloody tree. After all, the man was a sailor, accustomed to dangling from high places. Adam wasn't overly fond of heights. He preferred the solid earth. It was one of the reasons why he'd chosen His Majesty's Army over the Navy.

A soot-covered face poked out the nearest window. "Eh, guv. I see y' made it." The lad spoke with the hushed tones of a practiced burglar.

Mac ruffled the boy's dark hair. "Aye, Reilly. Is it clear?"

"Aye, Capt'n. Other than a cook in the kitchen and a man sittin' by the front door, the household's tucked in their quarters. No one's about on this floor. The gent's bedroom is next door. On the other side is a fancy readin' room."

"Good work," Mac said as he traded places with the lad, stepping quietly inside the house. "Back to the tree, now. If anyone comes, give us a warning."

Straddling the windowsill, Adam watched Reilly dart along the ledge like a jackrabbit. "Amazing the boy doesn't break his neck. How old is he?"

"Six or seven, I imagine. The lad knows his business. When we're done, he'll lock the window again and leave the same way he came in. No one will be the wiser."

"The fact you know a person or can find a person with these particular talents substantiates my opinion that you need a different line of work." Adam stepped into the room as well, closed the drapes and pulled two small candles from his pocket. He lit both and handed one to Mac. The study was cast into an eerie mix of light and shadow.

From the looks of the room, Jeremy Oswin was a fastidious man, one who paid great attention to detail. Sparse in furnishings but richly designed with comfort in mind, the room reminded Adam of his own study at Kerrick Castle.

"He's not much for clutter, is he?" Mac whispered. He checked the side door to Oswin's bedroom, then locked the door leading to the hallway.

"I was thinking the same thing. Which should make our job easier." Adam crossed to the desk in the center of the room. Aside from a marble inkwell, a pen and a brass table lamp, its top was bare. This was where Oswin worked.

But at what?

Somewhere outside the room and down the hall a clock chimed. Midnight. There was plenty of time to search these three rooms and return to the masquerade ball.

Mac peeked behind a series of paintings, looking for a safe or secret cabinet. "Find anything?"

"Not yet." Adam concentrated on the items in the top desk drawer. There was certainly nothing that incriminated Oswin. "The two bottom drawers are locked."

Mac tiptoed to Adam's side, pulling a thin metal object that resembled a lady's hatpin from his coat pocket. Within moments, there was a click, and the first drawer opened. Mac immediately went to work on the second. When Adam frowned, Mac said rather proudly, "I'll have you know, this particular talent has come in handy any number of times."

"Which makes me question your line of work even more." Adam rummaged through a collection of papers, mostly legal documents and ledgers regarding Oswin's properties. The bottom drawer contained papers particular to France, various maps, mundane correspondence with the War Department and a journal of sorts. Everything appeared disappointingly in order.

Adam tapped the walls, searching for a secret

space. Mac probed every surface of the stuffed chair and the mahogany table beside the fireplace. Together they sifted through the books on the small shelf, taking care to line up the leatherbound tomes in the same precise order as before. The carved sphinx perched on a side table was pure marble. There was nothing more.

Reilly suddenly appeared at the window. "Two blokes just arrived."

Adam cursed as Reilly scrambled inside. Quite by accident, the boy tumbled to the right, upsetting a three-legged stand upon which a celestial globe was perched. Adam shot to Reilly's side to catch the small ball before it crashed to the floor. An odd rumbling noise came from inside it. Adam and Mac exchanged curious looks.

"It might be a loose bolt or something," Mac said.

"True," Adam said skeptically, his eyes fastened on the wooden ball no more than twelve inches round.

"Reilly," Mac snapped, "unlock the door. You should be able to see to the foyer below. Tell me everything you see and hear."

While Mac held his candle close to the globe, Adam probed the edges of its metal crossbar until he found a tiny button. He pressed inward. Between the constellations of Cancer and Leo Major, a crack appeared and the sphere opened like a small treasure box. Inside was a velvet bag. Curious and even more excited, Adam loosened the silk string. He slowly emptied the contents onto his hand.

"I'll be damned."

Mac hovered at his side, a question on his face. "Isn't that your—"

"It most certainly is." A thrill of adrenaline shot through Adam, the familiar surge of satisfaction he felt after a successful campaign or battle. He wanted to shout with joy. By God, he couldn't believe, couldn't hope. If ever there was proof, this was it. Lying in his palm, its familiar red ruby winking back at him, was the Kerrick signet ring. The last time Adam had seen this ring it was on the hand of a dead Frenchman. He felt the disjointed compartments of his life click back into place.

"They just came in, Capt'n," Reilly whispered.

Mac nodded. "Take the bloody ring and let's get out of here."

Adam started to put the ring in his coat pocket. "Wait. If I take the ring as proof, Oswin can claim he never saw it before. Yet, if I leave it here and he disposes of it, then where would I be? Damn, I wish there was something more."

"Well, you had best make up your mind," Mac warned. "We haven't much time."

"They're giving their coats to the butler," Reilly said from the doorway.

Adam paced to the window. "If I want to catch Oswin, the proof has to be found on these premises. Then again, what is there to keep him from saying I planted the ring myself?"

"As I see it," Mac said, "the ring, along with the paintings and Seavers's help, would be enough to make people question your guilt. They won't hang you if they only *think* you're a traitor. They need proof. And, tomorrow morning, if you're still worried, I know a damn good forger who can create whatever documents you need to incriminate Oswin."

"That would make me the same kind of vermin as he."

"For God's sake. Smack in the midst of house-breaking is a fine time to remember your bloody code of honor. The bastard thought nothing of framing you. He spied for France. He even tried to kill you."

"Exactly. Why?"

Mac scooted to the door to peek over Reilly's shoulder. Then he checked the room, rechecked it and said, "Why the hell what?"

"If Oswin is the Leopard, as we believe, why did he try to kill me tonight? He already planted the evidence in my belongings in France. The authorities already believe me to be guilty. Why didn't he simply turn me in?"

Mac eased the hall door shut and darted to the window. He extinguished his candle and let the smoke billow into the cold night air. "That's a question that has to wait. They're coming up the stairs." Mac was halfway through the window before he realized Adam was back at Oswin's desk. "Didn't you hear me?"

"One last thing. Open this drawer again."

Bristling like a hedgehog, Mac did as Adam requested. "Make it bloody fast. You have about one minute to be on this ledge before our company arrives. I'm afraid our presence would be a tad difficult to explain." Mac pulled a pistol from the waist of his trousers. Reilly waited beside him, watching the door expectantly.

Lifting one of the ledgers from the middle drawer, Adam studied its first page. He flipped through the book until satisfied with what he'd discovered. He replaced it and closed the drawer. As Mac used his magic fingers to click the lock back into place, Adam tucked the ring inside the velvet bag. He tossed it to Reilly, who slid the bag back into its hiding place, then set the globe back on the stand. Extinguishing the last candle, the two men hustled through the window.

"Reilly, lad," Mac said, "lock the window and go out through the bedroom. We'll wait for you at the end of the lane. Hurry now."

Rain fell harder, making the ledge slicker. As quickly as possible without breaking his neck, Adam scooted behind Mac. He hadn't come this close to success to ignobly die in the thorn bushes below. The yellow glow of a light shone through the window they'd just left. Mac leapt to the closest tree limb. Adam did the same.

Just as Adam's toes touched solid ground, the study window opened. He leaped behind the nearest hedge and lay flat on his belly.

Above, Oswin scanned the ledge and the gardens, going so far as to lean out and glance down at the street. He cocked his head to listen. After what seemed an eternity, he slowly closed the window and pulled the drapes.

Adam wasted no time dashing across the sodden lawn to the street, where Mac waited. Neither spoke until they reached their carriage.

Once tucked safely inside, Mac asked, "So what the devil did you find that was so damned important you nearly got us killed?"

Adam grinned. He could practically taste victory. "Every month Oswin received a payment of two thousand pounds. There is no indication as to what or why."

"You think that's his payment for spying? That's crazy."

"Do you keep records of your cargo, your profits?"

"Yes, but . . ."

"Exactly. Thief, spy, smuggler—everyone keeps track of his money, especially a man given to detail."

"Well, then, it seems tonight's escapade was worth the effort. What now?"

"You keep a watchful eye on Dogface. See where he goes. I will talk with Seavers. I might even have Edward pay a visit to Oswin. By tomorrow night, Adam Hawksmore should be able to show his face in London. My reputation may take a while to mend, but this is a beginning."

The gallery walls stretched for what seemed miles, lined with paintings of every imaginable shape and size. Becca's head began to pound. There was no immediate escape for her and her aunt. Especially if Lady Grayson detailed every single picture as she had the first eight, three of which had been portraits of her. Art patroness or not, Lady Grayson was being downright tedious in her explanations. Becca swallowed her yawn with a tight-lipped smile.

"This is my favorite," Lady Grayson said. "I think Sir Lawrence captured my essence most realistically."

"Undoubtedly," Becca agreed enthusiastically, noting the woman's hair was a shade redder and her bosom a tad larger in this picture than in any of the other paintings. She also doubted the matron would appreciate such observations, so she kept silent. After all, she only suffered this ordeal to retain Lady Grayson's continued support.

"Indeed, Eleanor," Jeanette crooned as she sipped her tea, "the candlelight was a stroke of genius. You positively glow."

"True." Lady Grayson tipped her head, mirroring the pose in the portrait. "Pity Mr. Cobbald could not join us today. Though an artist with words, he might have found inspiration here. What did you say demanded his attention?"

"Nothing important," Becca answered with an irony only she could appreciate. Only clearing his name, saving his reputation and capturing the infamous French spy, the Leopard. *Leaving me behind. Again.*

The wall clock struck five. By now, Adam would have arrived at Lord Seavers's town house. Since he still believed the danger too great, he had actually forbidden her to accompany him. She sulked. Her father was given permission to call on Lord Oswin and ask a few questions, Mac was following Dogface. But they were men, according to Adam, equipped to handle unexpected danger.

So here she was, with her aunt, listening to Lady Grayson's endless prattle. Her single consolation was that Adam's good name would soon be cleared.

Then they would talk. He had issued the promise with such solemnity, she wasn't sure she wanted to hear what he had to say.

Becca feigned interest in a serene landscape of snow-covered mountains wrapped in mist. "Francis mentioned an outing. He offered no details."

"Typical behavior for a man. And artists can be even more temperamental. Are you prepared to deal with his moods and idiosyncrasies, the brooding of a complex man"—Lady Grayson lowered her voice suggestively—"a man with special needs?"

If she wasn't, Lady Grayson was; that seemed to be the implication. Becca shuddered. "Our love for one another will see us through. During the rough times, I am sure my fiancé will make an excellent teacher. He is unique."

"This painting is lovely," Jeanette enthused, thankfully redirecting the conversation.

Lady Grayson turned. "The artist, John Constable, has talent. . . . If only he could master his inspiration. And his father. I was thinking." Lady Grayson paused. "A small party in honor of Mr. Cobbald might be in order."

A party? What did this dragon lady have on her debauched mind now? Becca wondered.

"I'm sure you have a dowry, but without a monthly stipend, Mr. Cobbald needs help furthering his career. I am more than happy to volunteer my expertise."

She would offer her expertise all right, likely in bedroom etiquette. While they passed two more landscapes and a battle scene with vivid splashes of color, Becca sought an appropriate answer rather than her instinctive response.

"What do you think of my idea?" Lady Grayson pressed.

Suicidal, Becca thought. "I think—"

Coherent thought scattered. Farther along the wall, hanging above a small table, was a painting Becca had seen all too recently, under less desirable circumstances.

She fought to keep her voice calm. "I beg your pardon, Lady Grayson, but isn't this a Rubens?"

"It most certainly is. It's my newest acquisition. Cost me a fortune, but I simply had to have it. Regarding the party, a tea perhaps? Of course, I should discuss the details with Mr. Cobbald first."

"Of course," Becca readily agreed. "Where did you acquire such a painting? My father has a love, an obsession almost, for the Old Masters."

"Pish-posh," Jeanette muttered. "The only paintings my brother enjoys are—" When Becca slammed the heel of her foot on Jeanette's leather clad toe, her aunt yelped. "Do watch where you're walking."

"Sorry, Auntie. Don't you remember just the other morning, when we were having that lovely family chat? Edward admitted he loved paintings, especially those by Rubens and Raphael."

"He did?" Jeanette rubbed her ear, obviously struggling to remember the conversation. Her eyes widened as understanding dawned. "Oh, dear. Oh, my. Dear me. You are absolutely right. How forgetful," she giggled. "Edward loves art, spends all his spare time these days at the museum, and—"

"—his birthday is approaching," Becca added. "If only we were able to find such a masterpiece for him."

Smiling like a cat with a sparrow in her sights, Lady Grayson said, "I might be willing to trade information if you can convince Mr. Cobbald to perform for me—just once."

"Mr. Cobbald would agree to any manner of things if he knew how to locate such a wonderful present for my father."

Lady Grayson practically drooled. "In that case, I will post a note to Lord Seavers today."

"Lord Seavers?" Becca repeated, her mind whirling. "Lord Seavers sold you this painting?"

"From his personal collection. I believe the poor gentleman is having financial difficulties. This is not to be repeated, mind you. I can post a note to him today."

Becca managed to nod. If Lord Seavers, not Lord Oswin, sold Lady Grayson the painting, that meant Lord Seavers had pilfered the works of art from Paris. *He* was the Leopard, not Lord Oswin. This was disastrous.

"Pardon me. I just remembered an appointment with the modiste. Mr. Cobbald will be waiting."

Stopping beside the brass inlaid table, Lady Grayson practically dropped her teacup. "You said you couldn't remember where he went."

"I did? It must be all this betrothal nonsense. Come along, Auntie." Becca grabbed Jeanette's arm and dragged her toward the door.

The stunned gasp of Lady Grayson and the rustle of linen and pattering feet were the only sounds in the gallery as they dashed from the room. This was no time for small talk or mannerly good-byes. Becca had to drop Jeanette at home with specific instructions to find Edward or Mac and explain the newest development, then she had to warn Adam. He was in trouble. He needed her.

Chapter Twenty-two

"The ring is exactly the proof I required," Adam stated, barely containing his exuberance. "And I'm fairly certain the ledgers I found will implicate Oswin as well."

Seavers poured himself another brandy, then sat across from Adam. With a concerned look on his face, he asked, "How can you be certain the figures pertain to spying?"

"A hunch. One I'm willing to risk." Adam scratched the whiskers of his beard. "It must be Lady Rebecca's influence. She seems to be having adverse effects on my thinking these days. Nevertheless, for some inexplicable reason, it makes sense. I've kept financial records since I was fourteen years old. Oswin's ledgers struck me as odd the first moment I saw them. They're precise, yet are missing descriptions on some of the entries."

"What do you want me to do?"

Adam sipped his brandy, baffled by Seavers's mood. They were about to catch the infamous French spy, the man responsible for countless sabotaged missions and the loss of innumerable lives, but Seavers wasn't nearly as excited as Adam expected him to be. Perhaps the man still had doubts.

Draping his arm across his knee, Adam explained. "Even if the funds are not linked to the Leopard, I am willing to stake my life that this money is to pay for some illegal activity. With the paintings from the warehouse and your corroboration on the events at the Red Goose Inn, there will be enough evidence to force Lord Archibald at the War Department to declare a new investigation into the case. Oswin will be the one who has to prove his innocence."

"I see. When do you plan to have this discussion with Lord Archibald?"

Rolling the crystal snifter between his hands, Adam concentrated on the golden liquid. "I plan to go directly there after you and I talk."

"Is that wise?" Seavers asked.

The door to the salon burst open with a resounding bang as the brass knob connected with the wall, tilting a large mirror precariously to the side. Barreling past an astonished butler, Becca stomped toward Adam. "You sniveling windbag, how dare you!"

He immediately stood, set his drink on the nearest table and crossed his arms. "What is the meaning of this? Are you all right?"

"Good afternoon, Lady Rebecca," Seavers offered cautiously. "Would you care for a brandy?"

"Humph! Men. Can you think of nothing else besides drink and debauchery?" With heaving sighs and grand gestures, Becca paraded about the room, gathering her wits. Now that she knew Adam was alive and well, she needed a way to free him from the clutches of Lord Seavers.

She couldn't very well announce that she'd seen the painting from the warehouse hanging on Lady Grayson's wall, or that Lord Seavers had sold the woman that painting. Perhaps her best option was a temper tantrum. After all, when confronted with an emotional and irrational female, most men sought the quickest escape, Adam included. He hated scenes of any kind.

She figured she had one minute to entice Adam from the room before he either strangled her or Seavers guessed her little game. Halting abruptly before him, she jabbed Adam in the chest. "There is no need to hide your deceit any longer. Lady Grayson revealed every lurid detail, the truth about that night in her garden."

Adam snared her wrist before she poked him again. "I have no idea what you are talking about. Perhaps if you tell me exactly what she said—"

That we've been had. That Lord Seavers is the traitor. "So you will deny the entire clandestine affair, ply me with lies? I think not."

"This is not the time for guessing games." He shook his head in frustration. "If you have no intention of telling me the problem, then why did you chase me all the way here?"

"I prefer privacy. I demand you come with me right now."

"I am moments away from clearing my name, and here you want me to run off and chat about a rumor you heard—without even giving me the benefit of a reason?"

And he considered himself a great tactician, the

dimwit. He wasn't grasping the gravity of the situation at all. Becca had to make him leave the room, at least long enough to warn him. Biting her lower lip, she dropped into the chair Adam had vacated, covered her face with her hands, and wailed. "If you loved me, you would come with me. I loved you. Trusted you. Treating me like a *priceless work of art*, you *stole* my heart. Then, without a second thought, you shattered my soul."

Art? Utterly dumbfounded, Adam stared at her. Becca was impulsive but not stupid or prone to cheap theatrics. She knew the importance of this meeting. And his directive this morning had been perfectly clear: Stay away. She was obviously trying to tell him something. But what? And why now of all times? A sense of foreboding lodged in his gut.

Adam knelt before her, searching her face, trying desperately to understand her motive. "I will be more than happy to mend your broken heart. *Later*."

Fisting the lapels of his jacket in her hands, she dropped her head to his shoulder. Wailing she slapped his chest, then muttered several unflattering comments. Somewhere in between the third slap and the fourth sob, she managed to whisper, "Seavers is the spy."

Surely his ears deceived him. Wherever had she garnered such a notion? Considering her performance, she obviously believed she spoke the truth. If this were an idiotic ploy, she would hear his opinion on this untimely interruption. However, if she was right, they had to leave as soon as possible. Glancing toward Seavers, who lounged against an ebony side cabinet, Adam shrugged his shoulders in silent apology, as any beleaguered male might.

"If I may be so bold, Lady Rebecca?" Seavers

Peggy Waide

calmly moved across the room and straightened the mirror. "Lady Grayson is a good friend of mine, and a notorious gossip who often misinterprets information. Perhaps I can help."

Sniffing most indignantly, Becca stood, wrapped a stranglehold about her purse and edged toward the door. "Thank you, but no. In this particular matter, I have every reason to believe her. I'm leaving. Are you coming or not, Adam?"

Turning, Adam noticed a calculated gleam in Seavers's eyes that had not been there before. A chill skittered down his spine. Time was short. He fought the impulse to reach for the knife tucked in his boot. His first concern was to see Becca to safety. "I promise to return to finish this matter once and for all."

"Before you seek Lord Archibald, I hope?" Seavers asked.

"But of course," Adam offered with a chuckle. He managed three steps before he heard an all-too-familiar click. One glance over his shoulder confirmed his suspicions. As Becca whirled, Adam automatically shoved her behind his back. He crossed his arms and stared down the barrel of the pistol pointed directly at his chest. "The Leopard, I presume."

Seavers's lips thinned to a cynical smile. "At your service, Lord Kerrick. Pity you didn't die in France, my friend. We can do this the easy way or not. The choice is yours."

"Let Becca go first."

"Can't do that. You see, I understand your kind. You're thinking you can overpower me, take the gun and perhaps kill me. Even you can't hide the vengeance in your eyes. No, I believe I'll keep Lady Rebecca around for"—Seavers raised one brow—"insurance."

To prove his point, Seavers leveled the gun at her head. Seavers was right. As long as Becca was in danger, the bastard held all the cards. Fighting the raging impotence he felt, Adam fisted his hands at his sides. "Free her and I will go wherever, sign any documents you like. You don't need her."

"Actually, I suspect your lady friend is as single-minded as you. She won't walk away and let me kill you anymore than you can abandon her. Love can be such a burden, a lesson I learned long ago. I may need one or both of you as bargaining chips."

Speaking with cool pragmatism, as if he discussed yesterday's dinner, Seavers pulled a rope from the drawer of his cabinet. "I really have no desire to kill either of you in my own parlor. Lady Rebecca, if you would be so kind as to bind his hands. A word of warning, Adam: Make one false move, blink the wrong way or breathe too deeply and she dies."

Adam felt a moment's panic. Since the day he'd been gagged and bound, forced to endure his parents' murder, he'd never allowed himself to be restrained. It was a silly weakness, a boy's fear, yet it was one he'd never quite overcome. A cold knot formed in his stomach, one he quickly dispelled. This was not the time for cowardice.

When Becca stood before Adam, he quickly extended his hands. He expected confusion, anxiety or maybe even fear in her eyes, but not the fury he beheld. She did as she'd been told, then unexpectedly swiveled on her heels and leapt at Seavers, raking her nails across his cheeks.

Adam lunged forward.

Seavers clamped Becca around the waist and

pulled her flush with him. He pointed the gun directly at her temple. "Don't be stupid, Adam. Back away." Satisfied, he freed Becca and slapped her hard across the face. "Do that again and I won't be so generous with my care."

"You won't get away with this, you know," she snarled. "By now my father has alerted the authorities and is on his way here."

Had she been a soldier in his company, Adam would have applauded her courage. But now he wished for an ounce of docility. "Be quiet, Becca."

Seavers looked none too happy with her announcement either. He moved forward, pushing Becca ahead of him, his cold, snake-eyed glare fastened on Adam. "In that case, we had best be going. Turn around, Hawksmore. Very, very slowly."

When he did, Adam felt the blunt end of the gun crash into his head. Darkness overwhelmed him.

Bloody hell, he had the mother of all headaches, but Adam blocked out the pain. After all, he'd suffered far worse on the Peninsula and still managed to stay seated on his horse. And then he'd been fighting for his country. Now he was fighting for his life—and for Becca's.

Hoping to gain a slight advantage, Adam remained perfectly still and concentrated on his surroundings. One breath of dank air coupled with the pungent odor of spice and wine, and Adam knew exactly where he was: the warehouse near the docks.

But where were Becca and Seavers?

Helplessness clouded his mind. He remembered Becca, wrapped about his body, on fire in his arms, her bold declaration of love. She'd charged into Seavers's study, prepared to save him. He hadn't been able to do a damn thing to help her earlier, and it didn't seem he could do much now. His trepidation grew as only silence surrounded him. Then there was a rustle of fabric and the shuffle of feet. A sweet floral scent floated among the mildew. Becca was near.

"You probably killed him," she said. "Did you have to hit him so hard?"

"I assure you, my lady," their enemy snapped irritably, "that he is alive. For now."

"Just you wait until he wakens. You'll discover that Adam Hawksmore is not an easy man to kill."

Relief coupled with inadequacy flooded Adam's body. The terror ebbed slowly from his shoulders and hands. There was a wary edge to her voice, but at least she was alive. Her blind faith was admirable. If only Adam possessed her confidence in his own abilities. At the moment, lying on the floor, tied and trussed like a stuffed pig, it was difficult to find a ready solution to their problem. At least his feet were unbound and the knife was still safely hidden in his boot. One thing was certain: He would not let Becca die because of his error in judgment.

He tried to guess Seavers's plan. The bastard wasn't fool enough to think he could stay in London—not with Edward, Mac and the entire British crown after him. Obviously he felt he needed Becca or Adam, or maybe both, to make his escape. Like any trapped animal, Seavers would be dangerous, lethal.

Peeking through slitted eyes, he saw Becca perched on a large box beside the doorway that led upstairs. Other than a ferocious scowl and a rumpled cape, she appeared no worse for wear. Seavers, on the other hand, wore a pained expression that had Adam wondering about Becca's behavior while he had been unconscious. The building above was quiet.

"I see you're awake," Seavers said.

Adam levered himself to a sitting position. "Nice place."

"It suits my needs."

Dashing across the room, Becca threw her arms around Adam's neck. Her purse, which weighed more than it should have, collided with his already bruised shoulder. She pulled back to stare into his eyes. And damn if she didn't wink.

Under ordinary circumstances, he might have been concerned. In this instance, remembering the tiny gun she sometimes carried, Adam was terrified. Lord only knew what she had planned. As difficult as it was, he pressed himself against the wall and slid up to his feet. When Becca shifted to his side, he asked Seavers, "What do you intend to do now?"

"Will I kill you? Will I kill Lady Rebecca? Maybe both? You're dying to know, aren't you?" He laughed at his own joke.

Cocky, self-effacing bastards like Seavers were usually predictable, eager to boast about their exploits. Adam hoped Seavers held true to form. The longer Seavers talked, the greater the chance for a distraction, an opportunity for escape. Stalling for time, Adam asked, "At least tell me why."

Leaning against the corner of the wall beside the stairway, Seavers said matter-of-factly: "I was about to be exposed. You, my friend, happened along precisely when I needed you. I guess you should have gone to the Duchess of Richmond's grand affair after all. When you told me that Oswin was at the inn, I knew I had to act fast. I knocked you out, left you with a friend of mine, planted the papers in your belongings and returned to the ball. The plan was quite brilliant, if I say so myself."

"Why didn't you kill me?"

"Old chums, and all that. Honestly, I'd hoped I wouldn't need to. After I planted the evidence in your tent, I figured that if you showed your face again, you'd hang. When the French forces fell at Waterloo, it was difficult to find you again. My partner had been killed. I thought I was lucky and you'd died. That was the first of two mistakes."

"What was the other?"

"Letting Oswin live." When Adam narrowed his eyes, Seavers chuckled. "I see you're surprised. Oswin is my counterpart, you see. He is an agent of his royal majesty and, to my dismay, tenacious to a fault. I found it quite ironic that you thought he was the Leopard."

"Then, in that case, he's searching for you as well," Becca crowed.

"Most likely." Seavers glanced at his timepiece. "Lady Rebecca, step away from Hawksmore."

"No."

"You think I won't shoot you?" A feral gleam slid across Seavers's face, shooting chills down her spine. "I've shot a woman before. You're a sight prettier than she was, but believe me, I have absolutely no scruples."

"Do as he says, Becca."

Her chest felt as if it might burst. She sucked in shallow gasps of air. The savagery burning in Adam's eyes terrified her more than Seavers's warning. It wasn't as if she wanted to die, but neither did she want Adam to do something foolish. As long as he was alive there was hope. Reluctantly, she stepped halfway between the two men. With trembling arms, she clutched her purse to her chest, her knuckles white on her fisted hands. She'd tried to reach in for her gun several times already, but Seavers had watched her constantly and she had lost her nerve. If only he were truly distracted.

"Why, for God's sakes?" Adam asked. "You had a title, several estates to inherit and a name men revered."

"A title?" Seavers snorted. "My father managed to squander most everything before I turned eighteen. I barely had enough to buy a commission and keep my estates afloat. And a man's name means little if he's bankrupt."

"You betrayed your country for money?" Adam shook his head in disgust. "You make me sick."

"The high-and-mighty Hawksmore, lord and gentleman. How noble you are. You cannot fathom how, or why, I would sell my soul to the very devil, can you? Causes are short-lived, and pretty gold medals mean so little in the overall scheme of things. Don't you see? Honor and all that rubbish, they're just traps for weak men like you."

"Thank heavens there are men like him," Becca retorted.

"No doubt." Seavers pulled a timepiece from his pocket. "Well, Lady Rebecca, our ship awaits."

"Let us go," she begged. "We won't interfere."

"I kept Adam alive this long in case I needed him. The problem is, he'll just as soon shoot my ship from underneath me. With you on board, he'd refrain from such nastiness, but the even greater problem is, he'll never rest until I'm dead."

Adam stepped forward. "You've got that right."

"You're just too damn predictable." Seavers pointed his gun at Adam's head.

Becca turned toward Adam, desperation in every fiber of her being. Her fingers tugged at the strings of her purse, twisting the silk into knots. She had to do something. "You arrogant clod! Let him go. I'll be damned if you'll get yourself killed because of me."

As if he understood her silent plea, he inched closer to her and shouted, "He stole nine months of my life, betrayed England and ruined my name. He can't just disappear, get away with it."

Seavers stepped back, amused, so Becca went on. "I don't give a damn about England."

"He struck you!"

With a menacing laugh, Seavers shrugged. "As touching as all this is, it is time to go."

The man grabbed Becca's elbow, but she jerked her arm away hoping for one instant, a single moment, that he might be caught off guard. It was all the opportunity Adam needed. With a ferocious growl, he leapt through the air like a wild boar, thrusting his shoulder into Seavers's belly. Both men fell to the floor in a tangle of legs, grunts and groans.

"Becca, get out of here," Adam ordered, trying his best to restrain Seavers even with his hands tied, keeping the man away from his fallen pistol and fighting to give her time to escape.

Not on your life, she thought. She struggled with her damn purse's strings, watching in horror as Seavers struck Adam in the jaw. Adam's head jerked sideways. He rocked back to his knees, but clasped his hands together and swung his arms like a club, landing a solid blow to Seavers's nose. Blood spattered the floor. Seavers toppled onto Adam, but not before Adam locked his legs about the man's waist. The two rolled to the right, crashing into a wine shelf that rocked dangerously back and forth. Seavers reached for his gun.

Adam went for him, but he wasn't quick enough; the gun went off. He crashed backward, blood burgeoning on his jacket.

Becca screamed.

"Shut up," Seavers snarled. Lurching to his feet, he jerked Becca by the arm and dragged her toward the stairs. She drew her gun from her purse.

"No," she said.

Turning, Seavers slapped it away from her with a laugh. "Yes, dear. It is time to go."

Fighting with all her might, she clawed his face and kicked his shins. She couldn't leave Adam. Not until she knew if he was alive or dead. She struggled all the harder. Seavers slapped her again, across the face, and she tumbled to the ground.

A whoosh sounded in her ears, followed by a gurgle. Looking over, she saw Adam's knife lodged in Seavers's throat. Blood spurted in the air. Burbling, he slid to the ground with a look of disbelief.

Becca turned away, the bile rising in her stomach. She dropped to her knees beside Adam, who now lay facedown and perfectly still. She carefully rolled him onto his back. Blood seemed to be everywhere. The icy fingers of fear strangled her. Stroking his face, she cried, "Adam? Please, darling, open your eyes." He lay deathly still.

Removing her cape, she pressed the fabric to his wound. She dared not leave him. Hot tears streamed down her cheeks as she screamed for help. Fate couldn't be so cruel as to rip the man she loved from her just when she'd found him. She'd trade her blood for his, mingle her breath with his, if it meant he would live. Life without Adam was unimaginable.

"Please don't die, Adam. If you live, I'll never argue with you again. I promise. And I'll forget everything I ever read by Mary Wollstonecraft. I'll be forever dutiful, the mirror of obedience: fetch your slippers, your brandy, serve you coffee in bed every morning without cream and sugar, of course."

She struggled to untie his wrists, the bonds now soaked with blood. His arms fell limply to his sides. "Live, and you can lecture me daily. I'll actually listen." She sobbed. "If you die, I will never forgive you."

A chokelike cough rumbled deep in his chest. His shoulders jerked and his body shuddered. His eyes opened slightly, then drifted closed.

Becca swallowed a sob. She barely heard the footsteps thundering down the wooden stairs. Crowded in the doorway, guns drawn, were Mac, her father, Lord Oswin and Dogface. She had never been so happy to see such a furious group of men in her entire life.

Damn all men to hell and back! Becca sat in the windowseat of her bedroom and cursed the gender once more for good measure. Banished to her room by her father while the doctor mended Adam, she had bathed, started to read three times and unbraided and braided her hair four times. She'd sneaked to Adam's room twice, only to be turned away by her mother. That had been over two hours ago. In frustration, she crossed to the windowseat and sat.

As a child, she'd spent hour after hour in this very same spot, conjuring the image of the man of her dreams. Never in a million years had she imagined him prostrate on the ground with blood oozing from his chest. She stood and circled her room for the hundredth time, ignoring the clothes scattered upon the floor.

Adam had promised to talk to her. He had yet to tell her he loved her. If he lived, what if he decided he owed her nothing? She scolded herself for such nonsense. Collapsing to her mattress, she hurled the abandoned book across the room just as the door opened. The lights from the hallway outlined a man's figure. The face was cloaked in shadow.

"Adam?" she asked as she crawled to her knees.

"May I come in?"

The velvety whisper raised the hair on her arms. She managed to nod, her breath trapped in her lungs. He pushed the door closed with his boot and stepped into the small circle of light beside the bed. The threads of fear and worry began to unravel.

His hair was damp from his bath and neatly trimmed above the nape of his neck. The white streak had been washed out, leaving a dark mass of curls that begged for her touch. The eye patch had been discarded as well. Clean-shaven for the first time since his return, dressed in black trousers and a white shirt, his arm wrapped in a sling, everything about him was perfect: the crisp hairs peeking from his open shirt, the innate arrogance in his face, the sensuality of his mouth, the raw power in his every step. Oh, yes, most definitely, he was perfect. And she meant to keep him. "You shaved."

He lifted his hand to his chin. "I never thought such a simple task would be so refreshing. Do you approve?"

Was he joking? He was more handsome than she remembered. She answered with a shy smile. "Are you all right?"

"Nothing a few days' rest won't cure. The bullet

lodged near my shoulder and was easily removed. It seems I smacked my head a second time."

Her gaze strayed to the closed door. "Are you free to stay? I mean, have the authorities dropped the charges?"

"Yes. It seems Oswin has been searching for me for the last few months. He suspected Seavers, but he lacked the proof and never gave up hope. I was to be the bait."

Her mouth fell open. "At Lady Witherspoon's, when he said he was looking for something he had lost—"

"That was me. Dogface is actually Henry Tithers. He works with Oswin from time to time. He found my trail in France and lost it once again in England. He was the one who found the woman murdered in Cherbourg. She was Seavers's accomplice."

Becca gathered a pillow in her lap and jabbed the center. "I hope you smacked Oswin in the mouth. Hard. You were almost killed."

He shrugged his good shoulder. "It might be difficult for me to strike him, but he's still downstairs with your father if you're up to the task." Chuckling when she sighed, he stepped forward. His gaze grew pensive. "We need to talk."

The seriousness of his expression aroused her fears all over again. Hysteria caused her stomach to roil so loudly, she was sure Adam heard. Pulling the sides of her robe together, she softly murmured, "I know."

"Is now a good time?"

It depended on his answer, she thought. Her mother and father had taught her to face a problem head-on. She would listen to what Adam had to say, and even if he didn't love her now, she would spend every hour of every day changing his mind. She slid to the edge of the bed. "I love you. What do you intend to do about it?"

"I've been giving that some thought." Adam gripped the bedpost with his hand. He had to be insane. His life would be utter chaos, filled with daily skirmishes that robbed him of all peace and solitude. Yet that accompanied something more compelling: the negotiations with Becca afterward. He imagined they would be highly pleasurable for both of them.

She wore a plain silk nightgown the color of violets. Her hair was braided with a few wisps about her face. Her eyes glinted with the odd combination of defiance and insecurity. And all of that made him want her even more. He wanted to start at the top of her blond head and kiss his way to her toes, worshipping every inch along the way to show her how he felt. Unfortunately, if he continued on this train of thought, he'd never speak his mind. And she deserved the words.

As if he had all the time in the world, he walked toward the window. He'd resigned his commission a half hour ago, given the papers to Lord Oswin without the least bit of remorse or regret. For the first time in his life, he felt as though he had someplace else he belonged. This was all new territory for him, and he had Becca to thank.

"I spent my life, it seems, as a soldier. I never imagined doing anything different. Not really. Truth be told, I'm tired. Duty is a fine thing, but it makes a cold bedmate."

"What are you saying?"

"Until you came along, I never realized how lonely I was. I'd forgotten how to care about anything beyond the next battle, winning the next skirmish, doing my duty. Now, I understand there is more than that to life." He stepped back toward the bed. "I want you."

"That sounds like your head. What does your heart want?"

"I was never sure I had one." When Becca groaned in frustration, he sat beside her on the bed, clasping her hand in his. He gently stroked the palm with his thumb. "Francis Cobbald has been officially put to rest. Thank heavens. The man was a bore. Adam Hawksmore is whom you see before you—straightforward, with simple needs, a man not very good with fancy metaphors or pretty words. I am what I am and . . ."

Nibbling her lower lip, she said hesitantly, "Three little words will do."

Adam clasped her face with his hand. "Rebecca Marie Marche, I love you. Thoroughly. Madly. You are my heart, my soul. Marry me?"

"Yes." She threw her arms about him, then pulled away.

Adam groaned. He hadn't realized he'd been holding his breath. Regardless of what the doctor had said, he wasn't leaving her side tonight. Ignoring the throbbing in his shoulder, he eased Becca backward until she lay beneath him on the bed, he kissed her with every bit of love he felt.

"My parents?" Becca managed to ask between gasps.

"We marry in two days. I have no intention of sleeping anyplace other than this. Do you have a problem with that?"

She glanced at his bandaged arm. "Are you certain?"

"I'm sure we'll manage."

"In that case, my lord."

He toyed with the small ribbon at the neckline of her gown. "There is one last item to discuss. I vaguely remember some promises about obedience and duty." Flashing a grin, he said, "I intend to hold you to each and every one."

A challenge twinkled in her eyes. Life would certainly be a conflict, but one of which he intended to enjoy each and every moment. Starting right now. He pressed his lips to hers as all was forgotten except the pleasure and ecstasy found in Becca's arms.

Epilogue

"How much longer must I wear this ridiculous mask?" Becca asked petulantly as she bounced on the leather seat. The carriage had struck yet another rut.

"My darling, surprises are best when savored until the very last moment." Adam nuzzled the tender spot behind her left ear of which he was so very fond. "Somewhat like making love. The longer I make you wait, the louder you moan." He leaned over and his tongue laved the hollow between her breasts.

"Good thing Mother and Father are in the other carriage," she gasped. Moaning, she arched her back slightly as Adam's hand found the already pebbled tip of her nipple.

"Indeed." At last, Adam kissed her fully on her lips. She responded with equal ardor, an unspoken invitation. Becca had blown into his life like a whirlwind and with one kiss, a gentle word and, now and again, a flying object, she had turned his life into one of pure joy. Today he hoped to return the favor.

Adam managed to loosen the top three buttons of her day gown before the carriage rounded the last bend. Sighing, he said, "Too late, darling. We shall have to finish this discussion later."

"Promises, promises," she whispered seductively against his lips. "May I remove the mask?"

"Not until I tell you."

She grumbled. He smiled. When the carriage halted, he slid his arms about her waist, fuller now with her pregnancy, and lifted her from the coach. The gravel crunched beneath his feet as he carried her—one of those chivalrous acts he'd come to enjoy. All because of Becca. Even now, he felt like a lovesick groom on his wedding day.

Easing her feet to the ground, he stood behind her, his hands on her shoulders. "Ready?"

With the impatience of a child at Christmas, she ripped the mask from her face and gasped. Her eyes misted. She glanced over her shoulder. "Adam, darling. What can I say?"

He gave her a meaningful look. "Say you're thrilled. That I have fulfilled your greatest wish."

Her mouth formed a disturbing pout. "But that would be impossible."

His jaw fell open. He stared at the exquisite yellow brick manor in front of him, an architectural dream by his estimation, a gift that had consumed two years of his life, of secrecy and planning. By God, she had better like it. "What the devil do you mean? Don't you recognize it?"

She swung about to fully face him. "Of course, I do. This is a replica of my dollhouse. The very same you gave me when I was five years old."

"Precisely," he said indignantly, completely baffled by her reaction. She wasn't responding at all the way he'd expected. But then again, she never did.

She traced a fingernail seductively along the edge of his open-necked shirt. "Adam, my husband, my lover, my friend, my poet. Don't you know that you gave me the greatest gift the day you said you loved me? Each and every day, my life grows sweeter and fuller because you exist. Though it's lovely, I don't need this house to make me happy. I love *you*, you foolish man."

With that she whirled about and dashed toward the stone steps that led to the front door. "And if you hurry and are very, very nice to me, I just might let you prove it to me before my parents arrive."

"Be careful, for goodness sakes," he shouted.

Her laughter floated over him like a soft caress, and he knew she loved what he had built. Then he was racing after her, determined to make her pay for teasing him. And she would enjoy her punishment. He'd see to that.

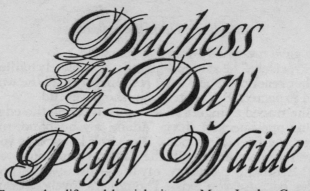

Duchess For A Day
Peggy Waide

To save her life and her inheritance, Mary Jocelyn Garnett does what she must. She marries Reynolds Blackburn—without his knowledge. And all goes well, until the Duke of Wilcott returns to find he is no longer the king of bachelors. As long as the marriage is never consummated, Jocelyn knows, it can be annulled—just as soon as she has avenged her family and reacquired her birthright. Unfortunately, her blasted husband appears to be attracted to her! Worse, Reyn is handsome and clever, and she fears her husband might assume that she is one of many women who are simply after his title. After one breathless kiss, however, Jocelyn swears that she will not be duchess for a day, but Reyn's for a lifetime.

___4554-0 $4.99 US/$5.99 CAN

Dorchester Publishing Co., Inc.
P.O. Box 6640
Wayne, PA 19087-8640

PEGGY WAIDE
POTENT CHARMS

She is the most frustrating woman Stephen Lambert has ever met—and the most beguiling. But a Gypsy curse has doomed the esteemed duke of Badrick to a life without a happy marriage, and not even a strong-willed colonial heiress with a tendency to find trouble can change that. Stephen decides that since he cannot have her for a wife, he will convince her to be the next best thing: his mistress. But Phoebe Rafferty needs a husband, and fast. She has four weeks to get married and claim her inheritance. Phoebe only has eyes for the most wildly attractive and equally aggravating duke. But he refuses to marry her, mumbling nonsense about a curse. With time running out, Phoebe vows to persuade the stubborn aristocrat that curses are poppycock and the only spell he has fallen under is love.

___4694-6 $4.99 US/$5.99 CAN

IONA

MELANIE JACKSON

Isolated by the icy storms of the North Atlantic, the isle of Iona is only a temporary haven for its mistress. Lona MacLean, daughter of a rebel and traitor to the crown, knows that it is only a matter of time before the bloody Sasannachs come for her. But she has a stout Scottish heart, and the fiery beauty gave up dreams of happiness years before. One task remains—to protect her people. But the man who lands upon Iona's rain-swept shores is not an Englishman. The handsome intruder is a Scot, and a crafty one at that. His clever words leave her tossing and turning in her bed long into the night. His kiss promises an end to the ghosts that plague both her people and her heart. And in his powerful embrace, Lona finds an ecstasy she'd long ago forsworn.

___4614-8 $4.99 US/$5.99 CAN

Dorchester Publishing Co., Inc.
P.O. Box 6640
Wayne, PA 19087-8640

Please add $1.75 for shipping and handling for the first book and $.50 for each book thereafter. NY, NYC, and PA residents, please add appropriate sales tax. No cash, stamps, or C.O.D.s. All orders shipped within 6 weeks via postal service book rate. Canadian orders require $2.00 extra postage and must be paid in U.S. dollars through a U.S. banking facility.

Name_____

Address_____

City_____ State_____ Zip_____

I have enclosed $_____ in payment for the checked book(s).

Payment <u>must</u> accompany all orders. ❑ Please send a free catalog.

CHECK OUT OUR WEBSITE! www.dorchesterpub.com

MANON
MELANIE JACKSON

Alone and barely ahead of the storm, Manon flees Scotland; the insurrection has failed and Bonnie Prince Charlie's rebellion has been thrown down. Innocent of treason, yet sought by agents of the English king, the Scots beauty dons the guise of a man and rides to London—and into the hands of the sexiest Sassanach she's ever seen. But she has no time to dally, especially not with an English baronet. Nor can she indulge fantasies of his strong male arms about her or his heated lips pressed against her own. She fears that despite her precautions, this rake may uncover her as no man but *Manon*, and she may learn of something more dangerous than an Englishman's sword—his heart.

Lair of the Wolf

Also includes the eighth installment of *Lair of the Wolf*, a serialized romance set in medieval Wales. Be sure to look for future chapters of this exciting story featured in Leisure books and written by the industry's top authors.

___4737-3 $4.99 US/$5.99 CAN

Dorchester Publishing Co., Inc.
P.O. Box 6640
Wayne, PA 19087-8640

Please add $1.75 for shipping and handling for the first book and $.50 for each book thereafter. NY, NYC, and PA residents, please add appropriate sales tax. No cash, stamps, or C.O.D.s. All orders shipped within 6 weeks via postal service book rate. Canadian orders require $2.00 extra postage and must be paid in U.S. dollars through a U.S. banking facility.

Name_____
Address_____
City_____ State_____ Zip_____
I have enclosed $_____ in payment for the checked book(s).
Payment <u>must</u> accompany all orders. ☐ Please send a free catalog.
CHECK OUT OUR WEBSITE! www.dorchesterpub.com